KIMBERLY DEAN
ELIZABETH DONALD
ANNA J.EVANS
EVE JAMESON
MARY WINTER

Sultry Summer Fun

ELLORA'S CAVE
ROMANTICA PUBLISHING

Hypnotica
Kimberly Dean

You are feeling very sexy…

When shy Copper Daniels is entranced at an Erotic Hypnotic show, her Caribbean cruise quickly goes from restful to restless. Encouraged to find the hottest man in the room—the one who turns her on more than any other—she chooses Nick Branson.

Nick isn't a saint. When Copper crawls onto his lap, he gives her what she needs—until he hears the hoots from the crowd. Angrily, he makes the hypnotist call off the spell. But it just doesn't take.

As their sun-filled vacation progresses, Nick and Copper quickly learn that whenever somebody says the trigger word, her inhibitions fade and things between them get hot. Blistering hot. Copper knows, because afterwards she can remember every kiss, every sigh and every touch.

Secretly, she hopes the spell never fades.

Tandem
Elizabeth Donald

Jericho Trail was too dangerous to hike alone—those were park rules. Hence two strangers hiking together.

Chris went to the woods to be alone, to think and find peace after a bad breakup. Reed went to the woods for a good time. But he had no idea the trail would be so difficult—or that he would share it with such an intoxicating woman.

Separated from the world, the dangers of the trail are nothing compared to the dance between two lost souls, forced together by circumstance but drawn together by the fire burning their blood.

Off the Deep End

Anna J. Evans

Caitlyn Saunders is looking for a little fun in the San Diego sun. But when she's caught in a spring storm and swept out to sea by a tidal wave, she's not really surprised. She and Fortune have never been friends.

Still, who needs Fortune when you can have a dark, mysterious stranger?

Lukas knows he has more pressing matters to attend to than pleasuring the mortal woman he pulled from the sea. But how's a man supposed to concentrate on royal intrigue when such a tempting woman is lying naked in his arms? Proving to this fiery redhead that he's the furthest thing from a mermaid — or a maid of any kind — is too decadently sensual a test to resist.

Saint Jillian's Rebel

Eve Jameson

In high school, Jillian Lawson had been nicknamed Saint Jillian by Pier's Point most infamous Rebel, Hunter Scott. Back then she hadn't known what to do with his erotic teasing except back away, keeping her good-girl image fully intact. Twenty years later, she's more than ready to accept his offer the second time around, even when she discovers he's been waiting a long time to teach his Saint a lesson in payback. But she has a few things to teach him, the first being that she's no longer a saint… Could their erotic interlude lead to more than a vacation fling?

Water Lust
Mary Winter

Grace Edwards lives on a private Caribbean island. More at home in the ocean than on land, she spends her time searching for the elusive man of her dreams. He fulfills her every desire, takes her to the heights of passion, and makes love to her every night—all night. There is just one problem. She really does only see him in her dreams. Come the dawn, reality rushes in and her dream man disappears back to wherever he came from.

Then, an old woman gives her the key to finding him.

Now that Grace has the information she needs, she's ready to find him and turn her dreams into reality. For Chemal, restricted for so long to only visiting the love of his life when night falls and he can make love to her as she sleeps, he's ready to prove to her that they have more than lust—that with her love they can have forever.

An Ellora's Cave Romantica Publication

www.ellorascave.com

Sultry Summer Fun

ISBN 9781419950926
ALL RIGHTS RESERVED.
Hypnotica Copyright © 2006 Kimberly Dean
Tandem Copyright © 2006 Elizabeth Donald
Off the Deep End Copyright © 2006 Anna J. Evans
Saint Jillian's Rebel Copyright © 2006 Eve Jameson
Water Lust Copyright © 2006 Mary Winter

Edited by Briana St. James, Mary Moran, and Sue Ellen Gower

Cover art by Syneca

Trade paperback Publication May 2007
This book printed by in the U.S.A. by Jasmine-Jade
Enterprises, LLC.

Content Advisory:

S – ENSUOUS
E – ROTIC
X – TREME

Ellora's Cave Publishing offers three levels of Romantica® reading entertainment: S (S-ensuous), E (E-rotic), and X (X-treme).

The following material contains graphic sexual content meant for mature readers. This story has been rated E–rotic.

S-*ensuous* love scenes are explicit and leave nothing to the imagination.

E-*rotic* love scenes are explicit, leave nothing to the imagination, and are high in volume per the overall word count. E-rated titles might contain material that some readers find objectionable—in other words, almost anything goes, sexually. E-rated titles are the most graphic titles we carry in terms of both sexual language and descriptiveness in these works of literature.

X-*treme* titles differ from E-rated titles only in plot premise and storyline execution. Stories designated with the letter X tend to contain difficult or controversial subject matter not for the faint of heart.

SULTRY SUMMER FUN

ʚɔ

HYPNOTICA

Kimberly Dean

Chapter 1

"Oh, look at it, Copper. Isn't it *gorgeous*?"

Copper Daniels looked up at the impressive sight of the cruise ship floating before them. With fourteen decks, three pools, a casino, a spa and all the food a person could eat, the *Allure* was awfully pretty. "She's beautiful."

"That's right," Jolene replied. "'It's a 'she'. Gotta remember that."

Copper didn't really care how her sister referred to the ship; to her it was a little slice of heaven. Seven days of sunshine, rest and relaxation. She could hardly wait. It had been a cool spring in Minneapolis and summer hadn't yet caught up. The thought of basking under the sun in warm Caribbean ports-of-call was the most alluring thing about the *Allure*.

Larry impatiently shifted the camera bag on his shoulder. "So are we going to just stand here admiring *her* or are we going to board *her*?"

Jolene let out a laugh and slapped her husband playfully on the shoulder. "You make that sound like something naughty."

He threw her a wink. "It is our anniversary, toots."

Copper felt herself blushing as the two shared an intimate look. It was their first anniversary, to be precise. That had been her one hesitation about joining them on the trip. "Are you sure I'm not going to be a third wheel?"

Jolene rolled her eyes. She looped their arms together and started heading toward the gangplank. "Puh-lease. That one might be handy in bed but he acted like I was torturing him when I wanted to go shopping on our honeymoon. That's why we both brought playmates this time. That way we can have fun during the daytime too."

"Golfing, golfing, golfing," Larry said happily as he followed along close behind them.

Copper let out a laugh. "You live in Miami. You can golf year round."

"No, he can't," Jolene said firmly.

"Golfing, golfing, golfing."

"Goofball," his wife tossed back.

"Golfing."

"Goofball."

The two kept going back and forth until it just got silly. By the time the photographer took their obligatory boarding photograph, the three of them were laughing so hard they were practically in tears. Copper quickly decided that it was best that she had decided to come along. As obsessed as Larry was, she just might be the one thing standing between him and strangulation.

"All right," she said good-naturedly. "If I have to, I'll be your stand-in. I'll shop, snorkel, play tourist and... Ooooh... Just stay here!"

She stopped to gawk. She'd been through all the brochures but nothing could have prepared her for the opulence of the *Allure*. It was like a floating four-star hotel. Make that an all-inclusive resort. She looked around in wonder. There were shops for every taste, a lounge with comfy-looking red velvet chairs and an atrium that stretched upwards forever.

"Let's find our rooms and then we can explore," Jolene said, whipping out their travel information. "Hmm... We're up two floors on the Empress Deck. Follow me."

Copper was still ogling the place when her sister pulled her onto the elevator. There were so many things to do.

Already she knew she wanted to get a facial at the spa, eat Pad Thai at the Purple Orchid and go shopping at the bookstore. Who needed a room?

Out of the corner of her eye, she caught her brother-in-law giving her sister's bottom a soft caress. Oh, that was right. Some people did need a room.

Unfortunately, she wasn't one of them.

Jealousy flickered inside her but she pushed it away. Her Larry was out there somewhere. Although to be honest, as painfully shy as she was, he was probably going to have to find her.

She just wished he'd hurry up.

Once off the elevator, she followed her sister down the long corridor until they found their adjacent rooms. Curious, Copper opened her door. Her smile broadened. The room wasn't all that spacious but the view was spectacular. The down payment Larry and Jolene had made on this trip during their honeymoon had been worth it. They'd managed to get balcony staterooms.

"What do you think?" Jolene asked.

"It's perfect." She loved the burgundy color scheme and especially the white cat sitting on the bed. If she wasn't mistaken, that was a towel. She glanced at the room to her right. "When is Murphy supposed to get here?"

"Oh," Jolene said, her eyes opening wide. "I thought I told you. Murphy can't go."

"Can't go?"

"Yeah, he called last night just before we left to pick you up at the airport. He was put on-call at the last moment and couldn't get out of it."

Well, that was just wrong. "So Larry's going to have to golf by himself?"

"Nick's coming instead."

Copper's head whipped around so fast, she nearly gave herself whiplash. "Nick!" she squeaked.

"I know. How lucky was that? I was surprised he could make it on such short notice. He's going to teach his early afternoon classes and then meet us."

"But... But..." Copper's mind was awhirl. Nick was Larry's brother—the quiet one of the bunch. The quiet, intense, sexy one. "Are you sure you want that much family along?"

Jolene cocked her head. "Funny. That's what Nick said until Larry told him you were joining us."

Copper was flustered. This was not at all what she'd had planned. Murphy was one thing. He'd grown up next door to them and was almost more of a brother than a friend. She felt comfortable around him. Larry too. But Nick Branson!

He wasn't the comfortable type.

She let out a puff of air. Her restful, relaxing vacation was quickly vanishing. She'd only met Nick twice before, first at the wedding and then at a Christmas family get-together. They'd hardly said boo to each other but those encounters had been enough for her to know that the man made her feel off-balanced. Tongue-tied. Self-conscious.

Whoa boy.

"Well, if you're sure," she said waveringly. She had to remember this was her sister's anniversary. She couldn't spoil it, no matter how fiercely her shyness was raring up inside her.

"It will be fun," Jolene insisted.

"Yeah," Larry said, joining his wife. He wrapped her in his arms and gave her a hug. "It will be a trip none of us will ever forget."

Copper didn't doubt that.

Seven days trapped on a ship with Nick Branson. Whoa boy.

* * * * *

He wasn't going to make it, Copper thought with relief. She turned the page of her book and reached for her strawberry daiquiri. Ahhhh. That was more like it. Warm sunshine, a pool and no unnecessary stress.

She savored the rum in the drink and gradually felt herself start to unwind. She'd been tense ever since Jolene had broken the news that Nick was going to come but he'd missed the boat. Literally.

She couldn't help but be a little glad, although her feeling of disappointment was surprisingly strong. For Larry's sake, probably. No. Not probably. Of course it was for Larry. Larry and his golfing. What else could it be?

The horn gave another blast signaling their four o'clock departure and she glanced towards the promenade. Jolene and Larry were waving goodbye to people on shore. She'd thought about joining them but she'd already scoped out her place by the pool.

And it was a good one.

Now that she knew the trip was going to be uneventful — relatively, at least — she could relax. Sitting up, she stripped off her cover-up and dropped it on the deck beside her lounger. Blissfully, she sat back and let the sun's rays warm her. After being wrapped up in layers of clothes for so many months, it was a treat to wear a bikini and not feel a chill.

"This is the life," she said under her breath.

Returning to her book, she found her place. She'd just begun to fall back into the story when the lounge chair next to her screeched as somebody opened it to the reclining position. Uneasiness tightened the back of her neck. Why did people do that? There were a dozen open chairs around the pool. Did this person have to sit so close, invading her space?

The encroacher sat down and self-consciousness pinched at her. It wasn't that she was ashamed of her body; she worked hard to stay in shape. She just didn't feel comfortable having people look at her.

And they *always* looked at her.

Automatically, she reached for her cover-up. She stopped midway, though, when her gaze stuck on something unexpected.

A dragon.

She loved dragons and the man who'd sat down beside her had the most amazing tattoo of one on his right calf. It wasn't a bad calf too, come to think of it. She tried not to stare but she couldn't help herself. A bad boy and a bad-ass dragon. She nearly licked her lips. The creature was twisting menacingly and its tail was flailing wildly. Best of all, the mythical beast was breathing fire out its nostrils right towards the man's knee.

In a word, it was awesome.

"Hi, Copper."

In a word, it was Nick.

Copper sat up so quickly her book tumbled onto her lap. When she realized it was the only thing that stood between her and his gaze, she lurched for it before it could hit the deck. Clutching it to her chest, she looked at him with incredulity. "You made it."

"I did."

She waited for him to elaborate but Mr. Effusive he wasn't. His dark gaze simply watched her lazily.

No, lazy wasn't right. She shifted on her lounger. There was nothing lazy about this man. She could feel his energy coming at her in waves. He just didn't waste it on talking.

"Oh. Well…" She struggled to find something to say. "If you're looking for Jo and Larry, they're over there throwing confetti."

"I figured they'd be nearby."

He glanced towards the spot where she'd gestured but his gaze eventually drifted back to her. She felt it land on her like a warm spotlight and her heart began to pound a little harder.

With all these people clustered around… With his own brother standing not forty feet away…

He'd spotted her first.

The question was out before she could stop it. "How did you find *me*?"

She never should have asked. Never.

That warm, lazy gaze started a slow tour down her body. Over her breasts, along her stomach, across the low-slung bikini bottoms and down her legs. It stopped on her pink toenails before meandering back upward. By the time it landed on her hair, she'd melted into a useless lump.

"How do you think?" he asked softly.

Her hair. He'd seen her hair.

Copper felt the heat of embarrassment start in her neck. Color rose upwards, betraying her. Quickly, she lifted her book before he could see her cheeks turn bright red. "I'm glad you made it," she mumbled.

"Me too." He casually tossed his towel across his lap before slipping on his sunglasses and lying back.

To anyone watching, they must have looked comfortable as they sat sunning quietly side by side. Companionable. Copper felt nothing like that. Inside, her heart, lungs and stomach were tying themselves into one big knot.

She didn't know how people could look on timidity as if it were a weakness. Something frail or fragile. In her experience, the emotion was ferocious as a lion. She could feel it clawing inside her now, making her distinctly ill at ease.

He was too good-looking. Too chiseled. Too male.

She stared fixedly at her book, trying to rein in her natural introversion. When she realized she was holding the novel upside down, she quickly turned it around. She threw a glance Nick's way. If he noticed, he didn't say anything.

If he noticed. Right. Nothing got by the guy.

She wanted to reach for her cover-up. Instead, she reached for her drink.

Ten minutes later, they were still sitting that way—her on the same page, him working on his already incredible tan.

On his incredible body.

With that incredibly sexy tattoo.

He seemed totally at ease with the silence but Copper was about to go mad. It was like this every time she got around him. At the wedding, he'd sat next to her at the bride and groom's table. Always quiet. Ever watchful. He'd hardly said anything to her but when the clasp on her bracelet had given loose, he'd swiped it off the floor before she'd even noticed it had fallen.

She'd definitely noticed when he'd put it back on her wrist though.

That had been the first time her heart had officially stutter-stepped.

Nothing had ever come of it though. Not then, and not at the Christmas potluck in December either.

She ran her finger over the corner of the page, trying to smooth a crinkle. If only he'd say something! The silence around them was churning, drumming in her ears and sending her blood pressure sky-high.

"Were you able to find somebody to cover for you on such quick notice?" she blurted.

His head turned slowly.

"For your karate school," she said inanely.

"It's called a dojo." He shrugged and the muscles in his chest moved sinuously. "I've got a couple of brown belts that can sub for me. It will be good for them."

"Dojo," she said, trying the word out. She tore her gaze away from his chest only to fixate again on the dragon at his calf. The knot in her chest squeezed tighter. "So you're the master, right? The... What is it? Ninja?"

He waited for a long moment but didn't laugh. He seemed to be looking at her contemplatively. "Sensei."

"Oh," she said. "I've heard of that."

Looking down, she swiped a drop of perspiration off her leg. She didn't know what else to ask. The conversation she'd managed with him so far was already an accomplishment.

He slipped his sunglasses onto his head and she wished he hadn't. Feeling his dark gaze upon her was one thing. Seeing that dark stare was another.

And all his concentration was on her.

She gripped her book to her chest more tightly, suddenly wishing that the tiny paperback were a full-sized hardback. She sat frozen as his gaze ran over her curves once again.

"You keep in shape," he observed. "Have you ever tried any of the martial arts?"

She bit her lip. "Does kickboxing count?"

He tilted his head. "It's a start."

"It keeps me warm," she admitted.

"Warm?"

"The Twin Cities get cold in the wintertime."

Something sparked in his eyes. "Ever think of moving back to Miami?"

Copper's mouth went dry.

"Nick! Hey, there you are. We were looking for you."

Slowly, he sat back in his chair. "Hey, Jolene."

Copper blushed. Of course. He meant to be closer to her family.

She sighed as her sister walked behind Nick's chair and ruffled his hair. Once again, she felt that twinge of envy. How could Jo be so easy with him? She'd managed to get a tiny conversation started but Jolene had always been the outgoing one, the social butterfly. Copper suddenly wished she could be more like her sister, more natural with people.

More *uninhibited*.

Jolene plopped down at the foot of her lounger and Copper tucked her legs against her chest. Her sister was so full of energy, she was practically bouncing.

"I'm so excited about this trip," Jolene gushed. "It's going to be twice as fun as last year."

"Hey," Larry protested. He nudged his wife as he pulled up another lounge chair and sat. "I think my manhood is offended."

"Sorry, honey." Jolene smiled, sharing a private joke. "It will be fun in different ways."

"You can say that again," Larry joked, wiggling an imaginary cigar at the corner of his mouth.

She giggled. "Pervert."

"Wild woman."

Copper felt herself shrinking. She knew the playful banter was all in fun but she was sitting right here! And Nick was right there! A blush started to rise up in her cheeks again. She had to make them stop before they got worse—because she knew from experience that they would.

"So have you two decided what you're doing for your anniversary tonight?" she said, hoping to change the subject. "Do you want Nick and me to make ourselves scarce?"

The idea was tempting. A night alone in her cabin with room service would give her time to figure out how to best handle the next six days. She hadn't been prepared for a weeklong vacation with Nick Branson. Just spending the last fifteen minutes alone with him had exhausted her. She needed to recharge.

"No, don't do that!" Jolene said, quickly twisting around. She tucked her leg underneath her as she bent over for her purse. "We found a dinner show we want to see. You two have got to come with us. It sounds like a hoot."

Copper's shoulders sagged. "Are you sure?" she asked, looking at Larry. "You don't want to be alone?"

A grin was already lighting his face. "The more the merrier." He winked at his brother. "Besides, I'm hoping to learn a few new tricks."

Copper felt a warning tingle at the back of her neck. "What are you talking about?"

"It's a hypnotist with a twist," Jolene said breathlessly. She finally found the brochure she was looking for. She whipped it open and thrust it out where both Nick and Copper could see it. Gleefully, she jiggled it side-to-side. "Erotic Hypnotic Show, here we come!"

Chapter 2

Copper played nervously with her purse as they waited for the doors of the dinner theater to open. The adults-only show seemed to be a popular choice for the evening's entertainment. The line stretched down the corridor but nobody seemed to mind. The newlyweds were cuddling together, lost in their own world. A group of single men were laughing at raunchy jokes and guessing at what they might see. The gray-hairs were more subdued but even they had a special sparkle in their eyes.

She just couldn't seem to get into the spirit of things.

Erotic Hypnotic. What did that mean? Just how far did people go? What did the hypnotist make them do?

"These things are so funny," Jolene said as she checked her look in a mirror. She snapped the compact shut and stuffed it into her purse. "We went to one when we first started dating, although it was just a regular hypnosis show. It's amazing how people can go under like that."

She snapped her fingers and Copper flinched.

"Some go under," Larry agreed. "You can tell which ones are just playing along."

"Yeah, those I can do without. It's the ones who slip under total control that just fascinate me."

Larry grinned. "Remember that librarian who started barking like a dog?"

Jolene's laughter tinkled down the corridor. "Tonight, we might get to see one humping like a dog."

Oh God.

Copper pressed herself closer against the wall. This just wasn't her sort of thing. Maybe she should play sick and go back to her room. It wouldn't be that much of a stretch. Her stomach was already doing weird flips.

She felt somebody touch her waist softly.

"What's wrong?" Nick asked.

His dark gaze was settled firmly on her face. Her stomach gave another flip, this time with a half-twist. She glanced towards Larry and Jolene but they were still chuckling and sharing memories. She looked back to Nick. "It's nothing."

"Tell me."

Was she that obvious? She twisted her purse more tightly in her grip but finally sighed. "It's just that I always get picked for these audience participation things."

One of his eyebrows rose.

Lifting her hand, she twirled a strand of her hair around her finger.

Understanding dawned on his face and his hand moved on her waist in what could only be described as a caress. "We don't have to go. You and I could go down to the Italian buffet."

She went still. The Erotic Hypnotic show or dinner alone with Nick Branson?

Her bashful side screamed. *What kind of choice was that?*

Jolene's laughter rang out like a bell and Copper's head dipped. "We can't. They've been looking forward to this all day."

"So? Nobody's stopping them from going."

The double doors opened and the dinner guests began to trail in. Automatically, Copper began moving with the crowd. "It's their anniversary. I don't want to spoil it."

His fingers started to tighten on her waist but he dropped his touch and fell into step beside her. "We'll sit at the back," he promised.

The assurance made her feel somewhat better—although his understanding helped more than anything. Copper was touched when he overruled Larry's choice of a table and moved them farther away from the stage.

"Okay?" he asked as he held out a chair for her.

"This is fine." Better than she'd expected. She felt some of her apprehension ease as she sat down. Nick took the seat next to her. When he pulled his chair closer to the table, she felt his pants leg unexpectedly brush against her shin. The unassuming touch was intimate. Cozy.

Goose bumps popped up on her skin. Had she just associated Nick with coziness?

Was she actually relaxing around him?

The moment she realized it, the comfort level disappeared. Had she forgotten what the show would bring? How was she supposed to sit in her chair beside this man while lewd and outrageous things were going on all around them? He noticed everything. Would he be watching her to find out what she found funny? Or embarrassing?

Her stomach did a double flip. Or sexy?

Oh God.

She glanced at her watch. Two hours. She just had to make it through the next two hours.

* * * * *

Nick felt Copper's tension increase when the lights went down. She'd done her best to hide her uneasiness over the course of dinner. She'd smiled when Larry had made jokes and nodded as Jolene had told yet another one of her stories. She'd even surprised the couple by pulling an anniversary gift out of her purse. Yet underneath her calm exterior, he'd felt her nervous energy running on high.

He was only starting to realize how much she did that.

"Oh goody," Jolene said when the show started. She scooted her chair closer to her husband so she wouldn't have to crane her neck to see the stage. Reaching across the table, she slid her cheesecake so it was in front of her.

Copper pushed hers away.

Nick stared at the lonely slice of dessert.

She was shy.

It hit him like a knuckle punch.

He didn't know why he hadn't seen it before. The blush on her cheeks… The hesitancy in her gaze… The tremble in her hands… The two times he'd met her, he hadn't been able to tell if she was quiet, stuck-up or just didn't like him.

But she was shy.

That put a whole new spin on things.

The hypnotist started the show with a few harmless parlor tricks, and Copper's nervous attention zeroed in on the man. Nick's protective instincts surged right along with her.

Yes, this put an entirely new spin on things.

He eased back into his chair, watching the beauty to his right more than the performer on the stage. The hypnotist knew his stuff, though; Nick had to give him that. He had just the type of easy-going attitude to draw in the crowd and make them trust him. Once he had their trust, though, he used it.

"Let's get some volunteers up here," the man said.

A spotlight came up and slowly started panning over the crowd. Nick felt Copper's nervous energy creep up into the danger zone but he didn't know what to do about it. He concentrated on channeling the negative feelings away from the table and a man down front with a bad comb-over was the first picked. A middle-aged woman and one of the loud single guys were next. The spotlight started to swing their way, though, and Copper cringed.

He nearly reached out to hold her hand before the light skimmed right on by them. "See?" he said, leaning close to her. "Nothing to worry —"

"Hold it," the hypnotist called. "Back it up. Right there."

The light was blinding.

"What about you, gorgeous? The one who's shiny as a new penny?"

"Oh! Copper, that's you," Jolene said with delight.

"All right." Larry started clapping. "Go on up there."

People at the tables next to them were smiling and nodding their encouragement. None of them seemed to see the look on Copper's face. She looked like a deer caught in the headlights.

"No," Nick said. This time he did reach out. He placed his hand over hers on the table. Her fingers felt like ice. "No," he repeated, this time towards the stage. "Pick someone else."

"Oh, come on," Jolene pleaded.

Copper looked mutely at her sister.

"For me?"

Nick couldn't believe it. Did Jolene not see what this was doing to her?

"She doesn't have to," he said firmly.

"It's...it's all right." Copper nervously licked her lips before they turned upwards in a forced smile. "It will be fun."

Fun as a root canal if the stiffness in her spine meant anything.

She pushed her chair back and the applause rose. Nick watched helplessly as she walked to the stage. The hypnotist met her at the bottom of the stairs and offered her his hand. He led her to the last chair where she sat and crossed her legs demurely.

Nick had never felt so powerless in his life.

She'd been right. He couldn't believe it. Her hair did draw attention—wanted or not.

He watched her as she sat under the hot spotlight. She looked so classy up there. So sweet. And that dress. The close-fitting green number with the tiny shoulder straps had nearly brought him to his knees when he'd met her in the hallway outside their rooms.

At least he was making progress. She'd wiped his feet right out from underneath him when he'd caught her in that skimpy blue bikini on the deck this afternoon. There was a reason he'd had to throw a towel over his lap.

But he was beginning to notice things other than her looks. Important things—like the way she was clutching the arms of that chair.

It was the same way she'd clutched that book beside the pool.

"Son of a bitch," he muttered, looking back at the hypnotist. The man already had the first three volunteers under. If that con artist so much as harmed a hair on her pretty head, he was going to find out just how much pain an eighth-degree black belt could dole out.

Nick felt the muscles at the back of his neck go taut as the man started talking to Copper.

"Your eyelids are getting heavy," the man crooned. His voice was soothing and encouraging. "You can feel a weight holding down your arms and those luscious legs."

The land shark.

"And sleep."

The other volunteers had relaxed at the word but nothing like Copper. She went under deeply. She slumped heavily in her chair and her head lolled to the side. She lay against the backrest as if she would sleep for hours.

Nick tensed, ready to go to her aid, but the hypnotist just smiled at the crowd and returned to the first participant.

Nick's mind raced. He couldn't let her be embarrassed. He wouldn't.

Something went flying off the stage and the crowd began hooting. Comb-over man had stripped off his shirt and was performing like a male stripper. The funny thing was that the guy wasn't bad. Hell, he was good. Some women at the front table stood up and began to gyrate with him. One was even waving a dollar bill.

Nick's gaze locked back onto Copper.

Don't even think about it, he telepathically warned the hypnotist.

The lights dimmed and the erotic element of the show increased. Giggles twittered through the crowd but curiosity was starting to come into play. Jolene was into it. She was absolutely delighted when she got her humping librarian — although under the spell, the woman admitted she taught tenth grade.

Once the hypnotist learned that, all bets were off. The rowdy single guy was next. It took nearly nothing to convince him that he was hot for teacher. The crowd was in stitches as the hypnotist had them dirty dancing all over the stage.

Nick felt a bead of sweat roll down his back when the man finally approached Copper. *Be careful,* he warned. *Be very careful.*

"And now for Gorgeous here," the man said. He rubbed his chin as he considered what to do. He turned to the crowd. "What do you say we play a game? Find out who this little beauty thinks is hot?"

Three of the single guy's friends were instantly on their feet.

"No, no," the man said, waving them off. "She gets to decide."

A catcall sounded from the table next to them and Nick nearly took a roundhouse kick at the man.

The hypnotist crouched down in front of Copper.

"Can you hear me, honey?" he asked in that singsong voice that was grating on Nick's last nerve.

"Yes," she said, not lifting her head.

"Is it warm up here under the spotlight?"

"Yes."

"Do you want to get off the stage?"

"Yes."

The hypnotist nodded. "Good, because I have an assignment for you."

"Okay."

"Did you see all the men who came to dinner tonight?"

"Yes."

"Were there any that you found good-looking?"

"Yes."

Nick's antenna went up.

"Good. Here's what I want you to do. When you hear the word 'gorgeous', you're to go find the best-looking one of the bunch."

"Best-looking," Copper murmured.

"I want you to find the sexiest man in the room, the one who makes you so horny you don't care who's watching."

"Over here, baby," somebody called.

The hypnotist waved the heckler off. "Once you find him, you're to show him just how aroused you are. You do and say whatever feels good until I tell you to sleep—or until you orgasm."

He winked at the crowd. "Sometimes I don't get there in time."

Laughter spread around the room in a wave.

"Do you understand?" he asked, directing the question back at Copper.

"Yes."

With a broad smile, the hypnotist bounded across the stage and down to the bottom of the stairs. "Okay. Come and get me, *Gorgeous*."

For a moment, Copper just sat there.

"She's not going to do it," Larry whispered.

He barely got the words out of his mouth before she slowly rose to her feet.

"Uh oh," Jolene said. When her sister started walking across the stage, she clamped her hand over her husband's forearm. "Maybe this wasn't such a good idea."

No kidding.

Nick's full concentration was on Copper, as was every other heterosexual male's in the place. A few sexually ambivalent ones too. He watched as she accepted the hypnotist's hand as she walked down the stairs. The look on the man's face was hopeful but she passed right on by him.

The crowd laughed at his comical disappointment.

The laughter quickly died. It was replaced with a heavy feeling of anticipation as Copper slowly surveyed the room.

Nick noticed intuitively that she was moving differently. More confidently. Her chin was held high, her back was straight and her chest was out. The sway of her hips, though, nearly caused one elderly man to hyperventilate.

She was a woman on the hunt.

Eyes that watched her became heavy-lidded. Mouths went dry and more than one man shifted in his chair as his cock stirred to attention.

Nick's was past stirring. He was so rock hard, he could hardly breathe.

"Larry, what do we do?" Jolene whispered.

Larry's verbalization skills had suddenly disappeared.

Breaths caught as Copper found her mark. She started moving across the room, not quickly, but definitely with purpose. The intrigue thickened and eagerness lit the place like a fuse.

Nick tensed, ready to stop whatever was about to detonate.

He couldn't move, though, when she turned her sights on him.

"She's not under," Jolene said with a heavy sigh as her sister headed to their table. She started to pick up her purse. "Let's get her out of here."

This time it was Larry who caught his wife by the arm.

Nick's pulse was pounding in his temples when Copper came to a stop directly in front of him. The look on her face was sultry. *Aroused.* She might be entranced but there was clear determination in her eyes.

She knew who he was and she knew what she wanted.

Watching him intently, she began working her close-fitting skirt up her legs.

"Oh my God!" Jolene gasped.

"Holy shit!" Larry said, his capacity for speech returning.

Nick was rooted to his chair when he saw black lace panties. He couldn't tear his gaze from them as Copper sexily straddled his legs and lowered herself onto his lap. Convulsively, his hands came up and clamped onto her waist. "Copper," he said through gritted teeth.

She leaned forward, rubbing her hands against his chest. Her cheek brushed against his as she whispered into his ear, "I like your dragon."

Nick's cock nearly burst through the zipper of his pants when she nipped his earlobe. God, how much was a man supposed to withstand?

A growl emanated from somewhere deep in his chest.

He couldn't deny himself.

He couldn't deny her.

Fisting his hand in her glorious hair, he pulled her back from where she was nibbling on his neck. Slanting his mouth across hers, he kissed her. He kissed her hot and hard. When she boldly met his tongue with her own, he jerked her closer.

She melted against him.

Nick felt his control vaporize. Her skin was soft but her muscles were toned. He slid his hand up her naked thigh and cupped her bottom. The skimpy panties were in his way. Backtracking, he slid his hand underneath the fabric and cupped her bare ass.

God, she felt good.

"Nick," she groaned as she pressed her breasts against his chest. Her fingers were threading through his hair. One trailed down his arm, measuring the strength in his biceps before sliding over to his waist.

Nick couldn't get enough of the feel of her — or the feel of her touching him. When her hand tickled his belly and started venturing down, though, he accidentally bit her lip.

Her gasp of pleasure finally turned on a switch inside his brain.

Or was it the gasp of the crowd?

Suddenly, he remembered where they were. Onboard a ship. At a dinner show. With too many leering onlookers.

"Copper," he said, catching her hand before all hope was lost. "Wake up."

She merely smiled seductively and thrust her hips against him.

Nick jerked so hard, he nearly bucked her off. "Copper," he said more firmly. This time, he caught her by the waist so she couldn't try that trick again. "Come on, honey. Snap out of it."

She threw her head back and ground her bottom into the hand that he couldn't seem to remove from her ass. Leaning back into him, she licked the sensitive spot behind his ear.

Nick came out of his chair so fast, it toppled over behind them.

"You," he barked at the hypnotist. "Bring her out of it."

Copper had wrapped herself around him like a clinging vine. Holding her close, he jerkily tugged her skirt down over her hips. Her hands were busy caressing his back. He caught them before they dropped too low and totally destroyed his determination.

For someone trained in maintaining control, his hold on it was tenuous.

"Remove the fucking spell," he barked at the hypnotist, who was rushing to their table.

"Calm," the man said. "You need to stay calm."

He wanted calm? Nick would show him calm.

Copper had just slipped one of her legs between his when the man got too close. With one hand, Nick had him flat on his back on their table.

Jolene and Larry jumped to their feet.

"Fix it," Nick roared. "Now!"

"Sleep," the man hissed, trying to catch his breath.

Copper didn't hear him.

"Sleep!"

She slumped so quickly, Nick was glad she was already in his arms. He caught her but she was like a rag doll. Bending his knees, he swept her up into his arms. "Wake her up," he said flatly. "Make it right."

The man had finally made it to an upright, seated position. He rubbed his throat as he looked at Copper lying so helplessly in Nick's embrace. "It was all in fun."

The look in Nick's eyes had him quickly scrambling off the table.

"I'm going to count backwards from five," the man said in a rush. He stopped to get his voice under control. "When I reach one, you will open your eyes. You'll feel alert and refreshed."

He glanced at Nick and swallowed hard. "Five, four, three, two, one."

Nick felt Copper's consciousness return. Her limp body slowly stretched. Her eyelids fluttered and then her brown gaze was looking up at him trustingly.

Until she realized where she was.

Her brow knitted. Slowly, her head turned. When she met dozens of rapt stares, the color drained from her cheeks. "Oh. No."

That was it. Moving around the table, Nick started heading towards the door.

"Oh God," Jolene muttered. "Grab her purse."

Larry swiped the purse from under Copper's abandoned chair and they were off after them.

Nick nudged the door open with his hip and carried Copper out into the empty hallway. She'd buried her face against his shoulder but the moment she realized they were in the clear, she pulled away from him.

"Put me down," she whispered shakily.

"Are you sure?" he asked. He didn't know what the aftereffects of hypnosis were. "Do you think your legs will hold you?"

"Put me down!"

The flare of impatience was the first unadulterated emotion he'd ever gotten from her. He liked it. Quickly, he put her back on her own two feet.

"Copper," Jolene said as she burst into the corridor. She pulled her sister into a hug. "I'm so sorry. I never should have suggested this."

"It's not your fault," Copper said quietly. She kept her face averted and busied herself with smoothing her twisted skirt. She was doing her best to hide it but Nick could tell she was mortified.

He could practically see the way she was turning in on herself.

Jolene helped her straighten her dress and handed her her purse. "Are you okay?" she asked.

He stood quietly to the side as temper surged inside him. He should have taken the guy out. Plain and simple.

"Are *you* okay?" Larry asked.

He threw his brother a cool look.

"Do you remember what happened?" Jolene asked, brushing back Copper's hair.

His look snapped back in time to see her face flush bright red.

Jolene's voice dropped to a whisper. "Why didn't you tell me you liked him?"

"I need some air," Copper rasped. Hastily, she pushed her sister aside and headed towards the doors that led on deck. Her steps were jagged and uncoordinated, as if she'd lost her sea legs.

Jolene started after her but Nick stopped her with a hand to her shoulder. "I'll go."

"But…"

Larry wrapped his arm around his wife's waist. "Let him talk to her."

Understanding lit her eyes. Still, she glanced with concern towards the door where her sister had disappeared.

"Go enjoy your anniversary," Nick said, already turning. "I'll take care of her."

He found Copper standing just outside the double doors, holding onto the ship railing as if it were the only thing keeping her upright. He took a deep breath. He wasn't good at these types of things but his mind couldn't get around one simple fact.

She'd chosen him.

Out of all the men in that room, she hadn't even hesitated. Shy little Copper had set her sights on him and come gunning.

His hands clenched into fists. He hoped like hell this stupid prank hadn't spoiled whatever chance he might have had, because it was no secret now that he had a thing for her too — a thing that was currently aching so bad, it was making him grit his teeth.

But there she was, looking as if she could die from embarrassment.

God, he hoped he didn't screw this up even more than it already was.

Gathering his control, he quietly approached her. When she didn't pull away, he bent over and leaned his forearms against the railing next to her. He'd just be here for her, he decided. Hell, the last thing she probably needed right now anyway was words.

She stood stiffly at his side, her tension winding tighter and tighter. "Don't you ever say anything?" she finally snapped.

Okay, maybe she did need words.

He glanced at her patiently. "I'm more of a man of action."

Her eyes widened but then her gaze skittered away. Obviously, they'd established that.

"How do you feel?" he asked.

She ran a shaky hand through her hair. "Humiliated."

"Other than that. Any side effects?"

"I'm fine. Good." She shrugged as if she didn't want to admit it. "My body is all light and airy, but I don't understand how I can feel this way."

Letting out repressed emotions could do that. He doubted she wanted to hear that though.

"I can't believe I did that!" she said, flinging her hand back towards the theater.

"You had help."

"Yes, but I didn't put up much of a fight when he put me under."

"I didn't mean him."

Her face turned practically crimson. Discomfited, she stared at her feet. "I'm sorry," she whispered. "About... you know."

"*Don't.*"

The irritation in his voice surprised her so much, her timid gaze flashed straight up to his.

"I wasn't exactly pushing you away. You're a beautiful woman, Copper." She started in surprised and he looked out over the dark water. The sky was clear and the moon reflected off the ocean's soft waves. "If anyone should apologize, it's me. I should have stopped it earlier."

Her mouth opened and closed three times but she never decided on what to say. Nick could feel her staring at him but he wasn't going to go any further than that. Let her figure it out.

They fell into a silence that somehow seemed even more intimate. They stood quietly side by side, each very aware of the other's presence. He could hear her soft breaths. He could see the way her toes curled in her flimsy little sandals. With the soft Caribbean breeze and the star-filled sky, the ambience was clear. It was a night meant for lovers.

And secrets.

Hers, unfortunately, had been let out of the bag.

"So you like my dragon, huh?" he asked softly.

She glanced at him worriedly but relaxed when she saw his smile. "I collect them," she admitted.

Ah, hell. Now why'd she have to go and do that?

He looked at her helplessly, his hard-on raring back to life.

She bit her lip when she realized the implications of what she'd said. "I'm sorry," she mumbled once again.

He caught her by the wrist before she could back away. "Don't do that," he said gruffly. "You don't have to be shy with me."

An older couple strolled by just then, oblivious to the tumult going on around them. The woman adjusted her shawl as she laid her head on her husband's shoulder. "Oh, Stan. Look at the stars tonight. Aren't they *gorgeous*?"

The moment the word was spoken, Copper's entire demeanor changed.

"Who's shy?" she asked. Tilting her head to the side, she let her hair sway provocatively. Seeing she had his attention, she stepped closer to him.

Nick stood frozen as she wrapped her arms about his neck and lifted herself up on her painted tiptoes. Her kiss was rocking him back on his feet when he realized what had happened.

She'd been triggered again.

Chapter 3

Copper wanted him.

Wanted him. Wanted him. Wanted him.

She pressed her body against his tightly and felt a hardness nudge against her belly. A thrill shot through her. He wanted her too.

She'd always wondered. *Hoped.*

Excitement gushed through her veins and she boldly reached for the zipper of his pants. She had to have him. She didn't care how. She didn't care who saw. She just needed him to ease the ache that was driving her stark-raving mad.

"Whoa," he said, quickly catching her hands. "Copper, quit it."

Quit? Was he kidding?

"No," she said, leaning in to nibble on his neck. She'd learned that he had a sensitive spot behind his ear.

It should get him going.

She smiled as she nuzzled against him. She liked it when he got going. She loved shaking up that steely control of his. Because when he lost it, he was like that fire-breathing dragon he wore like a badge of honor.

Just thinking about that tattoo made her wet.

"Oh, hell," he said, trying to twist his neck away. "Don't do that."

She'd felt him shudder though. The little feeling of power turned her on even more. "Don't you like it?"

"You know I like it." He caught her hands behind her back but that just made things more interesting. She shimmied against him and he cursed. "Damn it, what did that guy say? Sleep, Copper. Sleep!"

Who wanted to sleep?

She wanted to make love.

"Take me, Nick," she whispered. "I want you inside me."

Goose bumps popped up on the side of his neck and she brazenly licked her tongue over them. His arms tightened on her so swiftly, he lifted her right up onto her tiptoes.

"Mmm," she sighed in pleasure. That was more like it.

"Honey, snap out of it," he said, breathing hard. "This has got to stop."

"No, it doesn't. It feels too good to stop."

"I know but your mind's not clear. That con man didn't get the spell removed." Thinking quickly, he looked towards the door that led to the theater. "Shit, I can't take you back in there like this."

"Take me any way you want," she said suggestively.

He looked at her, his dark eyes blazing. "You don't know what you're saying."

"Yes, I do."

She was very clear on the matter. She needed him. Badly. Her breasts begged for his mouth and her pussy ached to be filled. It didn't matter how—his tongue, his fingers, his cock— she'd take whatever she could get.

But only as long as she was with *him*. "Please," she begged, letting her desperation shine through.

"We can't," he said, his voice strained.

"We have to." The need was getting unbearable. She couldn't stand here so close to him and not have him touch her. She needed to do what made her feel good and this didn't feel good. She slipped one of her legs between his. Not even trying to be discreet, she rocked her hips forward and began to ride his leg.

"Christ! Copper!"

She ground her mound against his rock-hard thigh and cried out softly. Oh, that felt good. Really good. She thrust herself back and forth against him, loving the firm friction against her sensitive pussy. It burned hot, making her feel like she was about to go up in flames.

"Baby, you're killing me." He swung her away from the door, hiding her with his body. Impulsively, he gave her a quick shake. "What's the problem? Does he have to be the one to say it? *Sleep!*"

"Only if you sleep with me." Her brow furrowed in confusion. Why was he making this so difficult? She had an assignment. She didn't know what to do if he wouldn't help her. Her head began to hurt. "Nick, I'm aroused," she said bluntly.

"I can tell," he muttered. "And you're not going to stop until he tells you to…"

He went still as comprehension suddenly hit. "Or until you orgasm."

With the word, Copper creamed so hard she worried that she'd wet his pants.

"Yes." She wanted him to make her come. She wanted to fly.

"Ah, hell." Pained, he looked again towards the theater. "What am I supposed to do?"

"Me!" The need to be with him was shredding her. She rode his leg harder and slid one hand down his heaving chest. Frantically, she cupped her hand over his raging erection. "Do me."

Their gazes connected and the night air sparked.

"Please," she whispered.

He took one deep breath. Then another.

"This isn't right," he said, his voice stern.

"Yes, it is." She squeezed his big cock and ran her thumb over its thick head. She hated all the clothes between them. "You're the one."

His hips rolled and sweat broke out on his forehead. The look he gave her was so intense, it felt as if he was looking into her very soul.

She let him look his fill.

Whatever he saw must have convinced him—or pushed him past his limits.

His head suddenly swiveled towards the bow and then the stern. It was darker and less traveled. "This way," he said, sliding his arm around her waist.

Copper hurried alongside him, her legs shaking with excitement. His strides were long and fast and it was difficult to keep up. The moment he rounded the corner onto the stern, though, he stopped. Turning into her, he pushed her back against the bulkhead.

Her breath caught when he stepped up close, his hot body leaning into hers.

She'd finally unleashed that fire-breathing dragon.

"Nick," she whispered.

His mouth came down hard, dominant and rapacious. His tongue swept deeply, rasping across hers. The contact was so intimate, so sensual, Copper shuddered. Molten heat exploded inside her and she raked her nails down his back.

Oh God. Yes!

This was what she'd wanted. This was what she'd needed.

Their bodies undulated together as the kiss went on and on, wild and voracious. There was nothing tender or seductive about the hunger. It just kept building, demanding more. When she felt her skirt riding high on her thighs, she realized he was gathering it in his fists, lifting it out of his way.

"Yes," she gasped, tearing her mouth from his. "Hurry."

She had to touch him.

Working her hands between them, she began tearing at his shirt. Somehow, she got it off him. It dropped to the deck beside them as his hands went to the back of her dress. The bodice sagged as he tugged down the zipper. He didn't even get it halfway unzipped before he began attacking the clasp of her strapless bra.

Copper felt herself spiraling upwards when he caught her bare breasts. The feel of his work-hardened touch was exhilarating. Knowing how dangerous those hands were, yet feeling the pleasure they gave her was beyond seductive.

Her nipples stabbed into his palms. She couldn't take any more foreplay. She was ready for him. Reaching down with anxious hands, she caught the tab of his zipper again.

His fingers tightened on her sensitized breasts. "Don't tempt me, honey. You're the one who needs to come, not me."

Hurt flashed through her. Didn't he want her? Of course he did. She thrust her hand inside his pants and caught his stiff cock. "That's a lie."

His hips jerked out of control and she banged back against the bulkhead hard.

"God damn it!"

He pulled back from her and she got her first taste of how fast the man could move. Using his foot, he tugged over a lounge chair that somebody had moved away from the pool. Before she could fathom what he was going to do, he flipped her.

"Ah!" she gasped. When the world righted itself, she found her butt in the chair with her skirt high around her waist.

Wide-eyed, she gaped up at him.

She'd never been so incredibly turned on in her life.

"Don't look at me like that," he warned. His hands opened and closed as he fought for some semblance of control.

At last, he gave one last precautionary look around the darkened stern of the ship. Convinced they were alone, he came down onto the chair with her. Pressing one knee onto the foot of her lounger, he reached for her panties.

"These just about put me over the edge back in that show," he confessed, his stare hot.

Her belly quivered as he traced the lace along her abdomen. He looked so predatory above her with the stars at his back.

Turning his wrist, he purposefully pushed his hand between her legs and cupped her pussy. "There," he crooned as her hips swung right off the chair. "Is that what you need, baby?"

"Oh!" she gasped. He was cupping her tightly. Possessively. And his thumb! She went a little lightheaded. It was sliding up and down, pressing the fabric into her slit and making it soak up her wetness. He did it over and over again until her clit was a hard pebble underneath the black lace.

She watched, heart thudding, as his thumb crept nearer to the sensitive bud. When he deliberately prodded it, her hips rolled.

"Looks like it," he said.

He fisted his hand in the crotch of her panties and began tugging them downwards. The garment bit into her hips. Breathing so hard she was almost whimpering, Copper hooked her thumbs under the constricting bands and helped him strip her bare.

He groaned when he saw the curls covering her pussy. "I'd wondered."

He let out a puff of air and softly petted her. "What's your real name, honey?"

Her name? Did it matter? "Connie."

"Copper fits you better," he decided. Opening his hand wide across her breastbone, he pressed her back against the chair.

Copper watched him, wide-eyed and breathless. The seatback was locked halfway into the upright position. She'd be able to see anything he did to her. Anything and everything.

Her breasts began to heave as he slid his hands between her legs.

"Easy," he crooned. Watching her closely, he opened her. He spread her thighs wide and gently draped them over the arms of the sturdy chair.

A flash of shyness unexpectedly jumbled her head. The position was too brazen. Too personal. Her chest tightened and her muscles instinctively tensed. Something familiar inside her told her to hide, to shrink back from his intimate gaze.

She roughly pushed the feeling of embarrassment away.

Being with him this way felt good. Everything with him felt good.

She couldn't stop.

"Touch me," she begged.

"With pleasure," he sighed, admitting defeat.

She lurched in surprise, though, when his head dipped.

He took one long deliberate lick and she cried out harshly. An answering sound escaped from the back of his throat. Hurriedly, he scooted down farther on the chair. Settling more comfortably between her spread legs, he began eating her out with a passion that was almost insane.

Copper's hand fisted in his soft dark hair. "Oh! Ohhhh!"

Every muscle in her body tensed as he licked and prodded and licked again. Her eyelids drooped but she couldn't tear her gaze away from what he was doing to her. She'd never seen anything so sensual in her life.

"Ah!" she cried when his hands unexpectedly returned to her breasts. His fingers were hard and demanding. They tugged at her aching nipples as his tongue kept plunging deeply, lapping up her taste.

"Nick," Copper gasped.

He was driving her up and up, too fast and out of control.

"Open wider," he said, his breaths hot against her. "Let it happen."

Forcing herself, she made her thighs relax, surrendering to his invasion. Seeing her acceptance, he reached down and pushed two fingers into her. Her bottom clenched.

"That's it!" he said triumphantly.

He pressed his mouth to her again, this time concentrating all his attention on her clit. When he took it in his lips and began to suckle, she was lost.

The stars in the night sky exploded. Copper's body arched against the chair but Nick wouldn't let up. He pressed his face harder against her cunt and curled his fingers inside her. Pleasure tore through her and her cries of completion drifted out with the *Allure's* wake. He kept at her, though, drawing out every last response she had to give.

At long last, her body went limp.

She didn't know how long she lay there, simply soaking up the feeling of utter fulfillment... rocking with the natural motion of the ship... and falling back to Earth.

The only thing she knew for sure was that she'd been well and truly taken.

"Copper?"

Slowly, she opened her eyes. Nick still hovered over her. He was watching her intently.

"Are you there?" he asked gruffly.

There? Of course, she was here. What was he talking —

"Oh my God!"

With a click, everything came into focus. She snapped back into full consciousness and abruptly became aware of her surroundings, her nakedness and her *lover*. Astounded at what she'd done—they'd done—she gaped up at him. "You...and I..."

It had happened again.

Her state of undress suddenly became unbearable. Shifting uncomfortably on the chair, she tried to tug the bodice of her dress back over her breasts. "What happened?" she demanded, panic starting to expand inside her lungs.

She was mortified when she felt him pull back and ease her legs down from the arms of the chair. "It appears that you've got a post-hypnotic suggestion still implanted in you."

"A *what*?"

"A trigger," he said concisely.

Her eyebrows fly upwards. "And somebody..."

"Set you off."

Copper had thought she'd known what blushing was all about. She hadn't had a clue. Blood pounded in her temples and heat lit up her face. Mutely, she looked around them. Their clothes were scattered about haphazardly. The ones they still wore were twisted and wrinkled, clear evidence of the way they'd pawed at each other. Worst of all, though, they were out on deck where anyone might have caught them.

And she'd done this.

Her.

Fitfully, she pulled at the hem of her skirt. It didn't even cover the copper curls between her legs.

"Lift," he said somberly.

She squeezed her eyes closed but lifted her hips so he could help pull her skirt back down. Mercifully, he made quick work of it.

Copper would have preferred to keep her eyes closed and ignore the reality of what had happened. She just couldn't. Taking a deep breath, she peeked through her eyelashes. She was surprised when she saw Nick sitting at the very foot of the chair looking tense. He dragged a hand through his mussed hair and measured every breath he took.

All of a sudden, she realized what this had done to him.

Or, more to the point, *hadn't* done to him.

Oh God.

"Nick," she said forlornly.

Forgetting her own discomfiture, she tucked her legs underneath her and moved closer to him. She started to reach for his shoulder but quickly decided better.

"Are you all right?" he asked in a monotone, not looking at her.

"I'm fine," she said, her throat tight. "Are... Are you?"

He stared out to sea and she could see a muscle in his temple twitching. "Regrets?"

He was asking if she regretted being with him.

Her natural inclination was to tell him yes. She was a private person and the way they'd cavorted together under the night sky, beneath the Caribbean breeze... It was perfectly scandalous.

Yet she'd loved it.

Coherent or not, she knew what felt good. She'd never climaxed like that in her life. Admittedly, sex had never been easy for her. She'd never been able to get herself to relax enough to trust a man the way she'd just trusted him.

But she had a feeling that was why her sense of fulfillment was so strong.

"Copper?" he said, concern narrowing his brow.

She twisted her fingers together. "I don't regret it—but I am sorry that I put you through it," she whispered.

His eyebrows lifted. "You've got to be kidding. You're sorry for me?"

Embarrassed beyond belief, she gestured to his lap. The evidence of his arousal was still plain to see.

He let out a long breath and looked back towards the wake. The moonlight glinted off the water, making it look like sparks were flying.

"I've never been that forward with a man," she said, her unease growing. She would have given anything at that moment to be able to snap her fingers and transport herself back to Minneapolis. "But I don't want you to think I'm a tease either."

He didn't say anything and an uncomfortable moment turned intolerable. Slowly, though, he turned back towards her. His look was considering. "Then kiss me."

"Kiss you?" she said, her head snapping back.

"Then we'll call it even."

"But... But..." She didn't know what to say.

He looked at her steadily. "That's all I want, a kiss from you to me. *With you clear-headed.*"

After what they'd done, the idea of a mere kiss shouldn't have sent goose bumps down her arms. But it did.

He sat there waiting patiently. He wanted her to do it with no prompting from him or the hypnotist. Copper felt her breaths go short. Unbelievably, she felt her nipples tighten and her tired pussy squeeze.

His lips flattened. "It's all right," he said, starting to stand up. "You don't have to."

Yes, she did.

For him and for herself.

Catching him by the arm, she pulled him back into the chair. Lifting herself onto her haunches, she leaned towards him. The air snapped as their gazes connected. Slowly, she looked down to the mouth that had given her so much pleasure. God, he was so sexy, she could hardly stand it.

Softly, she brushed her lips against his.

Lightning shot through her core.

Oh, that was so good.

Unbidden, she kissed him again, this time deeper and with more assurance. His arms came around her and it was the most natural thing in the world when he pulled her onto his lap. His cock pressed hard against her hip but she liked the feel of it. She liked knowing she'd done that to him.

She wrapped her arms around him and his heat seeped into her. The kiss remained slow but the desire grew with every touch and every sigh. When she finally pulled back, there was pure carnal lust in his eyes.

Unsureness hit her again. Should she... *offer?*

Abruptly, he caught her by the waist and stood. She felt shaky as he stood her on her own two feet and he steadied her. "Let's go find that hypnotist."

She caught her purse when he shoved it into her hands but hesitated. "Are you sure?" she asked meekly.

Something crossed his face but then he leaned close and kissed her cheek. "We're more than even," he whispered into her ear.

He swept up their remaining clothes and shrugged back into his shirt. Copper looked at her panties in distaste. There was no way she was putting them back on. Embarrassed, she shoved them and her bra into her purse. He said nothing but caught her hand and began leading her back to the theater.

When they got there, though, the show was over. Nick asked the clean-up crew where they could find the hypnotist but nobody seemed to know.

Concerned, Copper pressed herself closer to his side. She didn't like feeling like a potential time bomb. She wanted this hex out of her head. "What are we going to do?" she asked.

He let out a long breath and looked at her. Finally, he squeezed her hand comfortingly. "Find the ship's doctor."

Chapter 4

"So… Copper, huh?"

Nick glanced at his brother from the passenger side of the golf cart. He'd been wondering when he was going to get around to that. Give the boy some credit; he'd made it to the eighteenth hole. "Yeah, Copper," he said, giving away nothing.

Larry set the brake and they both got out to select a club. "Did she settle down all right after you went after her last night?"

"She's fine." Brother or not, Nick wasn't going to talk about it. Last night had been private.

With a capital P.

"Jolene's worried about her," Larry confessed as he pushed his tee into the soft Bahamian earth. He looked up from under the bill of his baseball cap. "You know how shy she is. That stunt in front of the crowd must have just about killed her."

The stunt at the hypnosis show or the incident on deck—it was probably a toss-up. "She wasn't happy about it."

"You, on the other hand, didn't look too upset when she crawled onto your lap."

Nick leveled him with a look.

Larry shrugged. "I'm just saying…"

"Hit the damn ball."

The grin on his brother's face faded as his shot sliced to the right. "Crap."

"You've been doing that all day," Nick said, eyeing the ball as it bounced to stop behind a palm tree.

"Yeah, yeah," Larry muttered as they switched places.

Nick set his tee, gauged the distance to the flag and took a practice swing. When he lined up and teed off for real, the ball flew off his club like a rocket.

"Damn," Larry said, squinting as he watched the thing fly. It bounced straight down the fairway, setting up perfectly for a chip shot onto the green. "And you've been doing that all day."

He cocked his head. "Working out a little sexual frustration perhaps?"

"Up yours, Lar," Nick snarled, although his brother was more on track than he could possibly know. Only one problem, there was nothing "little" about it.

That kiss. Damn.

He concentrated on wiping down his club but his mind was on last night.

After seeing Copper back to her room, he'd had to jack off in the shower just to get his cock to ease up. Not that he hadn't enjoyed getting a taste of her; their little tango on the lounge chair had scrambled his brain. It had taken everything inside him to not whip out his dick and ram it into her. It was definitely what she'd been begging for…

He'd just wanted something more.

He sighed. He'd wanted the real Copper. The shy, sexy lady—not the man-eater. When she'd timidly settled onto his lap afterwards, though, that was exactly what he'd gotten.

One heated kiss and he'd nearly come in his pants.

He shook his head. He couldn't think about that. Not here and not now. "Let's go find your ball."

Larry knew when not to push. He slid his three-wood into his bag and hopped into the driver's seat. He hit the gas and they went scooting cross-course. Nick's cell phone rang just as they drove off the nicely mown grass and into the rough. Turning around in the seat, he unzipped his golf bag. His brow furrowed as he looked at the caller's name. "It's Jolene."

Larry rolled his eyes. "She better not have maxed out the credit card. I warned her."

Nick punched the send button. "Hello?"

"Nick!" Jolene said in a rush. "Where are you?"

"On the last hole. Why?"

"You've got to get back here. I don't know what to do."

He felt a tingle at the back of his neck—the kind he normally got when an opponent was about to strike. "What's wrong? Is it Copper?"

"Hold on."

The phone was muffled but he could catch smatterings of what was happening on the other end of the line. "No, no, hon... He's not there...back to the ship...be all right."

"Jolene," he barked.

"I thought you said a good night's sleep would take care of this," she barked right back.

He went still. "That's what the doctor said. He told us that the subconscious suggestion would fade on its own."

"Well, it hasn't."

The kick in the gut was worse than Nick had expected.

Copper had been triggered but he wasn't there.

"Copper, walk normal," Jolene hissed, once again muffling the phone. "You're going to throw a hip out."

He threw a fierce look at Larry. "We've got to go back."

"But we're almost done."

"Now!" he snapped. He wiped a hand across his face and tried to think. "Jolene, what happened? Exactly."

His sister-in-law's breaths were ragged. "We were shopping at the Nassau straw market. Everything was fine until some teenager saw a bag she liked and said the g-word!"

Nick closed his eyes. Shit. That meant that Copper was doing exactly as she'd been told. She was searching for the best-looking guy in the place, the one who made her so horny she didn't care who was watching.

His fist clenched around the cell phone. "Has she..."

Hell, he couldn't even say it. "Has she chosen someone yet?"

"No, you idiot! She's looking for you!"

That put him right back in his seat. "Me?"

"Don't act so surprised. Just get your studly ass back to the ship," Jolene demanded. "I'll try to find the hypnotist but you need to get here to...do whatever it is you do."

"I—"

"Don't tell me," she warned. "I might have to rip your ears off."

Nick turned to his brother. "Floor it."

* * * * *

There was no hurrying on island time. By the time they made it back to the ship, Nick's nerves were on edge. Leaving Larry behind to find a porter for the clubs, he rushed to the Empress Deck. Jolene was pacing in the hallway, waiting for him.

"There you are," she said when she spotted him.

"Did you find the hypnotist?"

"I couldn't leave her like this." She gestured uncomfortably towards Copper's room. "She's not in good shape."

"What's wrong?" Nick demanded, his voice hard.

"She's… Oh, for God's sake, you know." She crossed her arms over her chest defensively. "If I didn't trust you…"

"I'll take care of her," he said quietly.

She pinned him with a stern look but finally nodded. Footsteps sounded down the hallway and her head snapped around. It was Larry.

"Let's go find that charlatan," she said, catching him by the arm. "My fist has some speaking to do with his face."

Nick watched them go. With the way they stomped off, the hypnotist better be ready.

And so had he. Taking a deep breath, he looked back towards Copper's door.

His cock got heavy. *She'd held out for him.*

But this wasn't right.

His hands fisted at his sides. He didn't want to see that look on her face again when she snapped out of that trance. On the other hand, though, he couldn't make her suffer. Who knew how long it would be before Larry and Jolene could get the hypnotist up here?

It was a moot point when the door suddenly opened. Copper appeared looking anxious and confused.

And naked.

His indecision vaporized. Catching her by the waist, he swiftly impelled her back into the room. "Honey, you can't be out here like that."

For good measure, he locked the door behind them.

"Nick," she sighed in relief. She began tugging at his T-shirt. "I looked for you everywhere."

Realizing he could either take the shirt off or have it ripped off him, he let her pull it over his head. She tossed it carelessly onto the floor.

"I'm here now," he said. He ran his hands down her arms, trying to soothe her.

She was past soothing.

"I need you," she whispered. Leaning forward, she began kissing his chest. Kissing and nipping and licking and generally sending him out of his mind.

"Copper," he said tightly. His hand fisted in her hair.

He hadn't let her touch him last night. Only now did he realize what he'd missed.

She was all around him. Her tongue played with his nipple as her own stiff nubs raked against his belly. And her hands! His were known for being dangerous but he had nothing on her. The way she stroked his back made his balls ache.

His control slipped a notch. Sliding his hands down her spine, he cupped her ass.

"Mmm," she murmured, wiggling into his palms.

His fingers clenched reflexively, digging into the nicely rounded globes, and she went up onto her tiptoes.

"Oh, that's nice." Tilting her head, she nuzzled against his neck — and kissed that spot behind his ear.

"Hell, yeah."

He was only a man.

He started moving them towards the bed, reveling in the feel of her naked body against his. Her muscles were toned and her skin was soft and warm. Inviting.

Just like her pussy.

He thrust his hand between her legs as she fell back onto the mattress. She was already sopping wet. He pushed two fingers into her and let them scissor back and forth. Groaning in delight, she pulled her knees towards her chest.

Nick couldn't tear his gaze from her. She was so beautiful as she lay on the burgundy bedspread. The afternoon sun shone into the stateroom, lighting every detail of her from her shiny hair right down to her painted toenails.

Add a blush to her cheeks and she would have been perfect.

His fingers stilled inside her.

This wasn't his Copper.

The thought was jounced from his head when her hands fell on the drawstring of his shorts. "Don't stop," she said breathlessly.

She scrambled to kneel before him on the bed. When her lips pressed against his racing heart, he was done for.

Reaching out with both hands, he cupped her breasts. Flinging her hair back over her shoulder, she looked at him with lust in her eyes. He flicked his thumbnails over her stiff nipples and her back arched.

"Harder," she gasped.

He loved the look of her perky breasts in his hands. He'd wanted to do this yesterday by the pool. There was no way he was going to waste the opportunity now. He gripped her more tightly and began to thrum her nipples with his thumbs over and over again.

Her breath caught but then she was attacking his clothes. "Off," she said succinctly.

All it took was two jerks and she had her wish. Her mouth drooped in disappointment when she discovered his boxers.

"Off," he said, letting go of her to strip. His clothes dropped to the floor and he kicked them aside.

His sandals went sailing when she excitedly reached for his cock.

"Copper!" he said, his hips automatically thrusting towards her.

There were no signs of shyness as she gripped him possessively. Her delicate fingers wrapped around his thick erection and pumped up and down. A bit of pre-cum escaped and Nick cursed. When her other devious hand reached down and cupped his balls, though, he knew he had to act—and fast.

Catching her under the armpits, he rolled her back on the bed.

With the way she had his cock captured, though, she was the one in charge. Showing amazing dexterity, she kept rolling until he was underneath her. Her eyes sparked as she climbed atop of him. "I want it inside me this time."

God, who was he to deny her?

Scooting up so his back was pressed against the headboard, he pulled her higher onto his lap. Her hips undulated as she tried to line him up. Wrapping his fingers over hers, he guided the head of his aching prick to her wet opening.

"Ahhh," she sighed.

Her eyelids went heavy as she slowly lowered herself onto his thick staff.

The penetration was full. Nick's eyes closed too as he felt her hot channel gripping him.

"Oh, that's good," she moaned.

It was better than good.

He settled his hands on her thighs and felt her muscles bunching as she gradually impaled herself. She was tight but she was slippery. She sank all the way down, taking him in right down to his balls.

Her entire body shuddered.

When she started to move again, it got even better.

Nick watched her, his eyes opened to barely slits as she started to rise and fall over him. Her movements were slow as she accustomed herself to the feel of him spreading and filling her. It didn't take long, though, until she was riding him raggedly.

"Faster," she demanded, even though she was the one taking him.

Nick felt his balls drawing up tighter as she bounced up and down. Her hands reached out to grab his shoulders and his gaze zeroed in on her breasts. They jiggled and swayed as she concentrated on what was happening down below. He reached for her to give her a little more to think about.

"Ahh!" she cried out when he pinched her nipples firmly. Looking down, she watched as he twisted her turgid nubs between his thumbs and forefingers.

Their bodies heated under the bright sunshine. Nick felt his climax roaring down on him but he held it back, letting her use him first. He concentrated on breathing and calming himself as she fucked him hard.

With as rough as she was being, it didn't take long. She was on one of her downward strokes when he caught her by the waist. Holding her hips immobile, he lodged himself deep. Then, looking at her, he began to grind her hips in a slow circle.

The sensation was intense. He could tell by the widening of her pretty brown eyes and the slacking of her jaw.

He didn't let up. He ground her onto him, putting pressure steadily against her clit until her body started to shake. The orgasm swelled up inside her and her head dropped back.

"Nick!" she cried out.

Her body shuddered hard and her inner muscles squeezed him tightly, trying to squeeze out his cum. Nick wasn't ready for that. Not yet. His fingers bit into her ass and she cried out once more.

At last, her body relaxed. Slowly, her head came up. Her gaze was languorous and hazy. "Mmm," she sighed, resting more heavily against him.

She started to drop her head onto his shoulder, but he caught her and made her look at him.

He knew the precise moment she came back into herself.

And that was what he'd been waiting for.

Not giving her time to think, he pressed her back onto the bed. Keeping their bodies linked, he switched positions. Her hands instinctively clutched at his shoulders when she found herself under him.

Watching her face closely, he adjusted his penetration, letting her take his weight.

Her startled eyes widened. "Oh!"

A becoming blush colored her cheeks and he nearly blew his wad.

There she was.

"My turn," he whispered. Deliberately, he pulled back, nearly out of her. He liked the surprise on her face, though, when he pushed back in.

Now, they were getting down to business.

"Copper," he sighed, settling into a steady toe-curling pace.

Her pussy fluttered around him and he groaned. She wasn't asking him to stop. He slid his hand between their bodies and took possession again of her breast.

"Nick," she groaned, arching into his hand.

Lowering his head, he took her nipple into his mouth.

Copper was shaking. It had happened again. She'd lost control and had done something wild, something totally against her nature.

But that wasn't what had her so stunned.

He'd waited.

He'd waited until she was coherent again before taking his own pleasure.

Redness stained her cheeks as she felt him moving deeply inside her, screwing her right into the firm mattress. Under the Caribbean sunshine, the intimacy was barefaced and shameless. There was no place to hide, nowhere to escape.

But she knew instinctively that he wanted it that way. Last night, it had been the kiss. She'd wondered, but this... this made it conclusive.

He wanted to be with *her*.

She felt his damp breath against her nipple right before he took it into his hot mouth. Her back arched when he laved the sensitive nub with his tongue. "Oh God," she gasped.

It felt so good.

He felt so good. His muscled body... his heavy weight atop of her... his randy cock filling her. She creamed around him when she realized *this was Nick*!

Yesterday, she'd hardly been able to say two words to him.

"Touch me," he whispered, his lips stroking the underside of her breast.

He looked up into her face and shyness gripped her. Then again, *this was Nick*!

He thrust abruptly, breaking his slow and sensuous pace. "It's too late for that."

It was. And she didn't want to be bashful with him. She already knew how wonderful it could be if she let herself go.

So she did — this time knowingly and willingly.

Boldly, she slid her fingers into his dark hair. Something in his eyes softened and he automatically turned his face back into her breasts and started suckling. The urgent tug was stimulating. Captivating. Copper couldn't keep still. She wiggled underneath him and raked her fingers down his back.

When she ran her toe against the tattoo on the side of his leg, though, he nipped her with his teeth.

The sharp pain made her buck.

"Again," she groaned, surprising even herself.

He looked at her sharply and her color brightened. She didn't back away though. Instead, she tickled the dragon again.

And, in effect, turned him loose.

Nick was all over her then. His mouth took turns at her lips, her neck and her breasts. His hands, though, found a home on her ass. His fingers bit deep as he lifted her hips up and began shafting her harder and deeper.

Fucking her for all he was worth.

Her own little dragon responded in kind. She wrapped her legs around his waist, giving his hips freedom to move. Her hands clutched at his muscled shoulders, his rippling back and his incredible butt—whatever she could reach.

Their bodies worked together on the bed, fully in sync and fully involved.

When her tongue found that spot at the back of his ear, though, time went short.

"Nick," Copper cried out.

The friction between their bodies heated. Their skin clung and their breaths formed dew on each other's necks.

She gripped his shoulders tightly. "Ah, ah, ahhhh!"

"Copper," he barked out, the muscles in his jaw clenching.

He buried himself deep and his hips convulsed in little jerks as he ejaculated inside her. She came hard, colors exploding behind her closed eyelids.

And then she melted.

Right there onto the bed underneath him, her body went slack. He was rigid for a moment more but then, at last, he came down atop of her. Silence filled the room as they both tried to catch their breaths.

Copper stared up at the ceiling, absolutely astounded.

She didn't feel uncomfortable. She wasn't embarrassed and she felt no need to reach for the covers. She loved being with him like this—and it was even better when she was in control of herself.

Oh, she remembered everything she'd done since he'd set foot in the room. It had been mind-blowingly good. It just couldn't compare to this. She had no safety net now, nothing she could blame for her behavior. She just wanted him.

Wanted him. Wanted him. Wanted him.

He started to pull back and she clutched at him—inside and out. Her arms came around him and her pussy clamped down hard. "Don't go," she whispered.

His head lifted. When he looked down at her, his eyes were hot.

He searched her face but she met his gaze steadily. Confidently.

"You need to move back to Miami," he said firmly.

Her lips curled upwards into a tiny smile. "I know."

His shoulders relaxed then and his head dipped. The kiss he gave her was sweet but spicy. He'd just shifted between her legs when the phone rang.

"Fuck," he groaned.

"No," she said, tightening her grip again when he started to move away. "Let it ring."

This time, he was the one who smiled. Her heart gave a flip.

"I can't," he said. "It's probably Jolene. She went in hunt of that damn hypnotist." His smile turned serious. "It's time we got that hex out of your brain."

* * * * *

Nick watched with his arms crossed over his chest as the hypnotist sat down in a chair in front of Copper. For her sake, they'd moved into his stateroom. She sat alone on the bed, fingers clenched tightly in her lap. Everyone else had been asked to leave. That had put Jolene in a royal snit but Larry had seen the wisdom of the move.

It would put Nick alone with the guy—and he already looked nervous.

He should be.

"Do it," Nick said sternly.

The hypnotist turned a sickly shade of gray.

"We all need to relax," he said. He looked beseechingly at Copper. "That's probably why we didn't get the suggestion removed last time. You weren't focused in on me."

Nick's muscles bulged. "This wasn't her fault."

"No, no," the man agreed. "I take full responsibility. She just needs to find a calm place and trust me."

"Trust you?"

"Nick," Copper said, her quiet voice cutting through the tension in the room. "Let's just give it a try."

He backed off but only because she'd asked. "Do as the lady says."

Every protective instinct inside him was screaming. She looked so delicate and vulnerable. She'd put her sundress back on but without her sandals, he could see her toes curling in anxiety.

He let out a long, calming breath. This had been some vacation for her. He'd make it better; he swore he would.

The hypnotist pulled out a pocket watch.

"Trite, I know," the man said apologetically to Copper. "But maybe it will help."

Dangling the watch by its chain, he began to swing it slowly in front of her eyes. "Concentrate on the repetitive movement," he said. "Back and forth. Back and forth. You're trying not to blink but it's oh so hard. Your eyelids are just too heavy. The more you try to keep them open, the sleepier you get."

There was that singsong voice that put Nick on edge—as if he could have been any more on the alert. He watched every move the man made. Still, he was surprised when Copper went under so quickly.

Her head sagged and her body went limp.

The hypnotist quickly got to work. "Copper, can you hear me?"

"Yes," she replied, her chin resting against her chest.

"Good. I want you to know that you've completed your assignment. Do you remember what it was?"

"Find the best-looking man... Do whatever feels good."

"Right. You succeeded."

"I know."

The hypnotist smiled up at him but Nick met him with a scowl.

Worriedly, he turned back to Copper. "I repeat, your mission is over. The word 'gorgeous' no longer means anything special to you. It's just another word describing something beautiful. Like you."

"Watch it," Nick growled.

"I'm going to count backwards from five now. When I get to one, you will wake up feeling refreshed and relaxed. Five, four, three, two, one."

Nick stepped closer to the bed as Copper lifted her head. She blinked before her eyes finally opened and her brown gaze met his.

His stomach tightened. "How do you feel?" he asked.

She reached up to rub the back of her neck. "Good."

Her gaze moved back and forth between the two of them. "Did it work?"

The hypnotist swallowed hard, his Adam's apple bouncing. "There's just one way to find out... *Gorgeous.*"

Her look turned icy. "Don't call me that."

Nick pumped his fist in the air. "Yes, that's more like it."

Turning, he clamped his hand onto the hypnotist's shoulder. The man instinctively recoiled. "The door is this way," he said coolly.

"Oh, thank God." The guy's relief was obvious. He hopped out of the chair and darted towards the exit. He stopped, though, with his hand on the doorknob. Hesitantly, he turned back.

"You both should know something though," he said. "Hypnotism is not a dark art. It's simply a way to tap into the inner consciousness."

He held up his hand when he felt their impatience. "What I'm trying to say is that you weren't a puppet on a string, Copper. Hypnotism can't make people do anything they don't already want to do. It's impossible."

A knowing smile slipped onto his face. "And don't ask me why, but you wanted to do him."

With a jerk of his thumb, he disappeared into the hallway.

Slowly, Nick walked over and locked the door. Turning, he leaned back against it. He looked at Copper sitting so quietly on the bed. Under the sunlight, her hair gleamed. "Is that true?" he asked.

She shrugged restlessly. "I like you, Nick." Her cheeks turned a pretty pink. "A lot."

"That's good," he said as he pushed himself away from the door and started towards her. "Because, honey, you've had me spellbound from the very beginning."

Also by Kimberly Dean

ഔ

Fever
On the Prowl

About the Author

ഔ

Kimberly Dean likes the freedom of imagination allowed in writing romantica. When not slaving over a keyboard, she enjoys reading, sports, movies, and loud rock-n-roll.

Kimberly welcomes comments from readers. You can find her website and email address on her author bio page at www.ellorascave.com.

Tell Us What You Think

We appreciate hearing reader opinions about our books. You can email us at Comments@EllorasCave.com.

TANDEM

Elizabeth Donald

Trademarks Acknowledgement

∞

The author acknowledges the trademarked status and trademark owners of the following wordmarks mentioned in this work of fiction:

Boy Scout: Boy Scouts Of America Corporation

Jeep: DaimlerChrysler Corporation

Lexan: General Electric Company

M&Ms: Mars Incorporated

Chapter

"You have got to be kidding." Chris stared at the ranger's impassive face over the scarred wooden counter.

"No, ma'am," the ranger said, his voice barely inflecting. "No one hikes the Jericho Trail alone."

Chris blew out her breath in frustration. "This is a state rule?"

"Yes, ma'am," the ranger said, his hatchet face impassive as if it had been carved from stone. "Too many hikers get lost or hurt out on that trail. Tell you the truth, they're talking about shutting it down altogether. It's not safe for a lone hiker."

Chris shot him a look. "Not safe for a woman hiker, you mean?"

The ranger didn't even blink. "No, ma'am, I turned down a fellow just about ten minutes ago," he said, pointing out the window.

Chris glanced out the window and saw a man about her own age talking on the pay phone right outside the ranger station. His back was to her, but the gestures he was making while talking to someone on the phone made his agitation real.

Chris turned back to Hatchet Face. "Look," she said, leaning forward. "I've wanted to do the Jericho Cliff Trail for two years now. I'm about to graduate, I'm moving away, this is my last chance."

"Sorry," Hatchet Face replied without hesitation.

Chris stared at him for another moment then picked up her pack from its resting place on the floor. She debated shouting the string of profanity that came to mind, but instead she merely hoisted the pack onto her shoulders. She glanced out the window again and saw the ranger Jeep that had brought her up here was already gone. "Can you at least call me another ride back down to the park entrance?" she snapped. The ranger nodded.

Outside, the cool breeze struck Chris' forehead and she could hear the distant chirp of birds and insects past the trailhead. Inviting and open, she could see where the path curved out of sight just a short way into the woods.

"Do you have any idea where he might be?" the guy on the pay phone said. He had turned a bit more toward Chris and she could see him more clearly. His brown hair glinted a touch more golden in the sunlight and his mouth was used to smiling when he wasn't shouting into the phone. His back and legs looked strong, she noted, but his pack was far too clean and new to belong to a seasoned hiker. Her own pack was covered in the dust of a dozen trails, one of the grommets mended and a busted zipper repaired with a safety pin.

"Just tell him to call me as soon as you hear from him," the twenty-something man about her own age said, and hung up.

"Hi," Chris said, feeling oddly shy. "You get stood up?"

"Yeah," the man said. "My best friend. Not like him at all."

"Chris Coleman," she said, holding out her hand.

He took her hand and shook it, a firm, warm grip that spoke of tempered strength. "Reed Miller," he said.

Just then the ranger came out of the station with a slip of paper. "Mr. Miller," he said. "A message just came for you."

Reed blinked in surprise and took the piece of paper. Scanning it, his face visibly fell.

"Bad news?" Chris asked.

Reed shrugged. "My friend Jack," he said. "He fell down his apartment steps on his way to meet me here. Broke his ankle. He won't be coming but he's okay."

"I'm sorry," Chris said.

"The Jeep's on its way," Hatchet Face said. "Please wait here."

Chris rolled her eyes. "What, you think we're going to sneak onto the trail?"

"No exceptions to the rules, miss," Hatchet Face said, folding his arms.

Chris stared at Reed for a second. "Hey, just a minute," she said. "You said nobody hikes alone, right? What if we hiked together?"

Reed's mouth dropped open.

The ranger blinked. "Well..."

"You said we just had to be hiking with someone," Chris said. "I'll look after Mr. Miller here and he'll look after me, and your ass is covered."

The ranger looked distinctly uncomfortable. "I don't know, that's essentially two single parties."

Reed raised his right hand. "I swear we will stick together the entire time and not get dead."

Chris smothered a grin behind her hand. Hatchet Face was clearly uncomfortable now, but nowhere in the regulation book he used for a mind did he see anything wrong with it, she could tell.

"All right," Hatchet Face said, pulling out his permit book. "On your word that you stick together. No funny business."

"None whatsoever," Chris said, grinning.

Hatchet Face tore off a permit slip and gave it to Chris. "In all seriousness, miss," he said. "Don't take chances. I've had too many young people never come back down from this cliff."

"I've been hiking since I was six, sir, I think I can handle it," Chris said, strapping her pack.

Reed pulled on his own pack with a little more difficulty. "Would you please get a message to this number, tell him to pick me up Sunday morning?" he asked, scribbling on the note and handing it to the ranger.

Chris cinched her hip belt on and felt the familiar shift of weight come off her shoulders and on to her hips and legs. The hiking stick was a notched wooden pole with a leather strap on the end she rarely used. The place where her hand rested, a few inches below the top, was worn smooth from long use.

"Ready?" she asked Reed.

Reed sketched a quick salute and she giggled. The trail lay before them, green and quiet with rustling leaves and the slight chatter of insects, unseen beneath the undergrowth. Chris waved goodbye to Hatchet Face the Ranger, who stood watching them as they stepped onto the trail.

* * * * *

The trail was easy to begin with. Wide and well traveled, this section was often used by day hikers in the park. Chris made good time, moving onward between the trees. The cool breeze kept perspiration at bay on her face and the rhythm soon warmed her leg muscles to an easy pace.

Reed was slower. Struggling with his pack, he was soon a good distance behind her. She quickened her pace and when she came to the clearing, she almost didn't stop. But she knew she needed a water break and she was determined not to be stupid.

So when Reed came lumbering up the path behind her, Chris was drinking from her water bottle and enjoying a patch of sunlight. Unbeknownst to her, the sun glinted strange colors in her tawny-gold hair, casually swept up behind her ears under the plain tan baseball cap she wore. Her battered pack lay beside her long, coltish legs, stretched out in the sun and already warm and tingling with adrenaline from the warm-up stretch she had just hiked.

Reed dropped his pack onto the ground and sat down heavily. "I hate to ask," he said, a little out of breath. "But could you go a little slower? I'm not as experienced at this as you are."

Chris glanced at him. "What, are you kidding?"

Reed shook his head. "Sorry."

Chris blinked. "No, that's not what I meant... I meant, of course we're not going to hike together. Did you think that was for real?"

Reed's mouth literally fell open.

"That was just to get the ranger off my ass," Chris said. "You hike whatever speed you want. I'll be happy to see you on the trail. But I'm doing this trail solo."

Reed pulled out a metal canteen and took a long draught before answering. "I don't think that's such a good idea."

"Oh yeah?" Chris asked, immediately defensive.

Reed stared into the grove. "Hey, the guy wasn't kidding. This is the easy part. Later, in the bluffs, it gets dangerous. You shouldn't be alone."

"I can take care of myself," Chris said.

Reed shrugged. "Fine, maybe I shouldn't be alone," he said. "Anyway, I gave my word."

Chris stared at him a moment. "What are you, some kind of Boy Scout?"

Reed held up his hand in a three-fingered salute. "Eagle Scout, I'll have you know."

Chris's laughter pealed through the woods and despite himself, Reed smiled. There was something infectious about her smile and he glanced down at her legs again before averting his gaze. *Nice, buddy, real subtle,* he thought.

Chris's laughter subsided. "Well, they sure failed on 'be prepared'," she said, critically viewing his pack. "You are way overpacked, for one thing. What are you carrying, fifty pounds?"

Reed shrugged. "I don't know, but the water weighs a lot."

Chris shook her head. "You didn't need to bring in that much water, we'll be crossing two streams that we can draw water from, if you brought iodine," she said. "Your sleeping bag has got to weigh a ton—it's way too thick for this climate. I don't even want to know how big your tent is—at least, that's what I'm assuming you've got strapped on top. You sure as hell won't need that folding axe—you can't cut down live trees in these woods. And a metal canteen?"

"Hey," Reed said. "Screw the rest of it but the canteen stays."

Chris held up her tinted blue water bottle. "Designed for backpacking. Weighs about an ounce and can't break. You can run this mother over with a car and it won't even crack," she said.

Reed held up his dented metal canteen. "Family heirloom."

Chris shrugged. "Okay, but just so you know, the sun's going to boil that water by noon. You'll be able to make a cup of tea, just setting it in the sun."

"Noted and logged," Reed said.

Chris stood and hoisted her pack onto her bent knee, slipping her arms into the straps and cinching the hip belt. Reed marveled again at her easy grace, particularly when he lumbered to his feet, the axe clinking against his canteen. "Just try to keep up," Chris said smiling.

The path started to curve upward between the trees. Reed was forced to watch his footing more and more, his breath laboring a bit as he tried to avoid the snakelike tree roots. Chris walked ahead of him, a slight exhale with each upward step the only sign she was exerting at all. He watched the play of the muscles beneath her skin, the strength in her legs as they moved forward, the light glowing against her arm where she gripped her walking stick. He caught himself staring at her rear more than once and nearly tripped over the roots.

"You still with me back there?" Chris asked.

"I'm here," Reed said, cursing himself.

"Hang in there, we're almost to the first stream," she said.

The path curved upward and leveled out. Reed hoisted himself up after her and saw the stream, its water darkly clear and rushing over rocks and a miniature waterfall, no more than three feet high. Chris unsnapped her pack and sat beside the stream. She pulled a bandanna from her pocket and dipped it in the water, running the wet cloth over her face. Reed watched the water droplets form on her forehead and slanted cheekbones, her eyes closed, enjoying the sensations.

Reed, what the hell are you thinking?

"Don't just stand there, get a rest already," Chris said.

Reed knelt down and gratefully dropped the pack. "This sure isn't like day hiking," he said.

Chris blinked. "You've never backpacked?"

Reed shook his head. "I've done a lot of rock climbing, hiking through state parks and even some free climbing. But it's a lot harder with all this stuff."

"So why start with Jericho Cliffs?" Chris asked.

Reed grinned. "What a challenge, man," he said. "Those cliffs are supposed to be incredible."

"Yeah, well, you walk them, not climb them," Chris said. She leaned back against her pack and drank from her bottle.

Reed felt like an idiot just sitting there. He pulled out one of the water containers he'd brought, drinking deeply from it. The water cooled his throat and he felt his muscles relax a little, warmed and full of energy. He caught himself glancing at her legs, long and smooth from the edge of her shorts to her well-worn hiking boots. He leaned his head back on his pack and closed his eyes, hoping it would keep him from thinking highly inappropriate thoughts.

Chris glanced over at Reed, whose eyes were safely closed. The sun cast a mellow glow on his rich brown hair, and she couldn't help noticing his shoulders, strong even in repose. She'd always been attracted to men with good shoulders—not too bulky and over-muscled, not thin and hunched, but easygoing and squared. Shoulders weren't just about muscles and skin, they showed how a man held himself, what he thought of himself. Reed seemed the perfect balance between arrogant strength and insecure weakness.

Chris, babe, what are you thinking? Remember Charlie?

Charlie. Chris shook her head in disgust. He had adamantly refused to come with her. They had planned it for two months and the night before they'd had a wowser of an argument. He told her there was no way he was going to miss a Thornbirds concert just to "go look at some boring-ass rocks". She told him they ought to "take some time off". That was Chris-speak for "My bag's already packed. Fuck off." He'd be tough to unload, she knew. Dividing the CDs alone was going to be a nightmare.

"You ready to move on?" Reed was looking at her and Chris realized she had been lost in reverie.

"Yeah," she said, getting to her feet and hoisting up her pack again. She glanced at the map. "We're maybe two hours out from a good campsite."

* * * * *

Chris was laughing at him again and Reed couldn't help it—he laughed along with her. "I give up," he said, waving a tent pole in the air. "I bow to your expertise."

Chris was sitting comfortably on the ground in front of her small backpacker's tent, stretching. Reed was surrounded by a vast pile of harsh-smelling plastic tent poles piled beside him. "I honestly wouldn't know where to start," she said truthfully. "Were there directions?"

"Possibly," Reed said, looking around.

Chris grinned. "But like any good male *Homo sapiens,* you threw them away without reading them."

"Of course. Directions are for wimps!" Reed proclaimed.

Chris shook her head and came over to him, poking at the plastic. "This thing is going to leak like a sieve in a rainstorm," she said, sliding a pole through a long sleeve and hoisting it up.

"It's got this rainfly thing," Reed said, looking around.

Chris grinned as she jammed a stake in the ground, stomping it with her boot. "That little beanie? It'll deflect about nine raindrops."

Reed shrugged. "It was thirty bucks."

"Beat me there," Chris said, handing him an expanse of plastic. "Mine was more like two hundred."

"For that?" Reed exclaimed, looking over at her small, innocuous tent. "Hell, you couldn't fit more than one person in that!"

"That's the idea," Chris returned, ducking behind Reed's vast expanse of slowly rising plastic. She jammed another stake in it. "Besides, you can fit two people inside if they're really cozy with each other."

"Sounds like fun," Reed said, adding a little eyebrow waggle that was probably lost on her.

"Can be," she said grinning. "Charlie thought so."

Reed's smile faded. "Your boyfriend?"

"Yeah," she said automatically, jamming the last stake into the ground. "There, let it go."

Reed stepped back and the tent remained standing. "Halleluiah," he said.

Chris looked inside. "Damn, what is this, the Taj Mahal?" she said. "You need all this space? It's got rooms!"

"That's for my harem. They should be arriving any moment," Reed cracked, and Chris smiled back at him. "No, remember I was going to have a friend with me?"

"And you'd both be a total mess if it rains," she said, plopping back down on the ground. She checked the single-burner propane stove, which was boiling water. "What were you planning to eat?"

Reed opened his pack and pulled out three slightly squashed peanut butter sandwiches. Chris grinned and poured the boiling water carefully into a foil pouch. She stirred it up.

"What's that?" Reed asked.

Chris looked at the label. "Stroganoff with noodles," she said, and tasted it. "Honestly, I bet your sandwiches taste better."

The tents were set up on a small clearing overlooking a bluff. The woods were falling into green-tinted shadows beneath them while a tapestry of color and light played across the darkening sky. Chris ate her stroganoff, watching the sun set and letting the cool breeze waft over her head. Reed wolfed down his sandwiches faster than she could spoon her stroganoff, which tasted like dried monkey turds but it fed the growl in her stomach. When she finished, she put the empty pouch in her trash bag and pulled out a gallon-size bag of gorp—good old raisins and peanuts—with an entire bag of M&Ms mixed in for a shot of chocolate.

Reed was watching her hungrily and she offered him some of the gorp. He grabbed a handful and grinned. "Guess I really was unprepared," he said.

"You didn't bring candy bars, did you?" she teased. "Because now they're lovely lumps of chocolate."

Reed cleared his throat. "So why did you decide to hike this alone? Isn't it more fun with a partner?"

Chris looked out at the colorful sky. "A lot of things are more fun with a partner," she said. "Doesn't mean you have one."

Reed looked at her funny and she felt the need to explain. "Charlie, my boyfriend...he didn't want to come."

Reed privately thought Charlie must be crazy. Chris was taking off her boots and socks, stretching out her toes and rotating her ankles. Her long, muscled legs were a mellow golden tan in the fading sunlight, and despite himself he wondered how her firm thigh would feel beneath his hand, whether her skin was as butter-smooth as it looked, how that strength would feel pressed against him, around him...

Then he realized he had better start thinking of something else or he would have to put his hat in his lap.

"It was supposed to be a romantic getaway, huh?" he said, trying to commiserate. There was this air of pensive sadness around her now and he wanted to puncture it, make it melt away.

She shook her head. "Just something I wanted and he didn't," she said. "What about you? Why were you and Jack coming here?"

"Something buddies do," Reed said. "Go off somewhere in the middle of nowhere, talk, laugh, all that stuff. Jack's big into the world of nature as spiritual enlightenment. He was also bringing the beer."

Chris grinned and reached into her bag.

"No way," Reed said incredulously.

Chris tossed him a dark bottle and popped one herself. "I only brought four," she said. "Too heavy. But they say you should always bring one luxury."

Reed popped the bottlecap—a very nice microbrew, he saw—and took a long draught. No beer had ever tasted so good.

Chris drank more of her beer as the last of the light faded from the sky. "Better get to sleep early," she said. "We've got to be up with the sun if we'll make it up Goat Cliff tomorrow."

Reed knew what he'd be dreaming about.

Chapter 2

The air smelled different in the morning. Cool and crisp with a touch of moisture that seemed to soak in to Chris' skin. She finished rolling up her sleeping bag and finger-combed her long tawny-gold hair back into submission. She found herself wishing for a hairbrush and mentally chided herself — what use is a hairbrush in the woods? Just because she was hiking with a hot guy didn't mean she was suddenly a different person.

Outside, Reed was already collapsing his tent. She peeked out the small mesh window in her tent and watched him, hidden from his view.

He hadn't put on a shirt yet. Those wonderful shoulders were working hard, rolling the heavy plastic up and pulling out the stakes. She liked the play of his muscles beneath the smooth skin, the way his back smoothed to the waistband of his shorts, the sun gleaming in light-gold tones in his hair…

He glanced over at her tent and she pulled back from the window just in time. No sense letting him see how much she appreciated his fine form. The thoughts she was entertaining…they couldn't be. It wasn't even Charlie stopping her — somehow she knew her relationship with Charlie was over and probably had been for a long time. But something about Reed made her back away in caution, a sense of something dangerous. It was crazy to think that about a guy who could barely make it along the trail, but somehow she felt there was something raw and uncontrollable in him. It was exciting and titillating but she couldn't go there. Could she?

Chris sneaked another peek. Reed was trying to jam the tent back in the stuff sack and she stifled a giggle as he swore at it. He shoved harder, his fist disappearing deep into the pile of plastic, vanishing up to the elbow. Those muscles were fascinating—not huge and bound-up like a wrestler, but taut and firm. The power he contained in his body was something he didn't even seem aware of and she found it immensely attractive.

Chris stepped out of her tent and knelt beside her pack. "Good morning," she said as she fished out her sunscreen.

Reed turned around and smiled. Chris was sitting down in front of her tent, pulling the cap off the sunscreen. "Good morning," he said.

Reed kept stuffing the tent into the bag but he watched Chris surreptitiously as she smoothed the sunscreen onto her arms and shoulders. She was wearing the same white tank top as the day before and it set off the golden tone of her skin perfect. The morning sunlight fell across the campsite and lit her hair, making it glow with a dull fire that seemed to reach across the campsite to him. He wanted to plunge his hands in that hair, to pull her beneath him and...he lowered the tent to waist level as he kept stuffing the tent material into the bag, hoping she wouldn't notice his sudden discomfort.

Chris stretched those long, firm legs out in front of her, smoothing sunscreen onto them. The white cream sank into her skin, disappearing into a soft sheen that soaked in the sunlight. She rubbed the lotion up her strong, firm calf to her knee then added more cream to the top of her thigh, rubbing it in. Her hand ran up the outside of her leg to the hem of her shorts. Then her hand slipped back over to slide up the inside of her thigh, smoothing the sunscreen along the tender skin there.

She started working on the other leg, rubbing sunscreen onto her calf, and Reed became aware that he had stopped moving, the tent lying half spilled across his hands. He went back to work but was helpless to stop stealing glances at Chris. As she rubbed the glistening cream up the inside of her thigh, his breath caught in his throat again and his hands clenched in the tent fabric. He'd never been this powerfully attracted to a woman, any woman, particularly someone he'd just met. Who had a boyfriend. *Remember that, idiot*, he told himself. An honorable man doesn't think about a woman who's taken.

But is she really? His mind argued with him. *If she were yours, would you let her walk this trail alone?*

If she were mine, I'd never let her go, he thought.

* * * * *

Chris stepped cautiously up the trail, choosing her footholds carefully. The trail wasn't really steep enough to count as a climb, but a wrong step could lead to a fall.

"Careful, Reed," she called down below her. "This ground's loose as goose shit."

"Hell of a phrase," he grunted, looking up at her. He was finding the climb a little harder than he expected, probably because of all the heavy stuff in his pack. But when he looked up at Chris' smile, he smiled back. She turned her attention back to the path ahead—or above—and the sun glinted off her tawny hair, making it glow in the sunlight. She moved farther and he watched the play of her thighs against each other below her shorts.

She hauled herself up the last few steps and stopped to take in the view. "This is a good spot for lunch," she said.

Reed pulled up after her and hoisted his pack off his shoulders with a sigh of relief. Only then did he stop to look.

The woods rolled out beneath them like a green carpet, moving and sighing in the breeze. A thin silver ribbon of a stream wound a crease through the velvet carpet of greenwood. There were the occasional chirps of birds and the rustle of unseen creatures in the shrubs below them, but there was blissfully no whine of mosquitoes. The sun shone clear and warm through the azure sky.

A good spot for lunch. Reed thought he had never seen anything so peacefully beautiful.

Chris sat beside her pack, pulling out more energy bars. Reed eyed them wistfully as he pulled out yet another mashed peanut butter sandwich.

"Enjoying yourself?" she asked, munching on an energy bar.

"Actually, yes," Reed replied.

She smiled. "You seem surprised."

Reed shrugged. "It was going to be just a guys' thing, bonding in the wilderness."

"Grunt, grunt," she snarked, grinning.

Reed smiled. "But this is...beautiful. Just so pretty and peaceful. I didn't expect it to be like this. I'm surprised so few people hike it."

"The ascent is the easy part," Chris said. "The descent is where it gets tricky."

She stood and stretched out her legs, bending her knees one at a time. Reed loved to watch her move, graceful and smooth. "Are you a dancer?" he asked suddenly.

She stopped stretching. "No," she replied. "I have two left feet. Why do you ask?"

He stood. "You look like a dancer."

Chris laughed. "You must have been out in the sun too long."

Reed extended a hand. "I bet you can dance."

She stared at him. "You're a dancer?"

He grinned. "Now you seem surprised."

Chris shook her head. "I just thought...you know, dancers seem so..."

"Hey, don't judge us by the tights," Reed said, grinning. "It's harder than sports. I know, I tried that for a long time."

He held out his hand again. Chris took it and he drew her toward him. He put one firm hand on her waist and held her hand with the other. Her free hand rested on his shoulder, light and tentative.

He began slowly, moving her with him in a slow two-step that swept her around the small clearing in the sunlight. She glanced down at her feet and bumped into him. "Sorry," she said.

Reed reached down and lifted her chin up toward him. "Look at me," he said. "Let your feet do what they want. Just look at me."

He swept her back into motion, moving together with coiled grace and strength. He could feel her tense muscles begin to relax, to key off his movements. She stared up into his eyes and he suddenly felt the hammer of his blood, stronger than ever. Her eyes were a dark cerulean blue, almost the color of cornflowers, and he swore he could see himself in them. She felt like the wind itself in his arms as they moved back and forth, and he was acutely aware not only of the swell of her breast and the curve beneath her shorts, but the luster of her skin and the strength in her arms. She felt like something featherlight and steel-strong at the same time.

Chris moved forward too quickly and she brushed against his shorts—and the hardened swell of his cock inside them. The sudden contact made him clench his jaw at the jolt of sensation. She moved back quickly and he knew she'd felt it. There was a sudden flush to her cheeks and she stopped dancing.

"We should probably keep moving," she said, her voice deep and husky.

"Yeah," he replied. But his hand didn't move off her waist. He wanted to slide it down over the curve of her ass, pull her close to him again.

For a moment, her fingers slid between his, touching the sensitive skin and flicking a fingertip across the back of his hand. Then she let go and stepped away without a word.

"Wait," Reed said.

Chris smiled impishly and danced away a bit toward a large tree that overlooked the view. It had long, low-lying branches and Chris hopped up onto them. "C'mon!" she said.

Reed followed, clambering up after her with easy grace. Chris hoisted herself onto a swaying, slightly U-shaped branch that almost seemed like a swing with a heavy branch behind it she could lean on. Reed climbed after her, bracing himself against the branches.

"Always climb a tree," she whispered. "It's a rule."

"Ranger didn't mention that one," he said.

Chris smiled and opened her mouth to say something smart-ass but Reed stopped her by leaning in close, his mouth capturing hers in a slow, languorous kiss that soon deepened into a dance of tongues, a gentle mating of their mouths that made Chris' legs tremble. They were suspended above the ground, almost like flying, and the longer they kissed, the more Chris wanted him in that primal, natural way a woman wants a man. She had never felt more powerfully attracted, more turned on, in her life. She arched her back toward him and his hands moved from her waist up to just below her breasts.

Reed slid his groin up against hers and she instinctively pressed herself against the hard cock she could feel through his shorts and hers. She rubbed herself against him like a cat in heat, all passion and primitive wanting. He was balanced carefully, pressed tight against her, and his hand slipped over her breast with a controlled strength that made her lose her breath.

He suddenly thrust hard against her and she cried out. But then he stopped, retreating a bit from her. He was fighting himself, she could see—fighting something that was keeping him from her. She wanted him and she tried to speak, to tell him so, but he was already climbing down the tree, away from her.

Chris stayed in the tree for a few minutes, alone with the heat in her blood.

* * * * *

They had hiked through the afternoon, talking about everything and nothing. Movies, books, music, the relative merits of the Jericho College baseball team. But through the easy talk, it seemed as though Reed was still holding himself back, as though something about her gave him pause. Now, as Chris stoked the dying fire one more time, she realized it was more than that.

Reed was waiting for something.

Chris had taken off her boots and socks, cleaning her feet with cleansing wipes she tucked into her refuse bag before slipping on camp shoes. On a whim, she put another bundle of branches on the fire from the stack Reed had collected.

"Are you cold?" Reed asked.

She drew her light wrap around her shoulders. "A little," she said. Reed immediately started to shrug off his jacket and she held up her hand. "Please, if I get really cold, I'll change into my spare pants."

Reed moved over beside her. "You shouldn't be cold, not on such a beautiful night," he said.

Chris looked up at the stars and realized he was right. She had been so lost in thought that she hadn't even noticed the stars, cold and brilliant in the clear night sky. As she gazed up at them, she felt Reed kneel behind her, pressing against her back, running his hands up and down her arms.

Suddenly Chris wasn't cold anymore. She could feel that coiled strength, held so tightly in check, bound in his chest and arms behind her. She shifted, a little uncomfortable at the way his powerful hands made her feel.

Reed inhaled behind her and she suddenly worried about how she must smell to him after a day on the trail. Those thoughts flew out of her mind in a flurry when he lightly kissed the side of her neck. The shivers ran through her entire body and she suddenly ached in a nearly painful swell between her legs.

"Aw hell," she murmured, and leaned back against him, baring more of her neck and the line of her shoulder to him. He shifted the wrap off her shoulder and his mouth moved on her skin, slowly and with heat. His large hands rested lightly on her hips, almost restraining her. She felt completely within his grasp.

Chris turned her head sideways and leaned back. Reed's mouth came down on hers with nearly bruising force, devouring her mouth with the pent-up power in his body. His tongue forced its way into her mouth, stroking along hers with insistent passion. She tried to break the kiss, to gasp for breath, but his hand wound its way into her hair and held her tight. The delicious pressure against her scalp combined with the moist heat of his mouth and she pressed harder against him.

Finally he broke the kiss and she gasped a bit as she reached toward him. Reed captured her hand in his and led it back by her side. He turned her to face toward the fire and its growing heat sank into her whole body, warming the front of her thighs, her breasts, her face, until the flush rose in her skin. The wrap was banished to the ground and Reed's strong hands caressed her bare arms, making her skin tingle.

He slid his hands around her waist, pulling her closer. She could feel his cock, hard and hot, pressing against her ass through their shorts. His hands slipped up from her waist to cup the underside of her breasts. They ached for release from the tight sports bra she wore beneath her tank top. When his fingers found her nipples, she groaned aloud at the sensation.

"Reed." She breathed his name and he responded by rolling her nipples in his large fingers. Any words she may have thought of saying vanished in the flood of ecstasy.

Reed slid his hands under her tank top, bold and insistent. *This is crazy,* Chris thought. She barely knew him. She wasn't a one-night-stand kind of woman. She wasn't in to stranger sex. But then his hands moved over her sports bra, her tightly bound breasts aching for release, and he pinched her nipples almost hard enough to hurt while he kissed the back of her neck.

Chris suddenly felt the need to reciprocate. She pushed her ass backward, rubbing against the hard branch of his cock. He pushed forward hard enough to shock her with the sensation of him pressing between her ass cheeks. He tugged at her shirt and it joined the wrap on the ground.

She tried to turn around again, to feel his chest and arms, to lick him and suck him as she wanted to. But those powerful hands of his returned her to where he wanted her—facing the fire, at his command.

Reed's fingers stole around to the front again, skating across the sensitive skin of the top swell of her breasts before reaching for the hooks that held her sports bra in place. With each hook he released, his fingers snaked between her breasts, teasing virgin territory into life. When the last hook sprang free, the bra fell back down her arms to her elbows. She started to shrug it free but he took the weight of her bare breasts in his hands and she threw back her head in sudden passion.

His fingers rolled her hard nipples, tweaking them again and again, shooting bolts of pleasure so high it was nearly pain. His mouth traveled along the line of her shoulder and down her back between her shoulder blades. He began to rock against her, his cock pressed against her ass. She rocked with him, small sounds escaping her throat despite herself.

Reed slipped one of his hands down to her firm thigh, slipping it between her legs without preamble. He groped without pause, and the sudden pressure on her clit made her groan aloud.

"Chris," he whispered, and the hoarse growl in his throat made her realize just how much he wanted her.

"I'm on the Pill," she murmured.

It was all the assent he needed. He lifted her to her knees and she knelt trembling before the fire. He slipped away for a moment and she heard his shorts joining their clothes on the ground. She felt exposed before the fire, its heat baking into her skin even as the cool air of the dark woods swept around them. He moved her shorts and panties down off her hips and she lifted one leg then the other, letting them vanish beneath his strong, smooth hands.

He swept her body with his caresses, sliding over her bare ass, down her legs and back up to flick at her clit before sliding his finger inside her, rubbing gently while he pressed his cock harder against her ass. Her hair tumbled to the side as he licked and sucked her neck. Chris had never felt so completely under a man's control, as though the coiled strength Reed used to keep himself in check now exuded control over her, and she was helpless beneath his hands.

He turned her sideways and pressed her down until her head rested lightly on the pile of clothes. She held out her hands to brace herself as he grasped her hips, pulling her back toward him. She could feel his cock pressing between her legs as he spread her thighs, his inexorable strength pushing her where he wanted her.

Chris cried out as Reed slid inside her, his cock hard and strong. He slid deep, so deep she could feel him everywhere in her. He moved slowly at first, rocking against her ass. There was little she could do to move, only brace herself as he moved inside her. Each slow thrust drove her into the pile of clothes. She couldn't see him or what he was doing, only feel him and his strength. She could feel the crackling heat of the fire sinking into her back, contrasted when Reed's fingernails scratched lightly down the sensitive skin. He reached down and wound his hands in her hair and she rubbed against him like a cat.

Reed was starting to lose that tight control, she sensed as he pounded into her. Their bodies made an exciting slapping sound as he thrust into her harder and harder. Now he was making sounds, cries of pleasure and hoarse, wordless whispers. He pulled her hair to bring her up to all fours, remaining inside her and forcing himself into her even harder. He draped himself over her back and reached around to grasp her breasts as he kept thrusting. She felt his breath, hot and moist, against her back.

Chris was close—she could feel it. Reed seemed to grow larger inside her as he straightened up a bit. His hands were on her hips, bucking into her over and over in a barely controlled frenzy. One of his hands stole beneath her to finger her clit, rubbing it in a rough circular motion that made her cry out. His other hand slid down her ass to rub a finger against her anus, teasing the sensitive skin even as he bucked into her.

"Oh God," Chris moaned, and he didn't let up, thrusting forward with brutal force as his fingers pressed against her clit and anus in unison. Once, twice, a third, and the fourth time he pushed into her she came in a stunning wave of shattering passion, crying out as she rode the wave and contracted against him over and over. As she broke, he let out a hoarse cry and she felt him pulse and explode inside her. His entire body seemed to expel itself into her, his hands leaving her for a moment only to clutch her hips to him, keeping her in place as he rode every last wave of pleasure in her body. Only when fully expended did he relax, letting his cock slip back out of her and releasing her down onto the soft pile of clothing.

Chris' entire body tingled. Reed pressed up behind her, his warmth covering her from behind as the fire warmed her from the front. His arms slid around her body, his hands smoothing over her skin. The cold seemed banished for a moment, nestled against him.

Then she opened her eyes. "Whew," she said, and immediately felt stupid.

"Yeah," he murmured, quiet behind her.

Chris suddenly felt uncomfortable and started to gather her clothes. "I should...get to my tent," she said lamely.

"Wait," Reed protested, reaching toward her. But Chris grabbed her clothes and held them tight to her front, dashing for her tent. She quickly zipped it closed, sliding deep into her sleeping bag. The fabric felt cool and strange on her bare skin, still tingling from the endorphins loose and raging in her body.

She dared a glance out the small tent window. Reed had pulled on his shorts, sitting alone in front of the fire. She suddenly regretted her mad dash. What was she afraid of? He looked so lonely out there. Did he regret it?

Did she?

Chris huddled back down and considered it. The fire in her blood told her no, she couldn't regret something that good. The first time with a new lover is never all *that* good, she thought. She needed time to get used to a new body, new ways of pleasuring, finding the little tricks that turn on one man and would do nothing for another. But this had been better than good—spectacular even—better than the first time with Charlie. Hell, better than the *last* time with Charlie.

So why the hell did she leave Reed by himself at the fire?

Impulsively, Chris flung off the sleeping bag. She unzipped her tent, intending to step out fully naked, bathed in the glow of the fire...

Reed was gone. His tent was zipped closed, his clothes carefully gathered up and put away.

Oops.

Chris went back into her tent, zipping it closed just before Reed looked out his window.

Chapter 3

The morning dawned cloudy and dull, threatening rain later in the day. They walked mostly in silence, only a few murmured comments warning about loose spots on the trail or passing trail mix back and forth.

They reached the first stop, the place where the trail emptied into a small spring. Chris splashed the water on her face, kneeling beside the spring.

"Wow, that feels good," she said.

Reed knelt beside her, testing the water. "Hey, it's warm."

"It stays warm most of the time in the summer, probably because it's shallow," Chris said.

There was a long silence that Chris tried not to see as uncomfortable. She wiggled out of her boots, rubbing her feet and checking for blisters.

Reed took a long sip from his canteen, unlacing and removing his own boots. "So, are we going to talk about it?"

Chris shrugged. "Talk about what? About last night? It was great."

"'Cause if I did something wrong, I'd like to know about it," Reed said, his voice neutral.

Chris felt like she was climbing an uneven trail with gravel that could slide away from her and send her toppling any second. "Nothing, you did nothing wrong," she said. "I just…"

"Really needed to get back into your tent," Reed finished.

"What, are you mad at me?" Chris said, smiling. "I thought that was, like, the male fantasy, a woman who doesn't need to be held for hours afterward."

Reed looked away and she regretted her flippant attitude. She leaned in closer. "Can I make it up to you?"

She sidled closer, running her hand down his arm. She felt him tense, the energy and power inside him roiling. "C'mon," she wheedled. "I think I need...a bath."

Chris rose to her knees and pulled off her shirt. The sunlight felt amazingly warm on her bare shoulders, warming her body inside the tight sports bra. Reed couldn't help looking as she ran her hands over her own skin, smoothing away the pressure points from the back.

Chris moved behind him, rubbing his back and shoulders in a gentle massage that grew more insistent. She tugged at his T-shirt and he let her pull it over his head, revealing his strong chest and back to the sun. She pressed herself against his bare skin, let him feel it against his back as she unhooked her bra and let her breasts press free against him.

Then she stood and let the rest of her clothes fall onto the ground beside the trail. She stepped away from him and slipped into the spring, the water just a touch cool against her skin. It washed away the dirt and sweat in a soft rush about her body.

"C'mon in," she said, reaching out of the water toward him.

Reed looked as if he'd been carved in stone, tense and rigid, staring at her. His face was hard to read, impassive, but with jaw clenched. For a moment, she was almost afraid—was he really angry with her?

Then he was pulling off his clothes and gliding through the water toward her, his hard, powerful body colliding with hers. His hands were everywhere at once—he did not so much touch her as plunder her, exploring every inch of her body unseen in the water. She could feel his cock press against her stomach and let her own hands move over it, caress it beneath the water's surface.

His hands rose out of the water and clenched in her hair, pulling her to him. He kissed her roughly, nearly bruising her mouth with insistent heat as his tongue thrust deep into her mouth. She drank him in eagerly, hungrily, letting him press her close as though taking her over.

Then Chris squirmed away for a moment, diving beneath the water. She brought her head down to him, taking as much of his cock in her mouth as she could manage. She felt him grow harder as the heat of her mouth contrasted to the cool water, swelling inside her mouth as she moved back and forth, bracing herself by holding on to his firm buttocks. She sucked him hard, knowing she had only seconds before she would have to surface for air. She felt his hands reaching down for her, to touch anything of her.

She released him and came to the surface for air. His face was no longer impassive—he was burning, his eyes were filled with something she recognized as primal and strong, and yet was strange to her.

He pressed against her and kept pushing her backward until her ass struck a mossy outcropping, a small ledge just below the place where the stream tumbled into the spring. He lifted her onto it and the stream water cascaded over her shoulder, running over her breasts and making her nipples stand out. He caught a nipple in his mouth, sucking it between his lips in a harsh contrast to the cooler water. His fingers slid between her legs, slid up into her, his thumb caressing her clit in a constant circular motion that made her writhe under him. He dipped his head lower, down to the water, below it to slide his tongue between his fingers and lick her clit in a slow, languorous caress.

Chris felt it beginning but she didn't want to come this way, not until she had felt him inside her. She pushed his head away and he surfaced with that strange expression on his face she had seen beside the stream. *He thinks I'm rejecting him again,* the part of her brain that was still coherent said.

Quickly, Chris wrapped her legs around his hips and used them to draw him to her. He came to her hard and strong, his cock sliding up inside her with a delicious pressure that was only uncomfortable for a second, the water providing a lubricant to replace what it washed away. He thrust forward hard and strong, the head of his cock pressing into places she had never felt before. She wrapped her arms around his neck, clinging to him, almost immobile against the rock made smooth with moss and water.

Cold rock behind her, Reed warm and hard against her, his cock deep inside her, she let out sounds that would have frightened away any who would have heard them. She wrapped her legs around his hips, letting him plunge deep. She let her eyes open, staring up at the roil of the clouds, and let the last reservation go. She felt him cry out against her neck, his hands clutching her ass hard as he swelled and came inside her. One more thrust and she shuddered into an explosion of pleasure, rolling up through her body until she felt tears spring to her eyes, riding the ecstasy over and over until she realized Reed had stopped moving, his powerful arms trembling as he held her close.

He gently pulled her off the ledge, his cock sliding out of her. But she held on to his neck, helpless to move, clinging only to him. His strong arms held her in the water, letting her float against him. She felt warm and languorous, floating in a cloudlike spell of spent passion, and was content to let him hold her. He was shaking a little but his strength held firm.

Then the instinct for flight came again, the urge to run, to dress herself and hide, to put on the invisible armor that kept her inmost self safe. She fought it, knowing it would upset him again, afraid to hurt his feelings. He had made her feel so good, so wonderful, she couldn't stand to do anything or say anything that would bring that strange look to his face again. She wanted to give him a beautiful memory of the woods.

Chris lifted herself up in the water and kissed him again, a gentle, warm kiss of tenderness and comfort more than passion. He responded in kind, his hands on her back soothing instead of inflaming her. They held each other that way for a long stretch as the breeze found its way between the trees to offer its own caress.

* * * * *

The trail winding its way back down the bluffs was loose as hell. The threatening skies made good with fat droplets falling onto the gravel. Chris pushed Reed and herself harder, hoping to get to the last campsite before it became really bad.

But when they reached the foot of the stream, she saw how bad it could get.

The mountain stream that had wound its way near the path all the way down from the spring widened into a smallish river, complete with rocks and a good pace to the flow. That flow had knocked away the small, ancient wooden footbridge. It lay half submerged in the water, splintered boards jutting every which way in the gloomy sunlight.

"Shit," Chris murmured. "Remind me to issue a complaint at the ranger's station."

"I'm sure they don't know," Reed said, coming to a stop beside her. "Hardly anybody hikes this trail anymore, remember?"

Chris gauged the depth of the water, murky enough to make the bottom hard to see. "Have you ever forded a stream?"

Reed shook his head. "Looks like I'm gonna," he said.

Chris reached around into her pack and pulled out a length of light rope. "Here's what you're going to do," she said. "You see the places where the wood is just under the water? Step on those with this tied around your waist."

Reed nodded, taking the length of rope and winding it around himself.

"Test each step before you commit your weight to it," Chris continued. "Unbelt your backpack so you can let it go if you fall."

Desperately, Chris tried to remember anything else about fording a stream. It had been years since she'd had to do it and that had been with a group of seven. Vaguely, she remembered something about removing her boots but looking at the jagged boards, she discarded the thought. They'd just have to have wet boots and they'd probably have that anyway after the rain, she thought. Warning bells went off in her mind but what choice did they have? There was no way down the bluffs except across this stream.

Reed, ever the Boy Scout, had tied the rope into a firm knot. Chris took the other end and wound it around her own waist. Reed was already going ahead and she stilled the protest that she should go first. Reed's natural grace served him well, his dancer's balance moving him slowly along the submerged boards.

Chris stepped out onto the boards herself, feeling the rotten wood sink a bit farther under her boots. Her third step broke through the sodden board and she caught her balance with difficulty. The line twitched and Reed glanced back at her, improbably balanced on a board no wider than six inches across.

"You okay?" he asked.

Chris nodded. He kept moving onward as the bridge boards sank lower in the water. The stream's current washed over their knees and Chris tried to balance herself by holding out her arms, letting go of the rope.

Reed had almost reached the far side when the board beneath Chris snapped. Her left leg plummeted down between the boards and she felt something stab her calf with a sudden lightning bolt of pain. She cried out, pinwheeling her arms for balance and lost. The weight of her pack pulled her down under the water, her leg still caught in the remains of the bridge.

The water cascaded over Chris' face and in a panic she tried to breathe. Water gushed down her throat into her lungs and she coughed hard, helplessly trying to expel it. She scrabbled, feeling her hands shoot up into the air, so close and yet beyond her ability to breathe. She tried to rise up again but the weight of her pack held her down and the board firmly entrapped her leg.

Suddenly she felt the line haul her up, a strong hand grasping her arm and pulling her up into the air. Chris coughed and spluttered, unable to speak. Reed was physically holding her in the air and she could not get her free foot under her to balance upright.

Reed pulled her up harder and the board jabbed even more painfully into her leg. Still incapable of speech, Chris pointed frantically at her leg, still choking on what felt like gallons of water. Reed looked down then looked at her, and she could practically read his thoughts—he would have to let go of her to free her leg.

She nodded and tried to grab a lungful of air but only ended up coughing again. The look on Reed's face was indescribable but he only hesitated a second. Then he released her and she slipped back under the water.

It was only a moment while she felt Reed's hands grasp down her left leg and pry at the rotten boards jabbing it. It seemed much longer but there was no panic. Somewhere, Chris was sure Reed would help her. He wouldn't leave her here in the cold, dark water. He was there for her as she would have been there for him.

That jagged bolt of pain stabbed harder into her leg and suddenly she was free. The line tugged at her waist and Reed was pulling her up into the air again. She gasped for air, coughing what felt like cupfuls of water out into the air. Reed lifted her into his arms, pack and all, and a moment later she was lying beside the stream, still coughing.

She felt Reed's hands unclasping her pack—stupid, how could she have forgotten to do that, after telling Reed to do it—and releasing her. She lay back against her pack, staring up into the sky, coughing and enjoying the relative newness of air in her lungs.

Reed's fingers were at her throat, his dear face hovering over hers. She looked at him and tried to smile. "Stupid me, falling in the damn stream," she wanted to say, but couldn't make her voice work yet. She tried to move and her left leg stabbed her with pain again.

Reed's attention was elsewhere now and Chris tried to sit up to see what was going on. A large, thick splinter of wood the size of a butter knife jutted from her calf. It wasn't in very deep but the blood was flowing freely, mixing with the stream water cascading down her leg.

Reed looked up at her. "I'm going to have to pull it out, Chris," he said seriously.

Chris tried to talk but only coughed again. She nodded.

Reed placed his hands on the wood splinter and yanked it out in one hard motion. Chris couldn't help it—she gasped aloud at the pain and that set her off coughing again. Reed was already scrabbling at her pack for the first-aid kit and she pointed to the right pocket. He cracked open the blue and white box as thunder galloped above.

Perfect timing, Chris thought, glaring up at the skies. *Hold off a few minutes, wouldja?*

Reed knew what he was doing. She didn't have to point to the antiseptic—he was already washing the river water and dirt out of the small hole filling with blood. It stung a bit but the pain was already easing. Reed staunched the blood flow with wadded gauze. Chris broke out in another coughing fit as he bound it tightly with a butterfly bandage, covered it with another gauze pad and taped it in place.

She leaned back against the pack, suddenly exhausted. The adrenaline dump was fading from her bloodstream and she felt sick and stupid. For the first time, she wondered what Reed was thinking of her, how silly and weak she must seem to him.

Then he was leaning over her and his arms pulled her close to him. He was shaking and suddenly she worried about him. Was he all right? Was he hurt? She whispered to him, "You okay?" and immediately started coughing again, her throat hot and glassy.

Reed pressed a kiss on her forehead, her cheek, his hands stroking her sodden hair. "I'm fine, thank God you're all right, you scared the hell out of me," he rambled.

The intensity of his emotion surprised Chris and almost frightened her.

"I'm okay," she insisted, pushing up to a sitting position. "Sorry I'm such a klutz."

"Wait, don't try to move yet," Reed said.

"It's okay," Chris said, testing her leg and coughing a little.

"Dammit, Chris, stop pushing!" Reed said, his voice a little rough. "Take a minute after nearly dying to, I don't know, recover or something!"

"Hey, thanks for the heroic rescue, but don't—" Chris stopped, not knowing how to finish.

"Don't what?" Reed asked. "Don't care? Don't worry?"

"Don't tell me what to do," Chris said, feeling a little lame.

"I'm not," Reed snapped. "I'm trying to keep you alive. Despite your best efforts."

Chris flushed. "Look, I already feel stupid, okay? I'm sorry I inconvenienced you."

Reed ground his teeth for a moment. "That's hardly... Goddammit, Chris, I love you but you're absolutely the most infuriating woman—"

Chris stared at him, her mouth agape. Reed stopped, suddenly realizing what he'd said.

That feeling swept over Chris again, that sense of needing to run away, to hide, the flight instinct that made her want to put some kind of armor between them, as if she were naked with him even with clothes covering her, exposed and vulnerable.

"Reed, I don't know what you're thinking, but this isn't... I mean, this is just a weekend in the woods," she said in a rush. "It's been great, it's been fucking spectacular in fact, but it's just that. Just a weekend. Just sex. You know that, right?"

Reed looked away. "Sure. Sure I do. I don't know what I was...never mind."

He stood and started to gather the remnants of their things as the skies cracked overhead. Chris wanted to speak, to say something, anything. But nothing came to mind and she began to cough helplessly.

* * * * *

The warmth of the fire wasn't a match for Chris' shivering. The rain had thankfully held off so far, long enough for Reed to haul their stuff down to the campsite and come back to help Chris from the stream to their last trail stop. Everything Chris had was soaked, and when she had fallen in, Reed had let his own pack fall into the water. They ate the food they could salvage. Chris took a few mild painkillers from the first-aid kit, letting the white-hot pain in her leg fade to embers that only flared when she moved too much.

Reed's tent was a near loss, soaked through. He flung it over a low-lying branch in the vain hope it could dry a bit before morning. He set up Chris' tent, which was a much better designed to dry quickly, and put on the rainfly in case the skies opened on them.

Chris was still shivering.

"C'mon, you need to warm up," Reed said. "Get these clothes off."

Chris' teeth chattered and still she tried to crack a joke. "You men are all alike," she said, grinning.

Reed didn't smile. He helped her shed her sodden clothes, flinging them over the sheltered tree branch. Her nylon stuff sack had mostly protected her sleeping bag and she crawled into it naked, feeling its cotton-soft warmth envelop her.

A moment later, before she could zip it closed, Reed slid up beside her, his own sleeping bag unzipped to allow him to press close to her. He had also shed his wet clothes.

"I knew it," she breathed.

"I read this is how to prevent hypothermia," Reed insisted.

Chris smiled. "If I had a nickel for every time I heard that line," she said, and Reed kissed her gently. His hands moved over her cold skin, warming her with his own body. She could feel his arousal but it was almost a reflexive thing, having little to do with what was going on. He was comforting her, protecting her, not trying to seduce her. She nestled close to his warmth and felt safe, insanely happy despite the grumbling thunder and the dull throb in her leg and her continued embarrassment at her clumsiness.

She rested her head against his hard chest, her body warming in places that had nothing to do with avoiding hypothermia. She slid her arms around his chest, running them up and down his back.

"Did I thank you yet?" she murmured.

Reed's voice was rough. "I think so," he said.

She licked the outer curve of his ear before breathing, "Not well enough."

"You're hurt," he breathed.

"Then be gentle," she teased, kissing the soft skin on the underside of his jaw, traveling down the side of his neck. His hands moved over her cool skin, warming her beneath him. His hand slid down the line of her hip and smoothed over her thigh. He kneaded her ass with his fingers, sliding them up and down in a motion that awoke the heat between her legs. She pressed up against him, feeling the hot brand of his cock against the curve of her stomach.

Reed dipped his head to her shoulder, nipping the tender skin and making her clutch him tight. His hand swept back up to cup her breast, teasing the soft nipple to hardened life. He kneaded her breast with gentle force before lowering his head to take it in his mouth. He sucked gently and the tugs of his mouth made her breath catch in her throat.

His mouth traveled back upward to catch hers, his tongue sliding into her mouth with gentle passion. They melded together perfectly, pulling tight to each other. She could feel his heartbeat against hers from their bodies pressed together, almost in unison. She broke the kiss and pressed small kisses down his neck and across his chest, teasing a flat nipple with her teeth before flicking her tongue back and forth on it. Her hand wandered downward, wrapping around the hot length of his cock and moving up and down in a quickening motion. She could feel him grow harder beneath her fingers and she teased the head of his cock with her fingers, rolling it back and forth.

Reed rolled onto her and she stifled a quick gasp at the bolt of pain from her leg. He froze in sudden guilt and she quickly distracted him by pressing her clit against his cock. Had she ever been cold? It seemed there was enough heat to set her small tent on fire, his body pressing down on hers as his cock slid into her. It was incredible, a fulfilling sensation like nothing she'd felt before. He moved slowly, delicious friction building and retreating as he pressed deep within her.

Chris ran her hands up and down his back, lifting her hips to meet his in the slow, warm, rocking motion. She savored the feeling of him sheathed inside her, the sensation of melding, of forging their bodies together. His breath was warm on her shoulder, his cheek pressed against hers as he whispered something in her ear that she didn't quite understand.

Then he stopped, still inside her. She pressed her thighs against the hard muscles along his hips, urging him onward, but still he remained motionless.

"Are you all right?" she murmured. "Please, Reed..." He moved a bit and her voice broke in the cascade of sensation. She lost her breath as the thunder cracked overhead He slid up and down and she was helpless to move or take control in any way. He began to move faster and whatever she would have said was broken into helpless breaths that sounded like his name, cried out over and over. His weight pressed on her but it felt good, felt large and comforting as well as inflaming her. He thrust harder into her and she tightened her thighs against him, her hands clinging to his shoulders as though to steady her.

It began, a swell of passion cascading up from the rocking motion of his hips against hers, his cock pressed deep inside her. It began there and rolled through her entire body until it must have shot out from her very skin. Uncontained, she let out cries that might have been his name, over and over as the waves rolled through her, enveloping her in passion the way the water had enveloped her in cold, with Reed on the other side, crying out her name as he arched into her in his moment of passion. He kept moving until the final wave had ebbed, and then he remained within her even as he grew soft. Only then did he slip out, but he stayed on top of her, only propping himself up a bit to alleviate his weight.

Reed pressed kisses over her face, soothed her trembling skin with his hands. She waited for the panic, for the need to flee into the night, and it didn't come. It felt almost as delicious as it had before they had made love—and that's what it was, Chris realized. It wasn't just sex. It wasn't just a weekend. She reached up to tell him that but at that moment he moved off her, rolling to the side and drawing her close.

His heartbeat slowed beneath her cheek, and she felt the coiled tension in his body finally ease. His arm lay around her shoulders, smoothing up and down her bare back in a gentle caress. He touched her as though she were something beautiful, something he treasured. Had anyone ever touched her like that? Any lover she had taken, had anyone ever looked at her, touched her this way?

She drifted, her mind flowing over random thoughts and images like the river flowing over the rocks, never quite breaking the surface into consciousness. She barely felt Reed's arm lying heavy with sleep across her back or the furred texture of his chest. She floated as though back in the spring, with Reed as the only thing holding her still in the tumult around her. She saw his face above hers in the branches of the tree, suspended in midair, above the world.

Thunder cracked overhead and Chris' eyes opened, coming back to reality. Reed was asleep or nearly so, his arm slipping bit by bit off her shoulder. Had it been minutes or hours? In the low orange glow coming from the embers of the campfire, it was impossible to tell. A breeze wafted through the trees, providing its own background music to the creaking song of the crickets in the woods.

Say something to him, she thought, but words wouldn't come. She had never been good with words, never been one to share her feelings or admit she had them.

But she could show him.

Chris pressed her body close to him again, keeping her hurt leg carefully still. Her hand slipped down his stomach to slide over his cock, soft and sleep-warm. With slow strokes, she smoothed her hand down the inside of his thigh and back up to cradle his balls, rubbing the sensitive skin behind them.

She felt him stir against her hand, more of a sleepy reflex than actual arousal.

She lowered her head to tease a flat nipple to life, flicking the tip of her tongue back and forth across it before sucking it between her lips. He moved above her and she realized he was fully awake now. Her hand moved back up to his cock, growing hard beneath her fingers.

She kissed her way down his chest beneath the sleeping bag. He reached after her, whether to stop her or encourage her she'd never know. She ducked his hand playfully and licked the tip of his cock with her tongue.

His whole body arched in response. She couldn't see anything in the darkness of the tent and the heat of the sleeping bag around her so went on by feel. Her hand slid over his cock and brought it to her mouth. First she tasted the tip, licking the head and sucking it gently between her lips. Then she took more of it in her mouth, keeping a firm suction and sliding her tongue over it. She let it slip out then slid back down over it again, taking even more of him into her mouth, sucking him in until he filled her mouth and pressed against the back of her throat, hard and full and growing larger.

Reed was making noises above her, his hands clenching on the sleeping bag above her as her head moved up and down. She had never so enjoyed this—it had always been a chore, something she did because men liked it. Now it was as though his pleasure were hers and she drank it in.

He was drawing close, rock-hard and unable to keep still beneath the caresses of her mouth and hands. But she didn't want it to end this way. She let him go with regret and slid back up his body, still teasing his balls with her fingers. When she broke into the air, he tried to speak and she laid a finger over his mouth.

Slowly, Chris slid her leg over him and gripped his hips with her thighs. Reed gazed upward at her and his hands smoothed over her back to cradle her ass, molding and caressing it with firm fingers. He drew the sleeping bag up over her, still trying to keep her warm. He needn't have bothered, Chris thought—she was warm enough with the pounding in her blood.

Reed lowered his head to her breast, sucking at her nipple as he kneaded the soft flesh. The sensations speared through her and she couldn't wait any longer. Gently, she slid downward, letting his cock press against her, and he thrust upward into her in one smooth movement.

For a moment, she lay still, his head on her breast, letting him be within her. Then she began to move, rising up and down, riding his body. He thrust upward and she met him eagerly, keeping her thighs tight against him. Her hands smoothed through his hair as she rose and fell, feeling him press deep inside her. His eyes met hers and for once she didn't look away, didn't close her eyes, didn't hide from the intensity in his gaze. She kissed him, slow and deep, and felt him speed up beneath her. She broke the kiss with a cry and he wound his hands in her hair, holding her at his face as he thrust harder inside her.

"Oh God, Reed," she cried, and he bucked again, his voice breaking into a cry that seemed huge and wonderful at once, exploding and filling her up body, heart and soul. She felt like glass shattered and formed again, tears forming at her eyes, and his gaze filled her even as he slowed.

"Reed," she tried again, and he moved again, shattering her voice. "Oh Reed…" He slid up one more time, deep and full, and she broke into shuddering pleasure, the wave that swelled and fell and swelled again until she drifted to a stop, letting him slip from her.

"Chris," he whispered. "Chris, I love you."

Chris slid to his side and nestled against his chest again, encircled in the warm strength of his arms. When the thunder finally gave way to the rain, she was already asleep in his embrace.

Chapter 4

The morning came with warm sunshine, the light falling with an effervescent clarity that made each leaf, every branch stand out in its own spotlight. Chris helped Reed dismantle the campsite. They were only a few hours' walk from the ranger station, even with her slower pace thanks to her injured leg.

Chris hoisted her pack onto her back, wincing a little. "Some serious rest and relaxation is in order," she told Reed as they walked down the trail.

"After a trip to the hospital to get that leg looked at," Reed said.

Chris grinned. "I've got a better idea. A bed and breakfast in Jericho, that town just below the bluffs. A night of relaxation before heading back to the city."

Reed didn't respond. Chris kept musing aloud. "A long bubble bath—that would be marvelous."

"Chris," Reed began, his voice tentative. "What happens when we get down to…?"

"The world?" Chris asked, smiling. "Our lives?"

"Boyfriends," Reed said.

Chris's smile faded. "Ex-boyfriend. Hopefully has finished moving his things out of my apartment while I was gone. If not, it should be a nicely unpleasant homecoming, complete with walking papers."

Reed didn't say anything.

"It's not for you," Chris hastened to add. She wished she could see Reed's face—talking to his back bothered her. "I made that decision before I even started down this trail."

"Glad to hear it," Reed said, his tone neutral.

They walked on for a while in silence until finally the chirp of the birds and rustle of the breeze grew deafening in its quiet.

"Come with me," Reed said quietly.

"We went over this," Chris said awkwardly, the panic trying to come back in the sanity of morning light.

"That was bullshit and you know it," Reed said, stopping and turning to face her. "This wasn't just some frolic in the woods, Chris. This is it, the one true undying whatever, and you only get a shot at this once or twice in a lifetime. I didn't know why I wanted to come here and I didn't know why I still wanted to do the trail when my buddy bowed out. Now I know I was coming here for you. I've waited my whole life for no one but you."

Chris couldn't speak. Her mind was a whirl of hissing static and no words came out.

Reed turned away and kept walking, faster now. "My friend will be waiting for me at the trailhead," he said. "You can come with me and we'll go into the town and get your leg looked at. And then we'll find that bed and breakfast and be together, for real in the real world. Or you can wait for the rangers to take you to your car and we'll go our separate ways."

Chris followed him in silence, her mind racing. All the blessed, sane reasons why this was totally impossible were whirling about her head like a tornado. They hiked on and she could hear cars again as they neared the trailhead with roads and buildings not far beyond the trees.

Ahead of Reed, she could see the forest thinning out toward the clearing where the ranger station stood. *Too soon,* she thought. *I haven't had time to think yet!*

Sure enough, a blue pickup truck was waiting in the parking lot, a young man with a cast on his left leg sitting on the flatbed reading a novel. "Reed!" he called, waving as he lumbered down. "You survived. Damn. I was going to swipe your CDs."

"Thanks, Jack, you klutz," Reed said cheerfully. "Jack, this is Chris Coleman."

"Miss," Jack said, nodding respectfully. "Can we give you a ride down to the trail lot?"

Chris met Reed's eyes. He tossed his pack into the back of the truck and faced her, waiting.

The moment stretched out in silence. Jack looked from one to the other, his mouth forming a silent O. Then he faded back to slide behind the wheel, leaving them alone.

Reed stared at her, his face impassive just as it had been in the woods when she'd hurt him.

And there was a touch of that sadness as he turned away toward the passenger door of the truck.

He laid his hand on the handle.

"Wait," Chris said.

Reed turned back and Chris came to him, pulling him against her and kissing him with everything in her. He held her close, the sun shone about them and the last of her fear melted away in its light.

They had come through the woods together and Chris had finally realized what Reed already seemed to know — they were bound together...partners, lovers. Walking in tandem.

Also by Elizabeth Donald

℘

Fever
On the Prowl

About the Author

℘

Elizabeth Donald is a writer fond of things that go chomp in the night. She is the author of the award-winning Nocturnal Urges vampire mystery series and numerous short stories and novellas in the horror, science fiction and erotica genres. By day, she is a newspaper reporter in the St. Louis area, which provides her with an endless source of material. Her web site is www.elizabethdonald.com, and readers can find out more by joining her YahooGroup at: groups.yahoo.com/group/elizabethdonald.

Elizabeth welcomes comments from readers. You can find her website and email address on her author bio page at www.ellorascave.com.

Tell Us What You Think

We appreciate hearing reader opinions about our books. You can email us at Comments@EllorasCave.com.

OFF THE DEEP END

Anna J. Evans

Chapter 1

Caitlyn had been dreaming about this vacation for four months. Since the last Christmas present under her lonely little tree had been unwrapped, she'd spent every moment anticipating the sun on her skin, the cool feel of a margarita in her hand, the sweet caress of a salty breeze. She'd been sure the soothing combination would finally banish the stress and sadness that had been her constant companions since her software company had transferred her to Anchorage, Alaska, last fall.

Geez…*Alaska.*

It was an extraordinarily beautiful state, but a horrible place to live if you happened to be an unabashedly fanatical sun worshiper. The subzero temperatures were bad enough, but the long hours of darkness were unbearable. Her coworkers kept telling her to hold out until May, and then she'd have seventeen hours of sunlight with highs in the balmy fifties, but she couldn't wait another month for a break from the winter weather.

"Fifty sch-sch-schmifty," Caitlyn stuttered, unable to believe anyone could consider a temperature under seventy-five balmy.

"Can I get you another towel?" the older woman working the cabana asked, probably noticing Caitlyn's teeth chattering over the reggae music.

"No, I'm f-f-f-fine, thank you." Caitlyn sighed, pulling her striped beach blanket more tightly around her shoulders and rising from her lounge chair.

It was nearly dusk, and there was no sense lounging when there was no sun to bask in. San Diego had been

pounded with spring storms since the day she arrived at the
Sand Piper Resort and Spa. The highs the past three days had
been in the low fifties, the entire staff of the spa had called in
sick and the restaurant by the beach had shut down due to
general lack of interest. Even the margarita machine was on
the fritz. Caitlyn hadn't been out of her hotel room for more
than an hour at a time. There was nowhere to go except the
lobby, and as much as she enjoyed listening to people answer
telephones…

"At least I can get some exercise before the rain starts in
again," she muttered to herself, pulling on her sandals and
setting off toward the beach.

Even with the dark gray clouds hovering on the horizon,
the white sand was calling her name. She'd spent the first ten
years of her life in Miami and never lost her love for beaches,
summer clothing year 'round and one hundred-degree days
with poach-your-brain-like-an-egg humidity. There was
nothing quite like wearing nothing but a sundress while you
walked down the beach, feeling sweat trickle between your
breasts as the bridge of your nose started to burn.

"You are *not* waxing poetic about sweat and sunburns,"
Caitlyn said, knowing she would have been able to muster up
a laugh at her own expense if she hadn't stupidly packed
nothing but sundresses.

Get off the beach!

The voice sounded in her head with enough volume to
make her jump. She had been talking to herself a lot since the
move, but she had yet to hear herself talking back. Especially
in a booming male voice that echoed between her ears.

"Maybe it's my inner masculine," Caitlyn said, struggling
to recall her college class on Jungian theory, while shaking off
the dizziness that had followed the mental shout.

Run back to the grass! Get off the beach, woman!

Before Caitlyn could yell at her inner masculine voice for
being chauvinistic enough to use the word "woman" as an

insult, a slap of cold water hit her mid-thigh and knocked her to the ground.

"Oh c-c-crap," Caitlyn gasped, the water so cold it immediately began to numb her legs and hands.

She floundered in the newly wet sand as the huge wave surged away from the shore, taking one of her sandals with it.

"No way," she gasped, still out of breath from the shock of the cold water, but determined to rescue her new, sparkly, on-sale-for-half-off gold sandal from the cruel clutches of the Pacific Ocean. She so rarely treated herself to anything frivolous, she couldn't bear to lose her fancy footwear before it even saw the light of a sunny day.

Run, damn you! Are you mad?

Something about the sheer incredulity of the voice in her head made Caitlyn take her attention away from her rapidly retreating sandal, and up to the wave in front of her.

"Oh. My. God," she whispered, her gray eyes growing impossibly large as she realized, with a strange mix of peacefulness and despair, that she was about to meet her maker.

Her last foolish thought before the enormous tidal wave crashed over her head was a regretful one. And for that, she was a little sad. Still, she couldn't believe God had taken her out without at least one final day in the sunshine. She had prayed for that day, prayed for it with every ounce of her being.

But if there was one thing she should have learned from her rotten childhood, it was that a great number of prayers went unanswered and that God probably didn't like red-haired people.

Or maybe it was just her.

* * * * *

119

Lukas swam toward the woman with all the power in his body. But even with over two hundred and fifty pounds of pure muscle on his six-foot-four frame, he doubted he'd make it in time. The water would be deathly cold to a mortal woman, especially one so terribly thin.

At least they should feed *their women if they won't let them rule.*

The ways of modern humans were a complete mystery to his people. The Illuminated had been led by female rulers since time immemorial, the crown always passing from mother to daughter. There was equality between the sexes, without a doubt, and most of their warriors were male, but there were just some things that the female of the species were more skilled at accomplishing.

A good ruler had to have the ability to multitask and juggle a variety of roles simultaneously. Most of the men Lukas knew, himself included, had a more limited focus. Males tended to fixate on the job at hand until it was accomplished, and Goddess forbid you asked them to do anything else until they were finished, whether it be tending to the needs of their lover, feeding their children or chewing a mouthful of seaweed.

A wave of bitterness as large as the one he currently fought against rose within Lukas as he thought of the father he had never known and the lifemate he himself had never spared the time to find. He was as bad as the man he had resented for abandoning his mother. Of course, in this situation, his single-mindedness might save this woman's life.

With a last ferocious kick, Lukas found himself within inches of the woman with the long, wavy red hair. Her already pale face was now a ghostly white and the curly locks that had looked so alive and vibrant when dry floated darkly around her head, twining about her neck as if to finish the job the ocean had started. Quickly, he let one arm encircle her narrow waist as the other swept the hair away from her throat. He pulled her close, fighting the urge to moan as her soft curves melded against him and the wave spun them in a swift circle, mimicking the spiral of desire that was beginning to grow low in Lukas' body.

The woman was near death. This was not the time to be thinking of how it would feel to part those pale thighs and slide his aching shaft deep inside her, of how perfect her softness would feel clinging to him, how erotic her fingers would feel clenching his buttocks as she helped him find the rhythm that would make her come. Goddess, it *had* been far too long since he'd felt the slick heat of a woman if he couldn't even keep his mind on the task at hand.

Still, there was no denying that she would be warmer without the clothes that clung to her small frame, if she were pressed tightly against his own bare skin, able to absorb his heat directly. As he deftly untied the straps that held her dress together, Lukas told himself it was purely concern for her life that motivated his actions, not the fact that he was suddenly half mad to see her bared to his gaze.

Sweet Goddess…

She was even more lovely without her covering—thin, but perfectly proportioned, with pale, peach-colored nipples that pebbled in the cold water, begging Lukas to taste them. His mouth practically watered at the thought and his traitorous cock pulsed with need despite the chill of the ocean, but there was no time to waste. Still, he had to struggle harder than he would have liked to ignore the fact that the waves had washed away the scrap of fabric human women used to cover their sex, and that she was completely nude as he pulled her bare skin tightly to his own.

Open for me.

Lukas spoke the words softly into her mind as he brought his face close to hers, brushing noses gently, teasing her lips with his using the softest pressure. There was still air inside her lungs, he could sense it in the buoyancy of her body. If she was conscious enough to take the Breath Kiss from him, he could make sure she didn't drown while they made their way to warmer waters.

For a moment, there was no response, not even the slightest shifting of her limbs to reveal that she was still fighting to stay among the living. Lukas felt desperation quicken his own breath. He couldn't lose this woman. She was a stranger, a mortal, but something within him demanded that she live. Perhaps it was because he had failed to warn her to safety, or that the wave and the battle that had caused it were entirely his doing. Or maybe it was simply that she fit so perfectly in his arms. Whatever the reasons, the overwhelming need to pull her back from death made him hold her tighter, made him plead with his mind for her to try, just a little.

Kiss me. Open your mouth and let me taste you.

Just when Lukas was beginning to fear that his command would be ignored, the mortal made a sound low in her throat and arched in his arms, pressing her lips to his own.

And what sweet lips they were. Lukas felt a primal sound of need burst from his body as he clung to the woman, his tongue parting her lips and tasting the sweet flavor of strawberries mingling with the salty ocean. Weak as she was, he was surprised when her tongue met his with equal urgency, swirling through his mouth before she suckled at his bottom lip, drawing her teeth over the sensitive skin with a fierceness that had Lukas' already stiffened shaft fully engorged and pulsing hungrily against her slim hips.

He felt her hands tangling in his hair and moaned again, giving in to the temptation to slide one hand down to her firm ass and clench his fingers into her flesh. She ground against him with a need that rivaled his own and Lukas wondered if they would make it to warmer water or mate right there in the middle of the freezing ocean. He was struggling to control himself, to make sure his temptress was safe from hypothermia before they took their mutual lust any further, when that unnameable essence within him suddenly burst from his chest, traveling down her throat, into her lungs, giving her the Breath Kiss.

He felt the change in the tension of her limbs immediately. She stopped her writhing against his cock, and her entire body grew limp and relaxed before her eyes opened, slow and sleepy, as if waking from a dream.

Unfortunately, it seemed she wasn't pleased with her present reality.

"Ahhhhhhh!" she screamed, her voice distorted by the water, but the expression of pure terror on her face clearly communicating her shock and fear.

Her thrashing arms and legs did a decent job as well, and soon Lukas found the heel of a ridiculous-looking piece of human footwear shoved roughly into his stomach.

I'm here to help you, don't fight me!

"Ahhh!" she screamed again, following the sound with another kick, this time hitting what she'd evidently been aiming for the first time.

Goddess of the Deep, I should have let you drown!

Lukas doubled over in pain, his cock screaming out in agony, a dull ache blossoming through his balls and up into his cramping lower belly. He moaned and let his temptress and her cruel footwear swim a few feet away as he struggled to overcome the agony in his nether regions. He suddenly recalled very clearly why he hadn't loved a woman in so very long.

Because they were insane. Every single one of them, mortal or Illuminated. They were grinding against your cock one minute and kicking you in the same seconds later. Little wonder he had become a warrior. At least men and swords were straightforward entities.

Come back, you'll freeze to death.

Lukas tried to keep his tone even, to seem as non-threatening as possible. Bruised...ego or no bruised ego, he had to get the foolish woman out of the ocean.

"Get away from me," she gasped as her head broke water, her voice remarkably strong, though the movements of her arms and legs were already growing sluggish.

Let me take you back to shore. I know where we can warm you.

"I don't need your warmth," she said, teeth chattering.

The Breath Kiss won't protect you from the cold, only keep the water from your lungs.

"Go away!"

You're making yourself colder by swimming.

"No, I'm n-n-not."

Your core body temperature falls more quickly with movement. You're risking a heart attack.

"Y-y-you are risking my f-f-foot in your face."

Ah. Well, that's preferable to your foot in my cock.

"Shut up, you're not even real," she said, her voice cracking and a sob echoing across the water.

Woman, let me help you. I'm as real as that vicious shoe on your foot. Come to me and I'll take you back to your people.

Lukas said the words gently, feeling like the lowest form of bottom-dwelling sea creature. The poor woman thought she was hallucinating. She was half drowned and freezing to death, he, on the other hand, had merely gone too long without a female in his bed. Of the two of them, he should have been the more reasonable.

"No, I'm not...I don't..."

Her words trailed off as her eyes fluttered closed. Lukas caught her immediately and pulled her against the heat of his body, feeling a strange wave of tenderness as her damp curls settled against his chest. Whether her face was animated with anger and passion or peaceful in rest, she was as fair as any female he'd ever seen. And there was no doubt that she stirred his blood in a way no woman had done in a very, *very* long time.

Now, if he could manage to avoid notice as he carried her nude, unconscious form to the warm bubbling water in the center of the human settlement, they might have a chance to discover if they could bear each other long enough to share a night of passion. She had desired him, there was no doubt in his mind, and it should be easy enough to convince her that he was as flesh and blood as she herself.

Though you certainly have more pressing issues at hand than bedding a mortal.

Lukas did his best to ignore his inner voice of reason. What could be more pressing than clearing his mind at this critical juncture in the history of his people? His half-sister, Queen Eleanor, had finally made an unforgivable error in judgment. After years of dancing the line with both her subjects and the High Council, her mad foolishness had finally threatened the very survival of their world. As a direct result of her command, a cursed race of serpents from their own enchanted seas had been loosed into Earth's oceans, endangering the human race—a sin that none among them would be able to forgive.

Whether it was merely legend or fact, their culture was founded on the belief that the Illuminated had been granted a chance at paradise by the ancient gods because they had vowed never to make war upon the human race. Unleashing monsters big enough to devour a small ship and forbidding their recapture most certainly qualified as an act of war in most minds, including those of the High Council. When they'd ordered Lukas and his men to subdue the beasts against the Queen's wishes, Lukas had known it was only a matter of time before Eleanor was asked to abdicate. He would need his wits firmly about him if he hoped to ease his half-sister from the throne without losing his own life in the process. Therefore, it would be in his best interest if he wasn't being distracted by the unsatisfied shaft between his legs.

Thin logic, soldier.

"But good enough reason for a few hours' enjoyment." Lukas smiled and increased the power of his strokes toward shore, thinking of several extremely pleasurable ways to satisfy his profound craving for this mortal woman. Not the least tempting of which was the thought of his face buried between the creamy thighs that floated on top of the water, revealing a thatch of auburn hair that called to him as seductively as any Siren's song.

Of course, any Illuminated man worth his salt knew Sirens were all talk and no action. But this fiery redhead seemed to have both areas covered, and he wondered what she would scream into the night when she came. He sent out a prayer to the ancestors that it would be his name.

Chapter 2

Caitlyn was back in the erotic dream, which was perfectly fine with her. Given the choice between the erotic dream and the freezing-cold-out-in-the-middle-of-the-ocean dream, she'd definitely take the former.

Especially if it involved that beautiful man. That's how she'd known it was a dream in the first place. No man like that had ever spared her a second glance, and would certainly never risk his life to save her from a tidal wave or start kissing her in the middle of the ocean.

"Oh yes," she breathed, her entire body tingling as the beautiful man's talented tongue swept lightly, teasingly, *perfectly* over her clit.

She couldn't recall the last time a man had kissed her there—okay, maybe she could, it had been exactly five years, seven months, three days ago—and it was so much more intense than she remembered. Waves of pleasure rolled through her body, her womb already pulsing with the prelude to orgasm, every nerve ending sizzling with awareness. It was as if he were telegraphing pleasure to every inch of her skin as he swept his tongue around and around her throbbing nub, building her need until she was dizzy and disoriented.

Goddess, you taste like the afterlife.

"Oh wow," Caitlyn gasped, opening her eyes and looking down between her legs, expecting to see the long, kinky black hair and startlingly gorgeous, velvet brown eyes of her dream man and instead seeing…water.

Bubbling hot water, to be specific. She must have fallen asleep in the hot tub nestled in the center of the Sand Piper's extensive gardens. Thank God she hadn't drowned. With as few staff members as the place apparently employed in April, her body could have floated there for days unobserved.

"Oh wow!" Caitlyn gasped again, her body arching in the hot water as the stroking between her thighs resumed. Her breasts grew heavy and full and her nipples tightened almost painfully, hungry for more than the swirling water to caress them.

Her first thought was that she'd somehow positioned herself on a water jet, but there were several things wrong with that theory. Firstly, that certainly didn't *feel* like water, it felt like a very talented, very thick and eager tongue. Secondly, there were definitely two warm hands on her thighs, gently but firmly spreading her wide, and thirdly, there was a dark shadow lurking beneath the water that she was fairly sure wasn't a hot tub shark.

And if that weren't enough evidence, she was completely naked and she sure as hell wouldn't have done that herself. She was a one-piece bathing suit girl, all the way. No need to draw attention to her barely B-cup breasts or shockingly white stomach with a bikini. Not to mention the fact that she hadn't even put on her swimsuit today.

Tell me your name, I know that you're awake. Tell me your name so I can know whose sweet cunt I'm tasting.

"Caitlyn," she said softly, more than a little shocked that the manifestation of her internal masculine used the word "cunt". But then, he wasn't at all what she'd expected.

She'd never had fantasies about men who were over six feet tall, composed of pure muscle. And even if she had, they'd never had deep mocha skin and dreadlocks down to their shoulders, or a little goatee that scratched delightfully against her lips when they kissed. Not that she wasn't open to dating someone of a different race, but no one had ever asked, and Caitlyn tended to fantasize about the familiar. That way she was less likely to long for things that were out of her league. Her mother had always made it clear that her daughter's shockingly white skin, bright red hair and freckles were thoroughly repulsive to most of the male population, so Caitlyn had learned at an early age not to get her hopes up.

Touch yourself, Caitlyn. I don't want this sweet cunt floating away from me or I'd do it myself. Put your hands on your breasts.

Shaking slightly, her breath growing more erratic as her dream man continued to work his tongue against her clit, driving her just to the edge of orgasm but not beyond, Caitlyn moved her hands to her breasts. It was a completely foreign thing for her to do. Even when she used her vibrator she rarely spent time touching herself, especially not cupping her own swollen flesh or erotically tracing circles around the aching buds of her own nipples.

But it felt perfect to do so with her dream man. Just a little bit wicked, but in the nicest, most pleasurable sense of the word.

"Oh," she heard herself cry out in a strangled gasp, the electricity of her own hands on her body shooting down to join in the riot of sensations as his busy tongue swept from her clit to her throbbing entry and back again.

When she felt him part her folds and slide one thick finger inside, she almost lost it—almost came with a ferocity that she knew she'd never experienced before—but instead she pulled her hands away from her nipples, sucking in air and struggling not to fall over the edge. She didn't want this to end so quickly, wanted to draw out this pleasure, to hold on to this dream and never wake up.

But you are awake, idiot!

This time, it was her own inner critic voicing its opinion inside her thick skull, the very *awake* skull that was resting on the rough concrete of the very real hot tub that was surrounded by the very real gardens of the very real resort where she was enjoying the weirdest vacation on record.

And where a very real and apparently telepathic man was presently challenging the record for underwater cunnilingus.

Come for me, Caitlyn, come on my mouth.

If the command hadn't been accompanied by the teasing nip of his teeth on her throbbing clit and the vigorous movement of two thick fingers between her thighs, Caitlyn might have followed her natural inclination and jumped out of that hot tub faster than you could say "strangers with candy". As matters presently stood, however, all she could do was come—long and loud and hard.

"Ohhh!" she screamed, arching into his mouth so deeply that her breasts rose from the water and tingled in the cool night air.

Her entire body shook with the power of her release, her thighs trembling as her hands thrust beneath the water to tangle in mystery man's hair. With an abandoned sound, she pulled his mouth closer to her, grinding her slick center against him with a shamelessness that nearly shocked her out of her pleasure.

This just wasn't Caitlyn Saunders. She was a computer geek with fewer notches on her bedpost than fingers on one hand. She sat shyly in corners, hid behind her mass of hair and blushed a shade of pink bordering on fuchsia whenever an attractive man so much as glanced in her direction. She did not touch herself in front of people, she did not have sex in public places with strangers and she did *not* press a man's mouth against her pussy.

Oh, sweet woman, I'll crave the taste of your come until I die.

His words, accompanied by the thrust of his tongue deep into her center, were enough to banish all doubtful thoughts and bring on a second orgasm that rocked her more thoroughly than the first. She was sobbing by the time the powerful contractions finally started to abate, tears of happiness rolling down her face.

She had been completely off base when she'd wished for one more day in the sun before she died. What she had really needed was one night with this man. Now she knew she could go to meet her maker finally understanding what all the damn fuss was about. *This* was what sex was supposed to feel like, *this* was what she'd read about in those books under her mother's bed, *this* was what the girls in the office were talking about when they said their boyfriends made them come so hard they nearly forgot their own name.

She could safely say that at this moment she had no idea who Caitlyn was, nor did she care.

"The next time, I'm going to watch you come," her dream man said, shaking his black dreads loose as he emerged from the water like some ancient god who ruled over oceans, rivers, streams...and probably women's vaginas.

"Next time?" she panted, still struggling to regain her breath after the orgasm-to-top-all-orgasms.

"I can't wait to be inside you," he said, his voice thick with need and colored by an accent she couldn't place.

"Oh well, I—" Caitlyn began, completely losing the ability to form language when his massive hands moved to cup her face and his eyes found hers.

No man had ever given her a look like that, a look that said she was a goddess come to Earth and that he would worship at the temple of her body until he shuffled off his mortal coil. He took her breath away and made her already sated body start to yearn for more of this man, so much more that they might need years to fit all the more in. They might even need a lifetime.

"I think you must have me confused with someone else," Caitlyn said, pressing back against the side of the hot tub, trying to distance herself from the man and the thoughts he inspired. She had never let herself get swept away in some happily-ever-after fantasy. She was a logical woman who knew that love didn't spontaneously erupt at first sight and that no man this gorgeous could really be interested in her. Unless, of course, he were completely insane.

"Are you...crazy?" Caitlyn asked, wanting to slap herself the second the words were out of her mouth. Crazy people didn't *know* they were crazy, and even if they did they wouldn't admit it. Especially if they were trying to score some ass.

Oh my God...*she* was the ass this unbelievably handsome nutcase was trying to score. The thought made her dizzy with pleasure, despite the fact that she considered herself a feminist and above taking advantage of the mentally ill.

"I am not the one without the sense to run from a giant wave," he said with a smile that reminded her of how perfect it felt to have her tongue in his mouth, to bite down on the firm pillow of his bottom lip. God, she wanted to suck that lip into her mouth more than she wanted a transfer out of Anchorage.

"Can you feel how much I desire you?" he asked, moving his hips forward and pressing what had to be the largest and throbbingest of all large and throbbing erections between her legs.

Caitlyn gasped at the intimate contact, a gasp that he swallowed as he brought his lips down to hers. His hand tangled in the hair at the back of her neck and fisted, angling her head so that his tongue could thrust into her. Within seconds she was moaning into the warm, wet cavern of his mouth, returning his rough kisses with equal passion, claiming him as surely as he claimed her — and shocking the hell out of herself in the process.

Shouldn't she be caring that she didn't even know the name of the man whose long finger traced the crevice of her most private of private places?

"I don't know —"

"You *do* know."

"You don't even know what I was going to say," she gasped, her nipples calling for an end to all this ridiculous talk as her breasts pressed into the planes of his smooth, hard chest. He felt like living, breathing marble, warm, dark marble that she wanted to smear with her suntan oil and slip and slide all over on the king-size bed in her hotel room.

"I know what your body is telling me," he said with a wicked grin as he slid a finger deep into her center. "Feel how slick you are?" he murmured into her hair as his finger started to fuck her with slow, sensuous strokes that had her womb clenching with need.

"Well, I did just come…twice," Caitlyn said, her voice beyond breathy as his lips brushed hers again.

This time his kiss was as tender and insistent as the hand between her legs, and the combination brought her near tears a second time. No one had ever touched her like this, no one. She'd grown up with a mother who'd handed out more backhands than hugs, and her few encounters with men had been rushed, furtive couplings that had left her feeling lonely and unfulfilled. She'd never dreamed another human being's touch could bring such comfort, could ease something in her heart even as it brought her body to life with unbelievable pleasure. She knew that if she and this man were to come together she would finally understand what "making love" really meant.

"Twice is not enough. I want you to come again. I want to feel your sweet cunt throb around my cock," he said.

"We're in the middle of the resort, someone could see," Caitlyn protested weakly even as she continued to return his slow, sensual kisses and ride the two fingers he now worked inside her. She knew she should care that they might be discovered, but for some reason the idea almost excited her.

"My people aren't ashamed of such things," he said, kissing the column of her throat before using his tongue to trace a path down to her breast.

"Oh yes, please," Caitlyn moaned, arching into his mouth as he kissed and nibbled her swollen flesh before sucking her nipple inside the wet heat of his mouth. His rough tongue swept across her tightened tip, again and again, with the perfect teasing pressure, quickly banishing any thought of protest.

"I can't wait to please you," he growled against her skin, making her gasp as his teeth bit down on her sensitive skin, the slight pain quickly giving way to exquisite pleasure.

And then, before her body could recover from the magic of his mouth on her breasts, his lips were meeting hers and his large, throbbing cock was meeting the slick entry to her sex.

"No, wait, we should—oh God!" Caitlyn cried, whatever sensible thing she'd been about to say flying from her mind as his cock tunneled deep inside her, stretching her to the limits of what her body could bear, filling her so completely that it nearly brought her to the edge of another blinding orgasm.

"No, *you* are a goddess. Look at me, let me see your eyes," he said, halting his thrust when he was buried to the hilt, pulling back to cup her face in his hands. "I've only dreamed of such passion. You are beautiful."

"Oh...God," Caitlyn sobbed, clinging to his shoulders and struggling to maintain the terrible intimacy of eye contact with a stranger.

"Am I hurting you? You're so tight, so amazingly tight," he groaned, his face clearly showing the restraint he was exercising to keep from ramming inside her. It was a gesture of concern that touched her, but not in the way she wanted to be touched just now. This was sex, fabulous sex and nothing more. The only thing stupider than fucking a stranger was falling in love with said stranger, and she wasn't about to add another notch to her stupid post today.

"You're not hurting me," she said, moving in to kiss his lips, more than ready for the soul-deep meeting of eyes to end.

"But you feel so—"

"You're not hurting me. I want you to fuck me. Please, fuck me now," she begged, wiggling her hips wildly, showing him how desperately she needed for him to move, to fuck her, to take away the worries of her heart with the passion of his body.

"With pleasure," he said, a dark note in his voice as he gripped her buttocks in his impossibly large hands and began to give her exactly what she'd asked for.

Caitlyn cried out and raked her fingernails down his muscled back as the tension low in her body built to an unbearable level. There was a hint of pain when he thrust his deepest, but it was far overshadowed by the heavenly feeling of his thick cock stretching her as he pounded in and out of her pussy, the crisp, curly hairs on his chest brushing against her nipples.

"I'm going to come, I'm going to—"

"Lukas, my name is Lukas. I want to hear you scream my—"

"Lukas, oh God, Lukas!" Caitlyn screamed, bucking onto his shaft as her orgasm claimed her. She'd never come with a man inside her before and it was more intense, more intimate, than she would have dreamed possible.

"You feel so amazing. You're going to make me come, fill you with—"

"No, you can't," Caitlyn managed to gasp out though her body still shuddered with the strength of her release, making it difficult to even remember how to breathe.

"I can. I will. Right now," he said, his words followed by a purely masculine sound of satisfaction as his cock began to pulse inside her.

Caitlyn sucked in a deep breath, shocked to find that she could feel the hot streams of his cum shooting against her womb, and even more shocked at how exciting she found it. She could be risking unplanned pregnancy or worse, but the sensation still made her indescribably hot. Without a second thought she squirmed her hips into tighter contact with his, taking his pulsing length deeper inside and rubbing her clit against the base of his cock until she felt the tension crest within her once again.

"Lukas," she moaned, wrapping her arms around his neck and holding on for dear life as she started to come again.

As the violent pleasure coursed through her body, Caitlyn somehow managed to keep her eyes open, gazing over Lukas' broad shoulder—and immediately wished she hadn't.

"Oh my God," she screamed, shocked to see two, maybe three, men hiding in the dense foliage at the edge of the hot tub, watching as her orgasm finished having its way with her. She was simultaneously embarrassed and incredibly excited, and then stunned when the walls of her pussy started to contract with even more passion, responding to the unexpected eroticism of having such a private moment become a public event.

"What's wrong?" Lukas asked, holding her close and nuzzling her neck as the waves of pleasure finally started to subside.

"There's someone there, behind the... Well, they were there a second ago."

"They? How many?" Lukas asked, turning to look where Caitlyn indicated, every muscle in his body tense as he quickly pulled himself from her body and protectively positioned her behind him.

"Two or three men, I'm not sure."

"No women?" Lukas asked, some of the tension easing from the arm that held her behind him.

"No, I didn't see one. Why? Do you know them?"

"I may," he said vaguely, then added with a devilish grin, "If I do, I'll be sure they know that you enjoy being observed."

"I do *not* enjoy being observed!" Caitlyn protested, suddenly embarrassed.

"The way your body milked my cock would say otherwise."

"I don't care what my body says, you need to listen to my mouth," Caitlyn said, starting to get more than a little annoyed.

"But women so often say no when they mean yes," he teased, taking her back into the circle of his arms.

"Did you just say women say no when they mean yes?"

"Are you hard of hearing? If so, I can speak directly into your mind," he said as he trailed kisses over her forehead. "It is no trouble."

"What's your name again?" Caitlyn asked, her tone as innocent as his was condescending.

"Lukas," he said, pulling back to give her another wide smile. "Don't tell me you've forgotten the name you screamed into the night?"

"Lukas, you are a jackass. No wonder you're hard up for pussy," Caitlyn said, shoving his hands from her body and pulling herself from the hot tub with a speed and strength that surprised her almost as much as speaking the word "pussy" out loud. But hell, why pull any punches when the jackass in question had just had his cock in said pussy mere seconds before?

"Where are you going?" he asked, his handsome face a study in complete confusion.

"Back to my room. *Alone*," Caitlyn said, looking around for her clothes. She'd settle for a beach blanket or used towel some other sun-worshipper had left behind, but there wasn't a stitch of fabric of any kind to be found. She was going to have to make a naked run for her room. Nothing like being forced to streak for the first time in her entire life to put the cherry on this melted-ice-cream-sundae of a day.

"I have offended you," Lukas said, his eyes troubled, his goatee seeming to wilt around his full mouth. "I apologize. I'm not familiar with your ways. It's been many years since I have interacted with humans."

"Wh-wh-what?" Caitlyn asked, her teeth starting to chatter again now that she was out of the warm water and away from all that hot, silken skin. She wanted to accept his apology, wanted to crawl back into the bubbles and lose herself in his strong arms. She couldn't remember the last time she'd felt so safe, let alone so sexually satisfied. Too bad he hadn't stopped talking after the word "apologize".

"Come back into the water."

"Did you say it's been *years* since you interacted with humans?"

I have visited this settlement many times, but always late at night when there is no one to observe me as I make my way from the ocean.

"The ocean?"

My people enter your world through portals under the sea.

"My world?"

Beautiful Caitlyn, I will not think less of you if you have weak ears.

"What?!" Caitlyn said.

We all have parts of our body that betray us.

"Like your brain?"

I am Lukas of the Illuminated People, First Officer of the Queen's Ocean Warriors and —

"Oh God, you really are completely crazy."

Crazy? My people were building civilizations when humans still birthed their children in the dirt!

His angry words echoed in her head as she turned and fled down the garden path, an unexplainable aching in her chest. She hardly believed in love, let alone love at first sight. But then, if there were such a thing, it made sense that she would fall for a bossy, overbearing man who thought he was some sort of mermaid.

"He is no *maid*, woman. He is a man, most assuredly," said the beautiful woman lounging against the railing of the wooden bridge not ten feet ahead of her.

"Excuse me?" Caitlyn asked, not sure what else to say, but certain that freezing where she stood would be a good idea. No need to get any closer to a person who practically radiated unfriendliness.

"Perhaps you were not enough of a woman to arouse our Lukas. He does have a reputation for bedding only the most beautiful, sensual women. You look to be hardly more than a girl. And an unattractive one at that," she said, the smirk on her face supremely unpleasant.

Whoever this was, she was a witch. She was at least six feet tall, with bottomless black-brown eyes and raven hair that flowed in wild curls down to her ankles. Her skin was nearly as pale as Caitlyn's own, but with a hint of olive that said she would tan well if she were to spend the afternoon in the sun. It looked like she hadn't had the time lately, however, since there wasn't a single tan line on her completely nude frame.

Was the Sand Piper a nudist resort? They hadn't said anything in the brochure, but this was California, and Californians were notorious for being very blasé about things that would completely scandalize the rest of the country.

"Are you deaf and dumb as well as ugly?" the woman asked in a syrupy-sweet voice that was, without a doubt, the bitchiest thing Caitlyn had ever heard.

She was usually cowed by women like this when she was clothed, let alone buck-naked with tears in her eyes, but something about the repeated questioning of her ability to hear or understand simple sentences got to her.

"I don't know, are you socially inept or just a raving bitch?" Caitlyn asked, crossing her arms under her breasts.

I've killed *for less.*

The woman hissed the words into Caitlyn's mind and started walking toward her with calm, measured steps. The menace in the air was palpable, and for the second time in less than twenty-four hours, Caitlyn was completely convinced that she was about to die. Given the choice between the ocean and the Amazonian mer-bitch however, she suddenly wished she had a couple of lungs filled with seawater. At the least the ocean wouldn't have taken pleasure in her death.

From the gleam in the soulless eyes now coming way too close for comfort, this lady was going to enjoy wringing her scrawny neck. She was going to enjoy it a heck of a lot and there was probably nothing Caitlyn could do to stop her. Self-defense courses relied far too heavily on attacking your assailant's groin. Just another example of sexism at work and she hadn't thought twice about it. Now she would pay the price.

She had no idea how to take out a six-foot woman and running far enough, fast enough, wasn't going to happen, no matter how many endorphins were pumping through her system. So she exercised her only option.

"Help me! Somebody help, call the police!!" she screamed, her voice echoing through the quiet gardens, a strident, terrified sound that made the evil woman laugh, firmly erasing any hope for a swift, painless death.

The humans are bespelled. They will sleep until you are dead and my brother imprisoned for treason.

"Lukas, help me! *Please,*" Caitlyn screamed again, squeezing her eyes shut as the woman lunged toward her with her claws bared. He'd helped her once before, maybe he would help her again. If not, she was royally screwed, and not by something one-tenth as pleasurable as his thick, pulsing cock.

Chapter 3

Lukas ran the second he heard Caitlyn scream, vaulting from the hot tub and cursing himself for letting her leave his side. He shouldn't have taken her words so lightly, shouldn't have assumed that his warriors were the only ones observing them—despite their history of spying on each other as they bedded mortal women. Eleanor had to know by now that the High Council had gone against her express orders. Her days of ruling were already a thing of the past, but Lukas knew his half-sister. She would never give up her throne without a fight, would seek to destroy the brother she considered the only possible heir.

The Illuminated had never had a male ruler, and Lukas had tried his best to convince Eleanor that he had no interest in being the first. No matter how much he disagreed with the often-cruel practices of her regime, he had no wish to violate ancient custom. He would have served her until the day she died, but she had given him no choice but to oppose her. Even if the High Council hadn't given the order, he would have gone after the serpents. They were a curse upon his own world, but they were the Illuminated's curse to bear. Endangering thousands of Earth species who were all but defenseless against such fierce, ancient creatures was unforgivable.

He could understand that Eleanor had grown tired of losing warriors and fishermen to the bloodthirsty beasts, but that was no excuse for opening the portal directly across from their nesting grounds. The serpents had always made their home in some of the Illuminated's most fertile fishing grounds, but even those rich waters couldn't compare to the cornucopia of succulent marine life found in Earth's abundant seas.

Eleanor had known the creatures wouldn't be able to resist traveling through the open passage between the two worlds and had ordered the portal closed as soon as the last serpent had roared away into the Pacific Ocean.

When she had expressly forbidden any of the Illuminated People to recapture the creatures, she had sealed her own fate, and forced Lukas into the position of rival to the throne.

He had known when he led his men through the Earth portal that he would have to face the Queen's wrath. He just hadn't expected it to be so soon, or that she would dare to take an Illuminated dispute to the Earth's surface. But there was no mistaking the cold magic that shivered across his skin as he ran through the gardens, and he sent out a prayer to the Goddess that he wouldn't be too late to keep Caitlyn safe.

How touching, the great Lukas praying for his scrawny mortal lover.

Get out of my thoughts, Eleanor. It is against our laws to violate the sacred privacy of the mind.

Careful, Lukas, or I'll make sure the girl dies more painfully than I had planned.

"Stop this, sister. You have no quarrel with the mortal woman. Let her go back to her people and we will settle this dispute between ourselves," Lukas said aloud, slowing his steps as he came to a clearing in the path and saw his delicate Caitlyn dangling from Eleanor's strong grip. She had scooped up the smaller woman by the neck and only Caitlyn's two tiny hands clenched at either side of Eleanor's fist kept the hold from turning deadly.

"So *now* I am your sister? I think not, Lukas. That was not a name you used when my father was still your mother's *whore*," Eleanor hissed, causing a strangled yelp to burst from Caitlyn's throat as her grip tightened around her neck.

"Your father was mad. He took you from our mother's home against the wishes of the family. You know that our mother searched — "

"Not nearly hard enough. Queen Laini didn't give a damn if I was ever found. She wanted her precious little boy to be the first male on the throne."

"Put the woman down, immediately," Lukas ordered, moving toward the sister he had always secretly thought at least ten times as mad as her sire. He didn't remember Eleanor's father, had been barely three years old when he'd left the palace, but surely his mother wouldn't have bedded down with someone so clearly out of their head as their present Queen.

"You do not give the orders! You will *never* give the orders for our people!" she screeched, drawing back her arm and hurling Caitlyn from her with a strength fed by her fear and madness.

Lukas lunged after his woman, determined to keep her delicate bones from connecting with anything more damaging than his own body. Whether it was rational or not, he already thought of Caitlyn as his, and the idea that a single flaming red hair on her head would be damaged due to her association with him was more than he could stand. He knew he would kill Eleanor, sister or no, if he didn't succeed in keeping his future mate from harm.

With a deep bend of his knees, he hurled himself into the air after Caitlyn, breathing a small sigh of relief as his hands closed around her waist. He spun their bodies so that his would take the impact of connecting with the ground. A few brutal scrapes and a bloodied back were nothing he couldn't handle—seeing his love in pain was a completely different matter.

His *love*? Had he really used the word? Was it possible to love a woman with such deep, insistent, immediate passion?

You know nothing of love!

Lukas snarled as Eleanor's voice broke into his most private thoughts and his body connected hard with the ground. Thankfully, he landed in freshly planted earth. A bit of dirt and a few broken flowers were the worst of the damage and Caitlyn appeared completely unharmed but for the bruises on her neck, bruises that strengthened the urge to kill his half-sister.

"Run back to your lodging. I will come for you when it is safe," Lukas said as he pulled them both to their feet and pressed a quick kiss against Caitlyn's forehead.

"I'm not going to leave you alone with her," Caitlyn said, her voice hoarse from the damage Eleanor had inflicted on her delicate tissues.

"Do as I say, woman. I will battle better when I do not fear for your safety."

"Quit calling me 'woman' and let me help you," she insisted, her eyes wide with fear as she watched Eleanor stalk through the plants toward them, but her small hands fisted in front of her as she prepared to defend him.

In that instant, Lukas felt the suspicion of love grow into an incredible certainty. How could he not love a woman who was brave and bold, as well as a clever goddess whose cunt he would gladly feast upon for the next several hundred years?

"Your newfound depth of feeling is touching, Lukas. It's a shame your little human will have to die before you can claim her," Eleanor said as she quickly closed in on their position.

"Stop this, Eleanor. Return to our world and await the judgment of the High Council, or continue to threaten Caitlyn and die. The choice is yours," Lukas said, moving to block Caitlyn's body with his own.

"You *dare* threaten your Queen?"

"We both know your rule is over, Eleanor, and through no fault of mine."

"No fault of yours? *You*, who have done all that you could to turn my own people against me?"

"I have done no such thing, your own actions—"

"My actions could have freed our people of the serpent curse forever. But you would rather see Illuminated People die than risk a single human life."

"You know the law as well as I."

"Damn the law, and damn *you*, brother. We'll see before this night is over how you enjoy seeing one you love ripped limb from limb."

"Do not threaten Caitlyn again."

"Do not threaten Caitlyn again," Eleanor mocked. "You're too large for her child's body in any event. You would break her, Lukas. But maybe that's what you enjoy.

"Ocean Women don't tear and bleed quite so easily as mortals, do they? I wish I'd known you had such bloodthirsty tastes, sweet brother. I would have invited you to come play with me much sooner," Eleanor said, stopping a few feet from where he stood, close enough that he could smell the sickeningly sweet scent of the Hawaiian reef fish she consumed on a daily basis. He would never understand why the woman insisted on ingesting hallucinogenic fish when she was already as crazy as a great white shark in a feeding frenzy.

"I don't know about *your* culture, psycho, but sleeping with your brother is considered pretty gross here," Caitlyn's voice piped up from behind him.

"Shut your mouth, mortal," Eleanor hissed.

"And I didn't have a problem accommodating Lukas. I'm actually really looking forward to having him inside me again, feeling his thick cock moving in and out of me until I come—"

"Silence!" Eleanor screamed, her face nearly purple with her rage.

Despite the fact that Caitlyn's unexpected words were making his cock surge to a state of maximum attention, Lukas could see the wisdom of her tactics. He'd never realized Eleanor desired him in that way, but the jealousy in her nearly black eyes was abundantly clear, and more than a little disturbing.

What was the word Caitlyn had used? *Gross.* Yes, it was completely *gross* to contemplate bedding your half-brother in their culture as well, but there would be time for shuddering with revulsion later. At the moment, he needed to decide how best to use his Queen's obvious distraction to his advantage.

"He's also really talented with his tongue. Too bad *you'll* never know how it feels to have him lick your pussy until you think you're going to die from pure pleasure," Caitlyn said as her hand slowly wrapped around his waist to close around his burgeoning shaft.

Lukas felt his breath hiss from his body as her soft hand stroked him to his full length, teasing him from the tip of his cock down to his base, pausing to fondle the heavy weight of his tightly drawn balls before moving back up to the head once more. There she paused, swiping away the pearl of his essence that had already beaded at his tip, and brought her finger up to her mouth.

He did his best not to be insanely distracted by the sight of her pink tongue darting out to taste his desire, but it was a difficult thing. Far more difficult than slaying demon serpents or managing the dynamics of his royal family—which only went to prove that he had completely lost his heart.

"Mmm. And he tastes *amazing*. I can't wait to take his cock in my mouth, to have him come down my throat as I swallow down every delicious drop," she said, the look of pure ecstatic anticipation on her face nearly enough to make Lukas come, and evidently enough to drive Eleanor completely out of the last vestiges of her right mind.

You die! Now!

The Queen's lunge at Caitlyn was clumsy, bringing her far too close to Lukas' own powerful hands. He intercepted her easily, grabbing her smaller wrists and wrestling her to the ground. His raging erection died a quick death as he landed atop his sister, but the rest of his body remained completely unharmed as he pulled her arms behind her back and pinned her to the earth.

"What now? Do I get a rope or something?" Caitlyn asked, her breath coming fast as she bounced lightly from one foot to the other, adrenaline obviously still coursing through her body, though a moment ago she had seemed as calm and collected as the most skilled seductress.

"I don't think a rope will be necessary," Lukas said, smiling at his clever girl as he sent out a mental call to his warriors, certain that at least a few of his men were still nearby.

I will kill you, Lukas. You and your woman. Set me free this instant!

"I don't know about you, but I'd feel better if she were tied up," Caitlyn said, nervously eyeing the still-raging Eleanor, who bucked beneath him with amazing strength, even for an Illuminated woman. Still, she was much smaller than he and it would be no challenge to immobilize her for a few more moments.

"I think I would feel better if you were tied to my bed," Lukas said with a wicked grin in Caitlyn's direction. "I hope your words were spoken for more than distraction's sake."

"Are you flirting with me? At a time like this?" she said, the smile teasing the corners of her mouth belying her stern words.

"Is there a wrong time to tell your woman you find her irresistibly desirable?" he asked, letting his eyes rove over her body, thrilled to see a delicate blush start to spread across her breasts and up toward her lovely face. Her nipples tightened and puckered, practically begging for the attention of his mouth, attention he couldn't wait to devote entirely to her and her complete satisfaction.

"You're crazy," she said, a smile lighting up her gray eyes, eyes as beautiful as the most peaceful, untouched depths of the ocean.

"Perhaps it runs in the family," Lukas said, his tone and heart amazingly light for a man who was getting ready to commit treason.

My people will not betray me. Your men belong to me, they will not —

I will not speak for the rest of our race, but we four are ready to follow our Prince's orders.

Lukas looked up to meet the stern face of Mercury, one of his dearest friends and the only man he'd want at his back in battle. They had soldiered together since they were both too young to know how to properly please a woman, and Lukas knew how little respect the man had for their present ruler. Mercury had specifically requested to be included in the mission to recapture the serpents and Lukas had no doubt that he would deliver Eleanor straight into the hands of the High Council.

"Seize him, men. Take him to the darkest holding caves and —"

Where would you have us hold her, Lukas?

"No, you do not follow his command! A man will *never* rule our people!" Eleanor screamed, her desperation clear in her voice as Lukas allowed two of the younger men to grasp her around the elbows and pull her to her feet.

"That is for the Council to decide. Ask them where they would have her, Mercury. I will not assume more than my station until the will of the people is known," Lukas said, coming to his feet in front of Caitlyn, conscious of the need to shield her nude body from the eyes of his men. The bastards had already watched them mating in the hot tub, but for some reason he no longer wanted to share her lovely form with anyone — at least not until he'd claimed her completely as his own.

"The people will be for you, Lukas," Mercury said. "We are an honored race to have such a man as our first King."

Lukas acknowledged the words with a nod, more than a little overwhelmed as the reality of his friend's words hit him full force. Whether he'd coveted the throne or not, it was highly likely that he was within weeks of being asked to ascend to it. He only prayed he could prove himself worthy of his people's confidence, and knew his own confidence would be greatly bolstered if Caitlyn would agree to be by his side.

The High Council will never accept a mortal as your consort, you will never —

"She won't *be* a mortal once the Breath Kiss is permanent," Mercury said, obviously enjoying the newfound ability to put the woman who had made nearly a hundred years of his life a living hell in her place. Lukas had endured enough hardship as a relative of the Queen, but he knew that those who hadn't shared her royal blood had fared much worse. "He's already given her a taste of the Kiss, *and* they've mated—I watched it with my own eyes. Now there's only one last—"

"So you were the men by the hot tub?" Caitlyn asked, poking her head around Lukas' torso to shoot a murderous look in Mercury's direction. The movement caused her breasts to press against the middle of his back, making Lukas struggle to keep from getting too obviously aroused as he wondered how long he would be forced to wait before bedding her again.

"We've been observing our captain since before the sun set this day. My apologies, Lukas, but I was concerned for your well-being and the boys were concerned with other matters."

"Ah, I see," Lukas said, shifting his gaze to the three other soldiers who managed to avoid meeting his eyes. "I assume there were bets made as well?"

"Only minor wagers, my captain," Mercury said, having the grace to suppress the teasing grin Lukas knew was pulling at his lips.

"Well, if the winners of the wagers will deposit their spoils in my mate's dowry box before our official joining ceremony, I will forgive them their indiscretion," Lukas said.

"And tell them I don't like it and to never do it again," Caitlyn said, standing on tiptoe to whisper the words into his ear, her breath on his skin making him long to turn around and take her in his arms, to ravage her right there on the newly plowed earth without a care as to who might decide to watch.

"She doesn't enjoy being observed and I will castrate the next man I find spying on us while we mate," Lukas said, making his words sound suitably threatening, even though he suspected Caitlyn might enjoy performing for an audience once she became more comfortable with the ways of his people.

"As you wish. We'll take our leave, captain, and await further word," Mercury said.

"Will you also *convince* Eleanor to release the humans from whatever spell she's cast?" Lukas said, fully aware that enchanting humans against their will violated their law, but secretly glad Eleanor had done so. If she hadn't, the tidal wave created as he'd banished the last of the serpents to the Illuminated realm would have drawn a great deal more attention. Part of the beach had been washed away, as well as many of the boats docked at the nearby Marina. Only the poor weather had kept more humans than Caitlyn from being swept out to sea.

"I will convince her, one way or another," Mercury said, the threat in his words making even Eleanor pale.

"You will live to regret this day, Lukas, I swear it by the depths of the seas of—"

"Quiet, Eleanor. You're embarrassing yourself," Mercury said, his use of her given name shocking the Queen into silence as they pulled her to the beach and out to the undersea portal that would transport them back to their home world.

"I can't believe this," Caitlyn murmured as she watched them go.

"It will become less fantastic with time. After a few months among our people you will forget that the Illuminated were ever something to find amazing," Lukas said, turning to Caitlyn and taking her in his arms, feeling his cock harden between their bodies as she shifted her hips against him.

"No, I mean I can't believe a bunch of men really watched me have an orgasm and run naked through the garden and everything else. I know the killer mermaid-Queen business should be bothering me more than that right now, but I'm just so embarrassed," she said, tears starting to gather in her wide gray eyes.

"Never be embarrassed by your pleasure," Lukas ordered, taking her face in his hands and willing her not to cry.

"I'm not embarrassed by my pleasure, I'm embarrassed that someone was watching—and that a part of me enjoyed it," she protested as tears started to spill down her pale cheeks and roll onto his much darker hands.

"There's nothing wrong with that. I'm proud to bed you, and proud to have others see me bring you ecstasy," Lukas said, a strange, out of control feeling starting to grow in his chest. "But if you want me to blind them all, I'll do it. I can't bear to see you in pain."

"No, don't blind them," she laughed, then looked up at him with a shy desire that took his breath away. "But I can think of one thing that might make me feel better."

"Anything," he said, ready to slay any number of demons of land or sea on her behalf.

"Take me back to my room and...stay with me?"

"There is nothing that would please me more," he said, a heated smile on his face as he lifted her in his arms and aimed them both in the direction she indicated. He couldn't wait to be alone with her, to remind her just how perfectly their bodies could come together in passion and, he hoped, in love.

Chapter 4

"Almost ready," Caitlyn shouted over the sound of the bathroom fan, wiggling her toes in the cooling bathwater. The truth was she'd finished bathing and shaving a good ten minutes ago, but for some reason she couldn't bring herself to leave the bathtub.

The man had already seen her naked, had already kissed her "where the sun didn't shine", and made love to her in front of a small crowd of his friends. So why was she so terribly nervous? Was it just residual angst left over from helping him take down his psychotic half-sister, or something a little closer to home? He had mentioned something about a dowry, hadn't he? What the hell did that mean?

Was he talking marriage? Love? Little mer-children with his mocha skin and her gray eyes? Was she ready for something like that? Sure, she lusted after him with every fiber of her being, and something deep inside her thrilled to be near him, but was that enough of a reason to run off to sea with the man? Was such a thing even possible? She *did* have to breathe air and all, which was no small obstacle. Not to mention her job and family and friends.

Okay, so her job was going nowhere fast, her only living family member was the abusive mother she'd run away from when she was sixteen, and her friends probably wouldn't even notice if she ran off for a few years. Well, they might notice, but she wasn't sure if they would really care. Caitlyn just didn't feel that she was that vital to anyone's existence, which made her wonder why this amazing man—a man who sounded like he was about to inherit a throne and kingdom, no less—would want her.

She'd already established that he wasn't crazy, so that had to mean there was another reason for his obvious interest. Whatever that reason was, she doubted her terminally low self-esteem was going to help her figure it out in the next few minutes. She was going to have to go out there and face him. Too bad the hard questions she had to ask probably wouldn't lead to the night of pleasure she had hoped for when she had invited Lukas back to her room.

But there was no way to avoid asking them now. She'd made the mistake of allowing her brain time to process information, always a big mistake if you were really interested in losing yourself in a night of hot, sweaty, delicious, intimate, loving, mind-blowing sex. She was completely sure it would have been all of those things, deep down in her soul.

"I'm well past ready," Lukas said as he loudly opened the bathroom door, causing Caitlyn to squeal in surprise.

"You scared the crap out of me."

"Who did you think I was? The Loch Ness monster?" he said with a wry grin as he stared hungrily down at where she lay in the tub.

"Is that a mermaid joke?"

"I'm an Illuminated man, not a *maid* of any sort. What do I need to do to convince you of that fact?" he said with another indulgent look, accompanied by the slow, teasing stroke of his hand up and down his rapidly swelling cock.

And lord, what a cock it was, thick and the loveliest shade of light brown, stretching all the way to his navel and graced by a fleshy head that was, without a doubt, the most gorgeous, plump top to a penis that she had ever seen. She wanted to put her mouth on him more than she'd ever wanted to do anything. She wanted to taste the salty, musky flavor of him against her tongue, wanted to feel him lose himself in her mouth and smear his essence across her lips. She'd never let a man do that before, but with Lukas she knew that it would turn her on, make her as hot to give him pleasure as it had to take her own.

"I told you I liked to wash in privacy," she said, covering her breasts with her washcloth—to conceal their aching tips more than to make any pretence at modesty. She couldn't let him know how aroused she was becoming if she hoped to have any chance at a rational conversation.

"You smell quite clean," he said, squatting down and plucking the washcloth out of the water.

"I was wondering if...your people could smell," she gulped, her words catching in her throat as his finger starting tracing delicate patterns on top of the water, inches away from where her skin nearly shook with need for him.

"We can. Exceptionally well, in fact. So well that I can catch the scent of your cunt even when *it* is underwater and *I* am not," he said, his voice husky and eyes homing in on said body part.

"I'm not sure if I like the word cunt," Caitlyn said, sucking in a deep breath as his finger brushed casually over her nipple before resuming its lazy movements through the water.

"You like the word. It makes you wet, makes you ache for my cock between your legs."

"You're very sure of yourself," she said, her entire body humming out the truth of his words. She wanted him badly, had been aching for him to slide inside her since he'd put his arms around her in the middle of the frigid ocean.

"No, I'm sure of your body's desire, but your heart is a complete mystery," he said, his eyes moving back to her face and nailing her with a look that was completely vulnerable and unsure, a look that said she had a strange sort of power over him that even he might not be completely comfortable with.

"Lukas, I'm not sure how I feel. This entire experience has been a little overwhelming. I don't know, can't even think—"

"Then don't think," he said, joining her with a swiftness that made water slosh over the side of the tub and Caitlyn cry out in surprise.

"You're too big for this bathtub," she whispered, struggling not to close her eyes and moan in pleasure as he braced his strong arms on either side of her head and lowered his body over hers, his knees gently urging her thighs apart so that he could settle between her legs.

"I think the fit is quite comfortable," he smiled, softly brushing his lips against hers as he lowered his hips and pressed the shaft of his cock ever so lightly against her pulsing clit. It created an electric connection between them that was unlike anything she'd ever felt. The sense of rightness, of comfort and safety, was almost her undoing. She suddenly wanted to weep as much as she wanted to beg him to push his thick cock deep into the aching slickness of her pussy.

Emotional and physical desire, tenderness mixed with a passion that was too powerful to be restrained, wasn't that what she'd always dreamed of? She hadn't believed it possible, at least not for her, but hearing a small choked sound escape from Lukas' throat and seeing the look of almost painful need on his face, she could almost believe that he felt the same way.

"I've never wanted a woman like this, Caitlyn," Lukas breathed against her lips before his tongue demanded entrance to her mouth.

Caitlyn wanted to tell him that she felt the same, but could only moan and open completely to him, lost in the commanding sweep of his tongue dancing with hers, in the frantic hunger that grew even stronger when his hands moved to her breasts, teasing her nipples until her breath came in desperate little pants and her hips bucked into his cock, demanding that he fill the horrible emptiness between her legs.

"Lukas, I—"

"Don't," he groaned, bringing the pad of his finger to her lips. "Let me show you how I feel for you before you speak."

"But I—"

"No, Caitlyn, feel this first, remember how right it feels for my body to be joined with yours," he said, using his free hand to spread her pulsing folds and slide just the tip of his thick cock into her body.

Caitlyn moaned at the wonderful fullness as her body stretched to accommodate his girth, and soon found herself gasping and writhing beneath him. Hungrily, she suckled the finger at her lips and stroked him with her tongue, mimicking the way she wanted to love him with her mouth if he'd ever stop being commanding and forceful long enough to let her.

But God, she loved that part of him, loved the way he demanded she abandon herself to the pleasure of their bodies together. She loved the way his brown eyes darkened to a shade that was nearly black, the way his jaw clenched as he struggled to move slowly, gently, into her tight sheath, the way his hands were tender and strong, giving and commanding all at the same time. She loved the expression of wonder on his face as he started to delve a little deeper into her channel with shallow little thrusts that had her aching, weeping pussy begging for more—more of him, *all* of him.

"I love you," she said, feeling the rightness of the words despite the fact that she'd known this man less than a day.

"Thank the Goddess," he moaned, her words apparently shattering the last of his control.

Caitlyn arched her back and cried out as his cock tunneled deep into her center, bumping against the entry to her womb before she claimed quite all of his length. There was a hint of soreness, as her body hadn't quite recovered from their first time together, but it was far overshadowed by a deep sense of relief as her most basic animal instincts cried out that she had finally found her other, her mate, the man who was made to fit her more perfectly than she could have even imagined.

"Be with me, come back to my home and be my partner for this life," Lukas said, holding his body still within her and looking deep into her eyes. "All that is left is for you to choose me, Caitlyn. The magic of the Breath Kiss is simple, but more powerful than anything I've ever known."

"Are you crying?" Caitlyn asked, feeling a little teary herself as she looked up into his soft velvet eyes, suspiciously shiny around the edges.

"I am a warrior with over a hundred battles behind me."

"And warriors don't cry?" she asked, brushing a hand down his handsome face, feeling a tenderness for him that went beyond desire.

"Only if their love says *no*," he said, dipping his mouth to suckle one of her nipples, teasing and stroking the tight, puckered flesh until Caitlyn was moaning, fisting her hands in his hair and doing her best to force him to move his cock in and out of her, to fuck her hard and fast, with all the passion that was thick and heavy between them.

"Yes. Yes! Lukas, please, yes," Caitlyn begged.

"Yes, you'll come with me?" he asked as his mouth abandoned her breast for her lips, his tongue plundering her so thoroughly that it was hard to breathe, let alone formulate words.

"Yes, even if I drown, nothing could stop me," Caitlyn said, shivering as a rush of energy surged through her body, a foreign charge of something "other" that reminded her of the first time she had kissed Lukas, out in the ocean. It raced through her cells and was gone as quickly as it came, leaving her feeling warm and content, but with the sense that something had been altered deep within her.

"You won't drown, my love. Now that the Breath Kiss is permanent you won't even feel the chill of the water," he said with a smile.

"That's it? The…magic is permanent? I can't believe it. Shouldn't there have been sparks or something?" Caitlyn asked.

"I'll show you sparks," Lukas laughed, sealing her mouth with his before he rolled them both under the water.

Caitlyn felt a brief flash of fear as the water closed over them, but then Lukas was moving hard and fast between her legs and she couldn't think of anything but arching to meet his thrusts.

Dear God, they weren't using a condom, *again*. The thought was almost enough to make her ask for a brief timeout, when the wonder of the fact that she'd gone a good five minutes without breathing finally penetrated her lust-fogged consciousness.

I'm not breathing.

Caitlyn heard herself speak the words inside her mind, the same way Lukas' voice had first come to her that afternoon on the beach.

Yes, you are, just quite a bit more slowly – it's the magic of the Breath Kiss. You'll need to surface every few hours to breathe, but that's more than enough time to reach the portals to our world.

So I'm really a mermaid?

How many times must I tell you that we are the Illuminated –

Don't take that tone in my head when you're fucking me!

I'd rather not take any *tone when I'm fucking you, I'd rather just fuck you.*

He followed those words with a swift roll in the water that brought her on top of his body, her breasts within reach of his unbelievably talented tongue. Caitlyn gasped as the need built between her legs, but no water entered her lungs. It was like an invisible membrane covered her body, giving her the sensation of being surrounded by water without it actually touching her skin.

This is amazing, will it always feel like this?

Only if my cock is inside you.

You know what I mean, Lukas, don't be —

Yes, my love, we are mated for life and the effects of the Breath Kiss are permanent.

Will I grow a fish tail?

Do I have a fish tail?

No, but you have a huge and wonderful cock. Have I told you how perfect you feel inside me?

Goddess, I don't know if a few hundred more years will be enough. I could fuck you forever.

Oh God, Lukas, I'm going to come.

Come, woman, I want to feel your cunt pulsing on my cock.

Don't call me woman!

Her last words ended with a moan as his deep thrusts finally tipped her over the edge, making her womb clench and her channel start to spasm with waves of pleasure that were unlike anything she'd ever known. Her nipples tightened and her hands clawed into the flesh of his ass. She pulled him deeper and deeper, twisting and thrashing beneath the water, feeling a second orgasm start to build before the first had thoroughly abated.

I love you, Caitlyn.

His words spoken softly in her mind, combined with the very primal, male sound he made as he came inside her, sent her spiraling into her second orgasm. This one they rode out together, her pussy milking the last drop of hot cum from his body as their fevered joining slowly transformed into a languid thrusting that allowed them to float to the surface of the water.

"I'm really glad this is a big bathtub," Caitlyn finally said as she shifted slightly to rest her cheek on the smooth planes of his muscled chest, sighing with the deepest contentment she had ever known.

"And you said it was too small," Lukas murmured as his hand leisurely traced a path up and down her thigh.

"It's definitely not too small. It's big and thick and—"

"Are you ready to be fucked again so quickly?"

"What if I were?" she asked, running a teasing hand over his spent member, which was still larger in its resting state than the other penises she had met in her somewhat limited acquaintance.

"I would do my best to rise to the occasion," he said, his cock twitching slightly in her hand and indeed starting to swell, though not to anything near its full glory.

"Now you're just showing off."

"Perhaps," he said, a smile in his voice.

"Lukas?"

"Yes, my love?"

"We didn't use a condom—either time."

"There will be no child unless we both consciously choose to conceive. It is part of the magic of our people," he said, hugging her close to his side. "But you do wish for us to have children?"

"I do, but not at this exact second. I want to make sure that we're going to last. My dad was never around when I was a kid and my mom was, well…I just want more for my son or daughter," she said, the words not as painful to speak as they had been in the past. Somehow, lying this close to the man she loved, old hurts didn't cut quite so deeply.

"My father was a stranger to me, as well," Lukas said, pulling her on top of him and planting a soft kiss on her lips. "We will do a better job. With two such brave parents, our offspring will not lack for guidance or love."

"You think I'm *brave*?" Caitlyn asked, surprised by his choice of words.

"Incredibly brave. You stood with me against Eleanor and are willing to venture into a culture that is completely foreign to you so that we can be together. Two very brave choices from a brave woman," he said.

"I'm not brave, Lukas. I'm afraid."

"Bravery is not the absence of fear, but the strength to act in spite of it."

"That's a nice thought, but what if it's not bravery, what if we're both just crazy?"

"Love is a crazy thing, but it is also a treasure I've longed for. I'll not pass it by simply because it came more quickly than I would have dreamt possible," he said with a shrug as he began to idly massage the cheeks of her ass, building her need for him more swiftly than she would have imagined possible after such profoundly satisfying sex mere minutes before.

"What if I can't stand the dark?" Caitlyn asked, finally giving voice to the thoughts that had been nagging at her since this whole under-the-sea life had become a possibility.

"The dark?"

"It's dark under the water and I've spent the past four months being so depressed because I can't stand the dark. I need sunshine and—"

"What are you laughing at?" Caitlyn asked, scowling as the muscles beneath her grew even harder as Lukas began to quake with laughter. Sure, he looked beautiful when he laughed, and all those wide, white teeth were bright in his dark face, but this was a serious problem. "Quit it, you're being a jerk."

"Our land is not dark. We occupy the uppermost level of Underworld, a land of great beauty with a sun more ancient than even the star that lights this Earth. It's a world our people believe was granted to us by the ancient gods."

"What?"

"We're from a different dimension, my love, an entirely separate realm. The portals to our home are under the sea, but we are not creatures of the deep. We still breathe as humans do, but simply need to do so less frequently. We still die, but live for hundreds of years longer than Earth people," he said, still smiling at her as if she were a simpleton as he moved one hand to her breast and began playing with her nipple.

"There's no need to be condescending," she said, though pouting was difficult when she was already squirming on top of him, half dizzy with the need to have him inside her again.

"I would never condescend. I'm just happy to be able to put your fears to rest. You will have all the sunshine you need, and anything else that is in my power to give you," he said, the truth of his words warming Caitlyn to the depths of her being.

"Right now, I just want this," Caitlyn said, rising up and positioning his shaft at her entrance, slowly impaling herself on his length until her auburn curls were snuggled against his dark brown ones, the perfect melding of their two very different bodies giving her hope that the meeting of their two very different worlds would find equal success.

"One more question," Caitlyn said, bracing her hands on his chest and staring down into his eyes, already dark with his love and desire.

"Ask anything and I will answer, if you promise to take your pleasure from me in the next ten seconds," he said, his hands coming to her hips and his fingers digging into her soft flesh as he thrust even deeper into her body.

"God," Caitlyn moaned, struggling to keep from starting to fuck him that very second.

"No, I was never a god, but a small island off the coast of Africa once made offerings to me as a way to appease the tides," he said with a wicked grin.

"I was going to ask if I'd get to come back to my world when I need to. Just in case I get homesick," Caitlyn said, gently slapping Lukas on his manly pectorals. Her future husband had the manliest chest she had ever seen, a detail that was almost as much of a surprise as the fact that he was a merman.

"Anytime you wish. I spend quite a bit of time in your dimension."

"You can't get enough of hot tubs and Earth women?" Caitlyn teased as she slowly began to ride the man beneath her, knowing with a peaceful certainty that she was going to be the last mortal notch on his bedpost.

"The hot tubs are nice, but it's the fishing that draws me. Underworld has nothing that can compare to Earth's deep sea spear fishing," he said, tightening his grip on her waist and guiding her clit into more intimate contact with his hips, which were now rolling in a circular motion that quickly brought her within reach of another mind-numbing orgasm.

"I like deep spearing," Caitlyn said, her laugh turning to a moan as Lukas caught her nipple in his mouth and the tension within her grew even higher, hotter, almost more than she could contain.

Is this deep enough?

Oh…yes.

Will you come for me now?

Oh God, yes.

As she did, Lukas pulled back to watch her face as he'd threatened to do in the hot tub. But she didn't feel embarrassed or ashamed, she felt beautiful, sensual, complete and more loved than she could have imagined possible.

I love you, Lukas.

And I you, my love.

Will you fuck me from behind now?

Goddess, yes, but don't speak like that again or I'll lose myself in your sweet cunt.

I like it when you lose yourself in my sweet cunt.

Caitlyn laughed when Lukas moaned with the effort it took to maintain his control, a smile still on her face as he flipped her over in the water and slid into her from behind. Then he was slowly thrusting in and out of her, his hands finding her breasts and clit, coaxing her to another orgasm before he spent himself inside her with a final deep thrust.

Still tangled in Lukas' arms, floating in the rapidly cooling bathtub water, Caitlyn fell asleep, certain for the first time in ages that she was exactly where she needed to be, and that morning was something she was definitely looking forward to — no matter what the state of the weather.

Also by Anna J. Evans

୨୦

Decking the Hollisters
Ellora's Cavemen: Dreams of the Oasis II *(anthology)*
Enchanted

About the Author

୨୦

Anna J. Evans is a multipublished author who thinks romance is sexier with a sense of humor. She loves reading and writing paranormal romantic adventures and is thrilled to hear from fans. You can visit her website, email her, or join her Yahoo group (Anna_Evans_lolsexy-subscribe@yahoogroups.com) for free reads, the latest publishing news, and monthly member-only give-aways.

Anna welcomes comments from readers. You can find her website and email address on her author bio page at www.ellorascave.com.

Tell Us What You Think

We appreciate hearing reader opinions about our books. You can email us at Comments@EllorasCave.com.

SAINT JILLIAN'S REBEL

Eve Jameson

Trademarks Acknowledgement

The author acknowledges the trademarked status and trademark owners of the following wordmarks mentioned in this work of fiction:

Dodge Viper: DaimlerChrysler Corporation

Neiman Marcus: NM Nevada Trust

Chapter 1

"Speak of the devil," Deidre Norton sniffed as she traced the top of her wineglass with a bright red fingernail. Jillian followed her friend's gaze across the crowded hotel ballroom. Hunter Scott's wide shoulders were cutting through the throng of Pier's Point alumni crowding around the bar set up near the back of the room.

An ice cube from her margarita stuck momentarily in Jillian's throat when Hunter turned and caught her gaze. For a breathless second the clatter of forced cheer and clinking wineglasses faded as her brown eyes met and held his dark-blue stare. A current of awareness, as strong as it was surprising, arced between them, snapping her body to full attention.

Damn it. She hadn't expected her reaction to seeing him to be so strong after all this time. The attraction had been an integral part of her high-school experience, even if it had been unrequited.

Once oxygen made its way to her brain again, she was sure that what she was seeing in his eyes was nothing more than a trick of light, too many margaritas and sentimental nonsense on her part brought on by her twentieth reunion.

A large bald man in a wrinkled suit—who she thought was the skinny punk rocker who had sat behind her in geometry and never turned in his homework—bumped into Hunter and he looked away, releasing her from the heart-stopping freeze-frame moment. "Who?" she asked Deidre, ignoring the sudden racing of her pulse and turning to focus on the woman who had been her best friend in high school.

"Hunter Scott," Deidre said with a disdain that belied the calculating spark in her bright green eyes.

"Didn't you used to have a crush on him?" Deidre shifted and her cleavage paid dramatic homage to the miracle of the push-up bra. "God, I bet you're really glad now that he stood you up after graduation. At least you never got your heart broken by him like every other girl in the senior class. He absolutely preys on women. At the last reunion, he left with *two* of them."

Jillian thought about explaining to Deidre that being stood up by Hunter *did* hurt—

especially after months of being half in love with him—but decided it wasn't worth it. Too much water had passed under that bridge and compared to surviving a shattered marriage, a teenage broken heart was a piece of cake.

As gossip about the man who had been the hottest guy of their senior class continued to dribble out of Deidre like vinegar from a cracked cruet, Jillian found herself wondering what had held their friendship together all those years ago. More than two decades ago she had left South Carolina for Savannah and never looked back. A month later, her parents moved to California, and there had been no reason at all to return until now. But when she was seventeen, she had been the new girl and Deidre had basically latched on and made her feel welcomed. For a shy girl whose father was transferred every one to two years, Deidre's immediate friendship was a godsend.

A residual feeling of gratefulness mixed with the guilt over their dropped relationship had pushed her toward attending tonight. Then when her ex decided to get remarried the same week as the reunion, her daughter got behind the campaign for her to go. No matter how many times she tried to explain to Meghan that her father's remarriage didn't bother her—though his last taunting phone call had pissed her off—her daughter had still worried and pushed her to take a week of vacation just for herself. "You need to get away, *Mom*. You haven't had a vacation in years, *Mom*. You need to meet some men, *Mom*. You deserve to have some fun, *Mom*." It was enough to send her rushing to a travel agent simply to get her daughter to shut up.

Unfortunately, now that she was sitting in the middle of one of the two hotels in this small town, she realized that there wasn't a whole hell of a lot to do in or around Pier's Point on a Saturday night.

The rest of the week was looking decidedly bleak as well. After reacquainting herself with most of her old classmates tonight, she was convinced that she did *not* want to spend the rest of the evening with them. Forget the rest of the week. There went her fun-in-the-sun vacation. Twenty years obviously went a long way to turning acquaintances she had shared lab tables and English projects with into total strangers. So much for Deidre's insistence that the big "Two-Oh" reunion was an experience not to be missed and never to be repeated.

Thank god for the last part anyway. Two hours into the ordeal, she had repeated her re-introduction mantra so many times she thought her head might fall off from boredom. *Living in Savannah. CPA. Happily divorced with one child who just graduated high school.* She'd listened to the same type of mind-numbing facts in return before being snagged by another person she didn't recognize and repeating the dog and pony show. Out of desperation she had grabbed a drink and tried to hide at the furthest table in the darkest corner. No wonder the bar area was so crowded. She completely understood the need for alcohol at an event like this.

"Oh my god!" Deidre's panicked whisper cut across her cynical thoughts. "He's coming this way. Do I have lipstick on my teeth?"

Jillian shook her head and glanced up. Hunter was indeed bearing down on their table with an unswerving stride that left everyone who tried to stop him sputtering in his wake.

Watching the drop-dead gorgeous man make his way toward them, she wondered if he still thought of her by the nickname he had labeled her with the first time she had shrugged off his sexual proposition. Years ago she hadn't known what to do with his erotic teasing except back away. Then, when she had finally worked up the courage to shed her good-girl image, he decided to go for a sure thing with Penny Jackson, leaving her dateless for the big graduation party and her reputation fully intact by default.

Like a force of nature being held unnaturally static, Hunter came to a stop next to their table. Shadows from the flickering candles on the table underscored the muscled expanse of his chest under his dress shirt when he shoved his blazer back and stuffed his hands into the pockets of his pants. Irritation flared briefly in his eyes as they darted over Deidre before they came back to her, unexpectedly turning her stomach into a loop-de-loop carnival ride and topping it off with a solid dose of old-fashioned lust.

Inwardly, Jillian sighed and commanded her libido to cool it. It wasn't as if he were laying out a welcome mat or anything. In point of fact, he looked pretty damn well annoyed. Out of habit, she pulled the corner of her bottom lip between her teeth. Immediately, his gaze zeroed in on her mouth. A moment later when he looked back up, his expression was sharp with desire. The heat between them that had surprised her from across the room was nearly setting her panties on fire with him so close. Long dormant desires leapt to life as she smiled in anticipation. She was on vacation and she wanted fun, sun and—*hell yeah*—sex. Not necessarily in that order.

* * * * *

A slow minute ticked by while Hunter tried to remember the exact line he had wanted to say the next time he met Jillian Lawson. He had managed to hold on to his wits until she smiled at him. Suddenly he was eighteen again, blindsided by an attraction that was more about the inside of a girl than her bra size. A situation he'd had no idea how to handle since he'd been convinced the only thing he had to offer a woman was what he could do to her body. A distinct disadvantage when wanting to impress a girl who within a week had earned the nickname "Saint Jillian".

And now, with those amazing bedroom eyes of hers looking up at him in the glow of the candles, rather than the thirty-eight-year-old businessman he was, he felt like the class hood from the wrong side of town screwing up his courage to ask out the "good girl". Again. When he had spotted her across the room, instinct had taken over and he had plowed through the horde of half-drunk ex-classmates with all the grace of a bull elephant crashing through the jungle. He hadn't even noticed Deidre sitting next to her until it was too late.

"Would you like to dance?" Shit. That was definitely not in the list of lines he had been running through his mind. And from the lift of her eyebrows, it had sounded just as fucking harsh to her as it had to him.

"We're not interested," Deidre answered.

Hunter felt the skin at the corners of his eyes pull tight as he cut a look in her direction. He'd had all he could take of Deidre years ago. "I wasn't asking you." Ignoring her exaggerated expression of shock that included a deep breath that brought her silicone mountains nearly popping out of her dress, he turned back to Jillian just in time to see a strange expression flit across her face. It came close to reminding him of the look his last girlfriend got right before she'd had enough and started her rant about his inability to commit. "Well?"

Shit, hell and damn. What was it about a woman that could scramble a man's brain so easily and reduce his vocabulary to single-syllable grunts?

Jillian opened her mouth to answer but Deidre interrupted again. "We haven't finished our conversation.

Besides, you know she's not your type." Had the woman's voice always had that shrill bitch quality to it?

Before he could answer her, Jillian rose from her chair. "Actually, I'd love to dance." She was more stunning than he remembered and it didn't hurt that the little black dress she was wearing clung to her curves in all the right places and then did a sexy fluttering thing around her thighs when she moved. Her high-heeled sandals called attention to her long legs—like they needed any help—and did amazing things to her ass. A fact he couldn't help noticing when she turned back to Deidre.

"I'll be right back," she said, "and then we can finish our conversation."

Jillian slid her hand around his arm, tilted her head to the side and looked up at him, waiting. He nodded and headed toward the center of the room where a dance floor had been set up. There were already quite a few couples dancing, thanks mostly to the free bar set up. Before the night was over, no doubt there'd be drunken renditions of the Bunny Hop, YMCA and the Macarena. He was planning on being long gone by then.

He turned and took Jillian in his arms. A slow song was playing and she stepped close enough to put her hands on his shoulders, but not close enough for full-body contact. Resting his hands low on her waist, he tried once more to think of one of the lines he had prepared, but it was futile with her hips swaying and the view he had of her breasts. Her dress was modest compared to most of the other women's, but the neckline still dipped down, revealing soft creamy mounds.

When he looked back up, she had a funny little smile on her face. "What?" he asked. Her lips moved, but against the tide of blaring music, he had no idea what she said. He shook his head and leaned in closer until her lips were next to his ear.

"I said, it's been a long time since I've caught anyone looking down my shirt."

"Shit," he hissed. He started to pull back, but she slid her hands up around his neck and held him in place.

"I'm not complaining. It's actually kind of flattering."

This time he did pull back. "How many drinks have you had?"

Her laughter floated up to him through the music as she tipped her head back and gave him an even better view of her chest. She wasn't making it easy on him, damn it. "I'm serious."

Stepping in close to his body, she stretched up to speak in his ear again and her breasts brushed his chest. "Don't worry. I'm old enough to legally consume alcohol in a public place. Thank you for rescuing me. I was about ready to bang my head on the table from sheer boredom. It's almost enough to forgive you for standing me up our senior year."

His head snapped up. "What?" But Jillian had turned and, grabbing his hand, led him to the center of the floor as a fast song started blaring over the speakers.

"Time to shoot the DJ," he mumbled. It wasn't that it was a hardship watching Jillian's curves bounce and gyrate, it was just that he was ready to put the next steps of his plan into action. This woman had kept a grip on his heart for too long now and it was time he exorcised her from his soul. For years he had consciously and unconsciously measured his accomplishments against the imagined censure of this one woman and it was past time to pry off her hold.

The irony of the whole goddamn mess was that for his entire life he'd had no problem shrugging off the rest of the town's scorn. Right up to the day he left fifteen years ago, he had accepted his place as the local bad boy, the one mothers pointed out to their daughters to stay away from. The same daughters who secretly sought him out for thorough fuckings every chance they got. He carried his reputation with pride as the shield it had become at an early age thanks to trailer trash parents in a brick-house-and-white-picket-fence town.

But Jillian had been different. She hadn't crossed to the other side of the street when she saw him coming, didn't snub him in front of her friends. What had gotten to him the most was her reaction when, in a moment of pure teenage spite at coming face-to-face with so much good to his bad, he had leaned over in the middle of chemistry class and offered to fuck her until she screamed. She hadn't slapped him or turned him in. Her big brown eyes widened, then she blinked, smiled and said, "No, thank you. Did you understand that last problem?"

He'd been half in love with her the rest of his high-school years until the night she humiliated him. And that was why he had been coming to these damn reunions every five years. Finally, she had shown up.

Chapter 2

Jillian had forgotten how much she loved to dance. After an initial spurt of self-consciousness, she realized that everyone was twice as drunk as she was and that Hunter Scott was a damn fine dance partner. Between the margaritas, the DJ's choice of constant 80's rock after the first slow ballad and the frequent brush of her body against Hunter's, she felt like she was flying.

Jason hadn't danced. Even at their wedding. It made him uncomfortable. So she hadn't danced. For years. She hadn't done a lot of things for years. And then when Jason decided to "spice things up" in their relatively staid marriage, he had called her a prude for balking at his insistence she play dominatrix to his submissive. But she had been forced to carry the responsibility of being the "adult" in the relationship in every other area and taking total control in the bedroom as well held no appeal to her.

Blame it on the romance novels she read as a teenager where the gorgeous pirate swooped in and carried off an innocent maiden, ravishing her and then falling hopelessly under her charms. Because though she knew that the dominatrix scenario worked for some people, she just wasn't one of them. She didn't *want* to tie up a man and flog him until he blubbered. She wanted to be swooped and ravished, dammit.

Spinning back around as the song reached a crescendo she was surprised to see Hunter glaring out over her shoulder. She stopped dancing and he looked down at her. "Thirsty?" he bellowed over the first chords of *YMCA* amid hoots and shouts from the pulsating mass.

Ducking a barrage of arms and elbows being haphazardly thrown about, she nodded and headed for the bar. Alumni stood four deep around the harassed bartender, shouting orders and sloshing liquid over the rims of their glasses as soon as they were handed them. A large hand wrapped around her upper arm and pulled her back into a solid wall of muscle.

"This is insane," Hunter growled into her ear. "Would you be against going someplace quieter?"

A shout went up from the center of the dance floor for a Rebel Yell pyramid. Jillian winced. The mental picture of Deidre taking her place as cheerleader captain on top of a pile of horny, inebriated middle-aged men and letting loose with that ungodly shriek in the name of school spirit made her shudder. "Think you can get us out of here in under three seconds?"

He grabbed her by the hand and flashed her a grin that shot sparks from her head to her toes. "Hang on."

By the time they burst through the double doors on the opposite side of the room, Jillian was laughing so hard she ran right into Hunter when he came to an abrupt stop in the middle of the hall. "Oh my god. I have got to take you with me the next time there's a sale at Neiman Marcus." He had turned to catch her when she stumbled and she was still smiling when she looked up at him.

Instantly the air was squeezed from her lungs and the hallway and roaring crowd they had left behind ceased to exist. The sheer power of Hunter's intense masculinity as he gazed down at her crashed over her senses, leaving her feeling incredibly feminine and yearning. He surrounded her with a strength and energy that was so primitive and animalistic that Jillian's pulse kicked into overdrive. An anticipation edged with fear. The thrill of playing with fire knowing you might get burned.

His scent, clean and wild, folded around her, holding her a willing captive as much as the arms encircling her. His large hands steadied her, the hard muscles of his chest and thighs pressed against her. Even as her body reacted at a thoroughly carnal level to each of these sensations, she might have been able to step away, make a joke about her clumsiness and untangle the situation. Maybe. But she had no defense against the primal magnetism that trapped her in his gaze.

Fierce indigo eyes glinting with undisguised lust stark and unashamedly blazing in their depths. Jillian had forgotten how it felt to be wanted with such determined intensity. It knocked her feet right off their pedestal of good judgment and common sense. Her fingers curled into the smooth fabric of his shirt, the heat of his skin tingled past her fingertips and spiraled through her body to land with a shower of sparks in her pussy. The sparks caught on the dry tinder of her recent sexual drought and in seconds, a full-blown blaze was racing through her veins.

"Oh my," she whispered, right before Hunter lowered his head and kissed her.

* * * * *

With Jillian's words brushing his skin, her body softening in his hands as he pulled her near and the flush of arousal staining her cheeks, Hunter forgot everything but the woman in his arms. His mouth covered hers in a kiss that went from zero to ninety in a quick breath. Her arms slid up around his neck as he shifted to hold her closer. One hand splayed over her back and his other hand started sliding slowly down to her ass.

He didn't want to push her too fast too soon, but when she licked inside his mouth and arched up so that his erection pressed hard into her stomach, he realized he just might be slowing *her* down. Slipping his fingers down and around the curve of her bottom, he gave it a gentle, testing caress. Jillian twisted his hair around her fingers and hummed in approving pleasure. A sultry, fuck-me-please sound if he had ever heard one—and he had heard plenty.

Desire knifed through his gut and he took a firmer grip on her ass and squeezed. He skated his other hand up her back to hold her head as she rocked her body into his. The kiss turned savage. Everything within him was driving hard with the need to get inside her lush body.

"Oh my god! *Jillian!*"

The siren in his arms suddenly went cold and jerked away. Deidre stood in the hall, her mouth open in shock.

"What the hell are you doing?" Deidre propped her hands on her abundant hips with a disbelieving huff. At first, he just assumed the bitch was harping at him until he realized that she was staring at the woman who had just tilted his world with a simple kiss. Automatically, he started to pull Jillian behind him, but she shook off his hand and stepped forward, mirroring Deidre's indignant pose.

"I beg your pardon."

Jesus, for being halfway to drunk, Jillian's voice was sharp enough to slice the balls right off a man.

"You were...were..." Deidre flapped a hand at them as she searched for words. He could only guess that she was trying for Jillian's benefit to find a tactful way of referring to the only-needs-a-bed-and-condom display she interrupted. Because she had never had a problem telling *him* exactly what she thought.

With a half-strangled squeak that sounded like a choking rodent, Deidre dropped her hand and raised her voice. "With *Hunter Scott*. In the middle of the *hall*."

A bright red blush rose to stain Jillian's cheeks. "Your point?"

Deidre actually took a step backward. Her shock giving way to a derision. "But he's…he's…*Hunter Scott.*" She couldn't have said *pile of shit* with any more contempt.

"Excuse me?"

Hunter glanced around. Jillian's outraged question should have started icicles forming on the walls. He didn't need her to defend him, but her effort still sent warmth twisting through his heart.

"It's none of your business what I do. I'm a grown woman, I'm on vacation and I'm going to have some fun. So if I want to make out with Hunter Scott in the middle of Pier's Point Hotel, I'm going to make out with Hunter Scott in the middle of Pier's Point Hotel."

Abruptly, the warmth Hunter had been feeling settled back into the cold shame he had known as a teenager. Good enough to fuck, not good enough to take home to the parents. Her comment cleared the last of the lust clouding his brain. Though she might have come to fuck an old classmate, he had come to settle an old score. But he was never against a good fucking. Especially when the fucking went hand in hand with payback.

Deidre snapped to a stiff-backed stance which thrust her boobs out almost a foot in front of her chin. "Well pardon me for trying to be helpful. I saw you leaving and thought you might want your purse."

Jillian leaned forward and snagged it out of Deidre's hand. "Thank you." She turned back to him. "Ready?"

He let his gaze wander over her body. Slowly and with intent. By the time his eyes returned to meet her gaze, there was no doubt in anyone's mind what exactly he was ready for when he responded. "Just waiting on you, babe."

* * * * *

·   The early summer night was what Jillian remembered of South Carolina coastal evenings—warm, breezy, smelling like salt. Stepping out into the fresh air had helped some to clear her head for a moment, but then Hunter stepped close and she discovered that a lust fog was just as potent in scrambling her thoughts as a couple of drinks.

Taking deep breaths, she let the comparative quiet outside the hotel work some calm back into her system as Hunter led her across the hotel parking lot toward a low-slung convertible. The black car glittered in the moonlight like a magic carpet waiting to escort her to all her favorite fantasies. When they reached his car, Hunter's hand shifted from the small of her back to her hip. Her shoulder bumped his chest as he leaned over to whisper in her ear, "Any requests for tonight?"

Jillian's breath stalled in her throat. She was glad they had already stopped moving when he asked his question with that low, sexy rumble she remembered so well. His words sent electricity zinging out from her stomach to flare in her pussy and through her breasts. With her knees nearly buckling, trying to take another step would have landed her on the ground.

"Requests?" Okay, sexual purring must be contagious because she was sure her voice had never sounded like that when she had spoken to Jason. Hunter turned her to face him and leaned into her, trapping her thighs against the car with his. The spicy musk of his cologne swirled around her and all thoughts of Jason disappeared.

Hunter kept one hand on her hip and slid the other through her hair at the base of her skull and used it to tip her head sideways, giving him easy access to the length of her neck. "For your vacation fling." His breath warmed the sensitive spot just under her ear and when his lips touched the same place, her hands shot up to grab his shirt for balance.

"Fling?" So much for the purr. That was the panicked squeak of a woman nearing forty who had slept with three men her entire life and none at all in far too long. The last of the bravado she had faced Deirdre with evaporated as Hunter pulled back to look down at her with a condescending lift of his eyebrows.

"What? This is your first affair?"

Something had changed since he had kissed her in the hall. The warmth that had been in his eyes had vanished and he was looking at her almost in anger.

"I have a teenage daughter at home and I am a responsible parent. I don't sleep around because I don't want my daughter sleeping around."

Hunter blinked and a little of the warmth returned to his gaze. Backing up half a step, his lips tilted in a slight smile. "Still Saint Jillian, huh?"

Her high-school nickname struck hard at a fresh wound. Every chance he got, Jason mocked her with similar monikers. Logically, she knew that it was because she had refused to play his particular brand of sex game. She also knew she was too old to be goaded into doing something she didn't want to just because of some stupid name-calling. But there was still enough tequila buzzing through her that her emotions trumped her logic — a rare thing.

She fisted her hands in his shirt and pulled him close. "I'm not a saint and I want to be fucked. Hard and repeatedly. If you can handle it."

Jillian closed her eyes and let the whipping wind snap her hair shoulder-length brown hair around her face as Hunter's Viper cut through the night. At the last moment she had regained some sanity as he had started the car and had the quick but necessary conversation about sex history and testing. For the first time to ask those questions in too many years to count, she felt fairly impressed with how she had handled it.

For his part, Hunter responded very seriously and reassured her that yes, he was clean. And then he had reached across the center console and kissed her until her toes curled.

Snuggling deeper into the leather bucket seat, she released the last of her reservations along with a deep breath. Her daughter had been right. She deserved to have some fun. Some *adult* fun. Meghan would be proud of her, if she ever told her—which she never would.

The car slowed and went over a small bump. Jillian opened her eyes in time to see a garage door open and Hunter pull into the empty spot next to a beat-up, blue pickup truck.

"Isn't that the same truck you had in high school?"

Hunter had turned off the car and come around to her side to open her door for her. "Yes. Doesn't look like much, but she still runs great." He took her hand and led her through a door to the kitchen. As they moved through the darkened house, Jillian got a dim view of leather sofas, dark carpet and the sleek lines of modern furniture. Stopping at the bottom of a flight of stairs, Hunter turned to look at her.

"Now's a good time to say you've changed your mind, because when we get to the top of these stairs, I'm going to fulfill your request."

"My request?" Jillian couldn't remember making one.

Hunter's eyebrows drew together. "Yes or no, Jillian."

"Yes." She took a deep breath. "Absolutely."

"Good." He started up the stairs, two at a time. Because he was still holding her hand, she had to scramble to keep up with him.

"What request?" she panted, slightly out of breath at the top of the stairs. He didn't answer but drew her toward the end of the hall where a set of heavy double doors stood slightly ajar. As soon as they crossed the threshold, he closed the doors and pressed her against one, using the length of his body to pin her in place. Lowering his head until their lips were less than an inch apart, he said, "Hard and repeatedly, I believe were your exact words."

Jillian didn't think her body could have reacted any more strongly to his words than if a lust bomb had been detonated in her pussy. She nearly came on the spot and put up no resistance to the assault Hunter launched on her mouth with a kiss that easily hit the top three she'd ever had. Twining her arms around his neck, she opened her mouth wider and swirled her tongue around his. A small part of her brain logged the fact that he didn't taste even a tiny bit like alcohol, just a hint of mint. And then his hands skimmed down her sides to her hips and back up to cup her breasts and she stopped trying to hang on to any type of rational thought at all.

Hunter pushed his knee between her legs and pressed his thigh against her pussy. Moaning into his mouth, she arched her back, widened her stance and rocked forward. The hands that had been kneading her breasts shot down to her ass and squeezed hard. She couldn't breathe. Digging her fingers into his shoulders, she tore her mouth away from the kiss.

He pulled her dress up to her waist and grabbed her ass again. "You have got to be fucking kidding," he whispered roughly against her temple as he traced the edges of her lingerie. "A garter belt and thong? Jesus woman, do you have any idea what that does to a man?"

"My daughter thought it would make me feel sexy." She was trying to get her hands between their bodies to undo his pants, but he had brought her flush against him and was holding her in place as his fingers wrapped around her thong and tugged. The material chafed her sensitized clit and she gasped.

"I'm going to make you feel sexier," he said. With a sharp downward yank, he tore the flimsy underwear from her body. Before she could protest—*as if*—he had two fingers high and deep inside of her and had bit down on the tendon stretched tight at the side of her neck.

With a loud cry she came at once, her cunt gripping and releasing the fingers that kept twisting inside her. The explosion was hot and fast, her skin flaming as ecstasy blazed into every nerve numbed since her divorce. Once the fireworks had cleared from her vision and she was able to see straight again, she realized Hunter had gone very still and was looking down at her.

Nervously, she cleared her throat. "Umm…sorry. It's been awhile."

"Jillian," he said, sliding his fingers free of her pussy, "never apologize to a man for making you come."

Something that had been bolted down in her heart started to shake free at the look in his eyes and the tone of his voice. But before she could identify it, a cocky grin eased over his face. "Otherwise, sweetheart," he said as he unfastened his belt and carefully slid his zipper down, "you're going to be apologizing all night."

Her mouth dropped open on a silent "Oh" at the promise in his words and she started to ease herself away from the door. Hunter stopped her with one large hand on her hip. "Where do you think you're going?"

"The bed?"

"Eventually." Taking both her hands, he wrapped them around his erection.

God, it felt good to touch a man like this again. Holding a hard, hot cock in her hands rated high on her list of sexual favorites — just under holding it in her mouth. When she adjusted her grip and started experimenting with different strokes, Hunter flattened his hands on the door on either side of her shoulders and a harsh breath hissed out between his teeth.

Almost immediately, he framed her face in his hands and tilted her head up to show her in a kiss exactly what she was doing to him. The harder he kissed her, the more sure and fast her strokes became. He growled into the kiss as she slid one hand lower to cup his balls. She had never had a man be so clearly transparent about his pleasure. It snaked a carnal thrill down her spine and made her bolder with her explorations.

Hunter's head jerked up. "Fuck."

"Mmm-hmm." She smiled with the knowledge that she literally held him in the palm of her hands. "Time for the bed yet?"

He moved her hands up to his shoulders and then grabbed her thighs, spreading and lifting her. "Time for Saint Jillian to be banged against a door. Move your dress out of the way."

Leaning backwards to balance herself against the door, she reached down and tucked the chiffon of her skirt behind a thigh and adjusted his cock so the head of it aligned with her open pussy. The smooth heat of it touching her swollen flesh made her moan and her hand automatically constricted around his shaft.

"Move your hand." The abrasive command was tempered by the urgent lust raging between them. Jillian had never felt quite so out of control or impatient. When she tried to wiggle down and take him in, he shifted his hands to keep her in place. Rolling his hips up a fraction, he pushed the head of his cock in. With barely there shallow thrusts, he stretched and teased her, staying just at her entrance until she was ready to scream. Her thighs clamped around his hips and she dug her fingers into the hard, flexed muscles of his biceps.

"Damn it, Hunter. What the hell are you waiting on?"

A sexy arrogance filled his eyes and she knew she had just given him what he was waiting on.

"For you to beg."

Okay, maybe not *quite* what he was waiting on. "I don't think so."

He slanted his hips in at a slightly different angle and instantly her clit was grazing part of his shaft every time he moved.

"Oh *god!*" She threw her head back and it hit the door with a thud she barely registered.

"Beg." His voice was raw, his tone dark and demanding.

"No." Hardly a whisper. She didn't know what had gotten into her, but she felt wild and wanton and understood instinctively that wild and wanton women never gave in until the last possible moment.

"You're dripping down my cock, Jillian. *Beg.*" Harsher. Darker.

Before she could rally the needed willpower to respond in the negative, he scraped his teeth down the side of her neck. When the *hell* had her neck become such a hot erogenous zone on her body? She held out for two more seconds, and then he sucked hard at that spot at the base of her neck just as it curved into her shoulder. The last possible moment had arrived.

"Fuck me, Hunter! God damn. *Please.* Fuck me. Right now —" Her frantic pleas were cut off by an instant loss of breath as his cock slammed inside of her.

Suddenly, everything froze. She didn't — couldn't — move. Hunter's body locked around her and the only sound in the room was his ragged breathing. She glanced up to find Hunter staring down at her with a stunned expression. Uncertain, she licked her lips. His eyes narrowed, focused on her mouth.

A soft curse preceded his brutal, fiery kiss. He seemed intent on overwhelming her. His tongue swept into her mouth, probing and taking. His hands slid from her thighs to her bottom and angled her pelvis to receive the full length of his impressive erection. Keeping her in position for the hard-driving rhythm he set.

Again and again, he rammed into her. Each time he filled her, she met his thrust by flexing her thighs, clamping down with her inner muscles and riding out each stroke. The rise to another orgasm was swift and scorching. Tiny tornados twisted violently through her until they coiled together in a tension too tight to maintain. One more hard deep thrust and her body went rigid for a split second as the final barrier to ecstasy was shattered. The ruthless pleasure of release claimed her, and Jillian did something she had never done before. She screamed out a man's name.

Chapter 3

Fuck fuck fuck fuck fuck.

The sound of Jillian Lawson crying out his name as she came apart with his dick buried deep inside of her sweet cunt was more than he could take. His plan for payback for something that happened years ago lost its appeal in the sweetness of the woman he held in his arms. Twenty years was a long time to hang on to a grudge. He had grown up a lot, changed a hell of a lot—in all but apparently one area. There was still one woman who could completely turn him inside out.

As her body shuddered through her orgasm and her pussy massaged him, Hunter didn't even try to slow the climax building in his veins and rushing toward his cock. With a shout, he joined Jillian in her flight over the edge of sanity.

"Shit," he whispered, his forehead dropping to bump the door. After his body had quit shaking and Jillian's legs had slid bonelessly back down to the floor, his brain cleared enough to realize that he needed to keep this purely in the "affair" category. Regardless of what he was feeling, Jillian only wanted a vacation fling and expecting anything else from her after all this time was worse than stupid.

But he could sure as hell make her remember this affair—and him—for the rest of her life.

When he was sure her legs were solid enough to hold her up, he slowly withdrew and stepped back. "Let's get you out of that dress."

She blinked at him, her dark eyes huge in the room lit only by the moon shafting through opened curtains. "Why?"

Goddamn the woman could make him smile. "For fucking. What else?" No one could have convinced him that her eyes could have rounded even more, but he watched it happen.

"Again?"

He turned her and unzipped her dress. She shimmied her shoulders and the dress fell to the floor with a soft *whoosh*. Hunter nearly swallowed his tongue. Against the dark wooden doors, her skin glowed a milky white. Her hair fell to just past her shoulders in soft waves, still mussed from the wind on the drive over and their recent fucking. Her waist curved in, her hips curved out and her ass curved around. Perfect. The black bra had lacy straps that matched the lace on her garter belt. Since he had removed her panties, the lace, straps and thigh-highs framed that perfect ass...perfectly. It didn't hurt that she was still wearing those fuck-me heels.

Jillian lifted her hands behind her back to unhook her bra, but he stopped her. "Just a minute." Quickly, he stripped out of his clothes and left them in a pile on the floor. Lightly, he ran the tips of his fingers down the line of her spine. Goose bumps followed his touch and he brought his fingers back up to her bra. With a flick of his wrist, the bra popped open and he slid his hands under the fabric and around her front to cup her breasts.

With a soft moan, she arched her back and her soft flesh pressed into his hands. He stepped closer so his cock could nestle in the cleft between her ass cheeks and pinched her stiffened nipples.

She hummed low in her throat and reached backwards. Grabbing his butt, she pulled him nearer and at the same time wiggled her hips so that his erection slid in deeper.

"You like to play with fire," he whispered against her throat. He loved the sensitivity of her neck and the way she shivered when he kissed her there.

"You started it," she said, leaning forward slightly and resting her head against the door.

He pulled her back to his chest. "Sweetheart, you started this twenty fucking years ago." Sliding one hand down over her stomach, he combed his fingers through her soaked curls and circled her clit. "And I'm planning on finishing it."

She let her bra drop to the floor and turned to place a soft kiss on his jaw. It was almost sweet, nearly innocent—and came so close to unlocking the emotion he had just shackled down, he decided that it was time to change tactics. She kissed him again and he heard the chains around his heart start to snap. *Now.*

Jillian let out a surprised shriek when he scooped her up and carried her to his bed. After tossing her onto the middle of it, he leaned over and flipped on the bedside lamp.

"Oh!" she said, slapping a hand over her eyes and rolling away from the light. "Warn me when you plan on blinding me next time."

"I want to be able to see every inch of you." Her response was muffled against the thick duvet when he grabbed her ankles and flipped her onto her stomach. She looked over her shoulder at him in surprise. Lifted one foot off the bed.

"Are you going to take off my shoes?"

"No." He ran his hands up her calves, the back of her thighs and then popped the straps of her garter belt against her ass. She tried to roll over, but he grabbed her hips and yanked her back to the side of the bed. Her feet hit the floor and just like that, she was bent over in front of him. "Straighten your legs and prop your ass in the air for me." All teasing banter was gone from his voice, replaced by a husky undercurrent that sounded a hell of a lot like a wild animal's growl.

Jillian balked and looked back at him. He might have grinned at her expression, but he was too turned on by the sight in front of him. And he sure as hell didn't want her backing away from him now. "What's the matter? Hasn't Saint Jillian ever been fucked from behind?"

Immediately, her eyes narrowed, but she didn't say anything. Instead she spread her legs a little more and then slowly straightened them. The look in her eyes turned to a dare, tempting him. With her pussy put on show like that, it was a challenge he was more than able to meet.

He smoothed a hand over the tight curve of the left side of her beautiful ass. She leaned into his hand, stretched her arms out in front of her and arched her back like a cat. Damn. Make that one hell of a sex kitten. Running his hands up the inside of her thighs, he brushed her folds with his knuckles. A fine tremor raced through her body, but she still managed a smug look.

"Is that all you've got?"

Her brash question spiked the lust he was doing his damnedest to keep under control. This time, it was his turn not to answer. He held her gaze as he knelt behind her, satisfaction flinging through him the moment he saw in her eyes that she understood what he was about to do. All signs of taunting were gone and the wide-eyed "oh-my-god" look was back.

* * * * *

Don't whimper. Wild, wanton women don't whimper. God, god, god. Jillian! Do. Not. Whimper.

As soon as Hunter knelt down, Jillian's blood crystallized for a split second before melting into a lava flow that threatened to scorch her from the inside out. Though she loved having a man go down on her, Jason had always avoided oral sex. Maybe because she had never *ordered* him to eat her out.

She watched Hunter's expression carefully, making sure that he wanted to do this. By the time he had moved out of her line of vision, the downright obvious lust in his eyes had her nearly shaking with anticipation. Her fingers gripped the coverlet and she turned her face into the mattress to muffle her moan as Hunter's palms skimmed over the back of her legs.

His hands were warm and slightly rough against her inner thighs. She felt the stretch of her skin as he pulled outward gently. Using his thumbs, he rubbed the outer lips of her pussy.

"Your skin's so soft here, sweetheart," he murmured. "Soft and slick. And damn, but I love seeing an open pussy. Wet and ready."

Hunter continued to run his thumbs around her labia with slow, teasing strokes. He was close enough that she could feel his hot breath on her swollen flesh. Jillian was dying. She could hardly draw in enough air to keep from passing out. Her clit was throbbing and the ache inside her cunt increased exponentially with each second that passed. Thought was long gone and only feeling and instinct remained. Closing her eyes, she let herself become totally focused on the sensations Hunter was bringing her.

She quit worrying about whether or not she moaned or whimpered. She didn't care if he heard what he was doing to her. Turning her head to the side, she took a deep breath that caught on a cry when he flicked her clit with his tongue.

"I love that sound," he rumbled in that dark, melted-chocolate sexy voice of his that could thaw an ice cube in an igloo. He pulled her pussy lips further apart and flicked her clit again. She jerked and cried out a second time. His hands tightened and held her in place and he began licking her faster. Concentrating solely on that one spot. His tongue circling, laving and flicking. It was the repeated, lightning-quick flicking that finally drove her over the edge. Right there. In that one — *oh my god* — spot.

"Oh *god!*" Jillian tossed her head back and screamed as her climax streamed through her. Her legs were shaking so hard her knees gave out. She sank like a boneless mass onto the bed, unable to hold her position for Hunter a second longer as the pleasure short-circuited the control she had over her own body.

"Oh no you don't. Put your ass back up here."

What? She could hardly move, barely think. "You're not done?"

Hunter chuckled. A sound made coarse by his desire. "Hell, no. How long's your vacation?"

Struggling to straighten her legs again, his last question jeopardized the small amount of control she had been able to reestablish. The thought of an entire week of sex with a man who knew how to use his tongue like that was enough to make her believe in fairy tales and Prince Charmings again. Even if happy endings were still solidly in the land of make-believe, Hunter could definitely provide happy comings for the next few days.

"I leave next Friday." His hands were kneading her butt. She arched hard and pushed back.

"Good," he said and lightly bit the back of one of her thighs. "That might give me just enough time."

She was about to ask him, "Time for what?" but then his tongue drove into her cunt and she couldn't remember her name, never mind a question she probably didn't want to hear the answer to. As his tongue darted in and out of her and her body started to shiver in the unique combination of need and rising ecstasy, a tiny shard of guilt cut through the tremors.

"Isn't it about time we turn this around?" she rasped.

He nipped her thigh again. "Don't worry about me, sweetheart." He kissed where he had just bit. "I'll get mine." And then he went back to working her pussy with his mouth, adding his fingers to tease her clit and Jillian's guilt disappeared in a sharp, sudden climax.

Her cunt seized with the first spasm of her orgasm and Hunter stood and thrust his cock fully into her. The unexpected switch from his fingers to his much larger cock rocketed her pleasure higher than she thought possible. He stood still, holding her fixed against him as she finished riding out her storm.

It wasn't until the contractions were fading that he started to move. His hands bracketed her hips in an unforgiving grip. She would have fallen, exhausted, to the bed but he kept her where he wanted her. Little by little, he withdrew inch by slow inch. When the head of his cock dragged over her G-spot, she gasped in surprise. She'd never fucked in quite this position before and had no idea a man's cock could do what his was doing. And so soon after she had just touched the stars. Again.

. A low, ragged moan rolled out of him and his fingers tightened around her as he pushed back in just as slowly. "Damn it looks sweet to see your cunt swallow me. Stretched tight and pink around my cock."

It seemed impossible that he could keep filling her, but he pushed in until every inner muscle was stretched and had started constricting.

"That's it, Jillian," he whispered. "Take me. Take all of me."

She was panting now. As he pulled back out and once again hit that *oh my god* place, she shuddered and her pussy gripped hard.

"*Shit*," he hissed. He moved so his thighs pressed to hers when he pushed all the way back in and started an unrelenting rocking. No longer pulling nearly out and then pushing slowly in, he was grinding against her. His balls slapping against her clit. His hips rotating so that his cock continued to put pressure on her G-spot.

This was unlike anything Jillian had ever experienced. Her climax started from deep within her, shaking loose her defenses and leaving her feeling exposed and vulnerable. Instinctively her mind fought its completion as desperately as her body raced toward it. The razor-edge dance of wanting more — wanting everything — and straining against the doubt and panic brought on by the powerful emotions flooding her.

"Hunter!" She twisted to look at him, searching. He looked up. Met her gaze. Kept fucking her with the determination of a tyrant set on conquest. His navy eyes flashed hot and hotter still.

"Come for me, Jillian."

"Oh god!" Her body shuddered. Shook with the tension as she held herself back from that sliver-fine edge. "Oh god, Hunter. Oh *no!*"

"Yes, dammit. Yes!" His fingers dug into her hips as he ground harder against her. She felt his balls draw up, watched his face turn granite-sharp. "*Come!*"

The last resistance gave way like a house built of sticks before hurricane-force winds. Her scream merged with his shout as his release poured into her. Writhing against wave after wave of bliss that sheeted through her body, Jillian forgot time, forgot place, forgot everything but the man and the explosive heaven he carried her to.

* * * * *

Hunter watched Jillian as she slept. Her lips barely parted for her steady, deep breaths. Her thick, dark eyelashes resting softly on her cheeks. He'd had no idea how dangerous it could be to a man's heart to watch a woman sleep in his bed. Much more risky than simply fucking her in that same bed.

After that last round of soul-shattering sex, they had both collapsed. He had rolled them around until they were under his comforter instead of sprawled across it. As soon as Jillian had wiggled out of her shoes, stockings and garter belt, she had snuggled up next to him and mumbled something about being better than a pirate. When he asked her what she said, she had shaken her head and yawned through a murmured, "Ravished by pirate fantasy. Much better."

Before he could get her to explain that interesting bit of information, she had rolled to her side, thrown her leg and arm across him and gone straight to sleep. His heart had done a slow stiff roll into a solid *thump* of falling hard when she had put her head on his shoulder. The realization that he wanted her right where she was for longer than just a week went a long way to clearing away his tiredness as he started formulate another plan for Jillian. It was no longer about payback but the future. He settled deeper into the pillows and let his heart lead his mind through the new options and possibilities of the next week.

The quiet brush of material against skin had Hunter looking up from the morning paper. The sight before him made him glad that Jillian wasn't telepathic, because otherwise she'd have known that at that instant, she could have asked for the world and he would have given it to her if it took his last breath to bring it to her.

Wearing just his dress shirt from last night with the sleeves rolled up to her elbows, she stood in the kitchen doorway looking a little lost, more than a little sleepy and a whole lot of what he wanted to see every morning over the top of his paper. With her hair mussed, makeup gone and the sun shining in behind her from the living room windows outlining her gorgeous body through the fine cotton material, she was so sexy it literally hurt to sit still when what he wanted most was to leap over the table and haul her back up to his bed.

When his gaze managed to go higher than her chest, he found her smiling a little uncertainly at him. "Hi," she said softly.

Such a quiet sound to have such a wrenching effect on his heart. Possessiveness roared through him with a desire to take her right here in the kitchen, right now. Instead, he folded down the morning paper and put it on the table. "'Morning," he said steadily. "Would you like some breakfast?"

She shook her head. "I don't eat breakfast very often. But I would like some coffee."

He gestured to a chair. "Have a seat. I'll get you a cup. Cream or sugar?"

"Just black." Taking soft, silent cat steps across the hardwood floor, she stopped when she saw the picture of Tyler and him on his boat. She picked it up and looked at it closely.

"Is this your son?"

"Yes. Tyler. He's fourteen. Lives with his mom in Charleston." He was also the reason Hunter had finally gotten his act together. He didn't want Tyler to ever feel ashamed of him the way he had grown up feeling ashamed of his own father.

"He's very handsome. Has your eyes."

That familiar paternal pride puffed inside of him. "Good thing for him that he got his mother's brains. He's a real sharp kid."

She replaced the picture. Turned and accepted the mug he held out to her. Propped her hip against the counter and took a small sip. "You were married?"

"Nope. She refused to marry me because she said I didn't love her." He shrugged. "I did care about her a hell of a lot, but she was right, and she deserved better." Leaning against the opposite counter, he picked up his own coffee cup and took a drink. "She got it. She's very happy with an insurance salesman."

A block of lead settled in his stomach as a sudden dread slithered through his mind. She hadn't been wearing a wedding ring last night, but he'd never actually *asked*. "Are you married?"

The shock that crossed Jillian's face gave him his answer before she shook her head. "No. Of course not. I wouldn't be here with you if I was." A soft pink flushed her cheeks and her gaze skittered away from his as she took a long drink. "So...besides not getting married, what else have you been up to over the last twenty years?"

Tilting his head toward the picture she had replaced on the counter, he said, "You've seen the most important thing that happened to me. Other than that, I take tourists fishing."

Jillian's eyebrows rose a fraction as she glanced around his spacious kitchen. "A lot of people must really like to fish."

"A few," he said with a shrug. "And you?"

"I haven't fished in years."

He smiled. "No, I mean the last twenty years. What have you been up to?"

Turning the mug so she could hold it with both hands, she grinned over the top of it. "Living in Savannah. CPA. Happily divorced with one child—Meghan—who just graduated high school."

His eyebrows rose at the way she rattled off the information. "Sounds like you've said that before."

Her grin widened. "About a hundred times last night. I think you're the only one who didn't ask."

"Your daughter's graduated already?" He found it hard to believe that Jillian had had a child so soon after high school.

Jillian shrugged. "I fell hard for Jason the summer before college and we married my freshman year. Then, a month later, some antibiotics and my birth control didn't mix well and I ended up pregnant."

"You still finished college?" When she nodded, Hunter's respect for her multiplied.

"It was rough, but I was young and didn't need much sleep. My mom helped by watching Meghan when Jason was at work."

Nursing her coffee, Jillian fell silent and stood shifting her weight from her right foot to her left foot. Hunter was content to simply let her finish her coffee and watch her stand in his home surrounded by the early morning light. And then she bit the corner of her bottom lip. A nervous habit she'd had for as long as he could remember. It affected him the same way today as it had the first time she had done it in third period when he had winked at "the new girl" in class.

Suddenly, a white-hot flame flashed over him. He set his cup on the counter behind him and stalked toward her. "About last night..."

As Hunter watched her eyes go big and wide all over again, he wondered if that was what had pulled him in from the first. Huge bottomless doe eyes that showed her emotions so plainly. He had grown up in a world where emotions were liabilities and demonstrated weaknesses that others could prey upon. From an early age he had learned to shutter feelings and turn a hardened exterior to the world. Jillian, on the other hand, opened her soul to you each time she looked at you.

Taking her cup, he set it down out of the way. He caged her in place by placing his hands on the countertop on either side of her hips. This close he could smell the remnants of perfume in her hair and the lingering scent of sex. Though the air conditioning was cool in the room, he felt hot and restricted by the T-shirt and cargo shorts he had put on this morning. Most probably from the furnace blast of lust that had fired to life between them with his last words.

"So," he said after dropping a light kiss on her lips, "do you have anywhere you need to be in the next five days?"

Jillian's tongue darted out and over her bottom lip. Hunter suppressed a growl. He had a new plan he was working here, and there was more at stake than just a few days of mindless sex. Or even mind-blowing sex. Though that was definitely *part* of the plan.

"I'm under strict orders from my daughter to have fun," she whispered.

A slow smile eased across his face as he thought how much he already really liked Meghan. "I think that can be arranged. Is there anyone you need to call this morning? Anything you need to do?"

She shook her head.

"Then what do you say about getting started on that fun right now?"

* * * * *

Jillian's breath stuttered out as Hunter stepped in closer. His voice had thickened on his last two words and made her shiver in expectation. The words she would have said evaporated when he brushed the tips of his fingers down the side of her neck. She leaned into his hand and hummed in pleasure instead of trying to speak.

He tilted her chin up with his knuckles until her eyes, half-closed with the weight of desire, met his. The look in his eyes brought back every lust-filled memory from yesterday screaming to the forefront of her mind. Not to mention the falling-out-of-the-sky feeling he was causing in her body. First thing in the morning and he was able to create serious hormone havoc. It woke her up better than caffeine.

"Are you sure?" There was something more than lust in the depths of his dark blue eyes, but she didn't want to try to figure it out. She wanted fun, and fun was what he offered. No promises, no expectations, no complications.

"Yes." He held her gaze a moment more. Searching. She didn't know what he was waiting on, but having him so close and not touching her the way she wanted tested the limits of her patience.

And then her world spun around crazily as he picked her up and tossed her over his shoulder. With a yelp, she grabbed the waist of his shorts to steady herself. Upside down as she was, it was a very disorienting trip out his back door, across his backyard and down a short dock to a waiting boat. The wind was blowing her hair around her face and if the arm that was pinning her thighs to his chest hadn't caught the tail of his shirt that she was wearing, she'd have flashed any neighbor who just might be staring out at the commotion he was causing.

"Wait! What are you doing?"

He didn't answer, but stepped onto the deck, opened a cabin door and stepped inside. The room was a combination sleep and dining area, the bed already pulled out and made ready. It was here that he flipped her off his shoulder. She landed on her back, arms and legs flailing. Her shirt had risen to her waist and before she could yank it down again, Hunter was on top of her.

"I seem to recall a certain fantasy you have of being abducted by a pirate." He held her wrists to the bed and took her mouth in a hard, conquering kiss that proved he was more than able to play the role of pirate. His body moved against hers, all demanding force and insistent pleasure. He nipped at her earlobe hard enough to sting slightly. "Ravished by a pirate."

Jillian's body instantly went liquid with need and she arched into him. "Oh god, Hunter. I—"

"Hell-lllo-o! Anyone on board?"

An arctic gale blowing though the cabin couldn't have chilled the mood more than Deidre's voice cutting through the air.

Hunter lifted his head and let out a low, extremely creative stream of obscenities.

"What's she doing here?" Jillian asked, trying not to feel jealous that Deidre was on intimate enough terms with Hunter to just show up and climb onto his boat.

"Hell if I know." He pushed himself up off her. "Don't move. I'll get rid of her and be right back."

As soon as he exited, Jillian got up off the bed, tugged down the shirt and moved to the door where she could hear.

"What the fuck are you doing on my boat?" The harshness to Hunter's tone surprised Jillian, and judging from the outraged gasp, it had surprised Deidre too.

"Well excuse me. But I was just checking on Jillian. No one's seen her since she left with you and I thought she might need my support."

This was too much. Jillian opened the door and stepped out onto the deck. Deidre was standing in front of the door, her back to Jillian.

"Besides, you're the one who announced you were only coming to the reunion to screw Jillian—the only girl whose pants you couldn't get into in high school."

The angry words that had been forming for Deidre died in her throat. Hunter looked up at her and his expression told her that this time, it wasn't just another false rumor Deidre was spreading.

Deidre turned and let out a shocked gasp. "Jesus! I didn't think you'd be here, Jillian. I'm sorry you had to hear that."

"Bullshit, Deidre." Hunter's voice was knife-sharp and slicing deep. "You knew exactly where she was. I don't know what you're trying to pull here, but it's over. Get off my boat."

Long red nails flashed in the sun as Deidre's hands fluttered in agitation. "You can't—"

"You have two seconds to decide whether you want to walk of this boat or be thrown off."

Deidre tossed her bleached mane over her shoulder with an offended huff and turned to Jillian. "Come on, honey. You can leave with me."

Jillian wrapped her arms around her stomach. "No, thank you." However hurtful Deidre's words might have been, she wasn't going to slink away again from Hunter Scott.

"What?" This time, Deidre's shock actually appeared genuine.

"Time's up," Hunter said, reaching for Deidre. She shrieked and jerked out of his reach. Scooting toward the dock, she cursed when she tripped getting out of the boat. Once on more stable footing, she turned and glared first at Hunter and then at Jillian.

"You're letting him make a fool out of you. The only reason he came to the reunion was to screw you and then brag that he's the only Rebel that ever fucked Saint Jillian." Hunter took another step toward her and with a final glare of fury, Deidre turned on her heel and stomped off.

Slowly, Hunter turned back toward her. "Jillian—"

Jillian held up her hand to stop him. "No. Don't. It's okay. I make my own decisions and it was just as much me fucking you last night as you fucking me. And whatever reasons you might have had, they don't matter to me. I'm not a teenager playing games here. If you want to fuck a series of women at your reunions, it's none of my business."

She started across the deck, but was brought up short by his confused look.

"What series of women are you talking about?"

She made a halfhearted sweeping gesture with her hand. "Two women together last time, Saint Jillian this time."

Now his confusion had turned into a frown. "What two women?"

Irritation at his obtuseness was a good substitute for hurt feelings that had no right to be hurt and Jillian grabbed onto it. "The two women you left with at the last reunion. Deidre told me all about your little orgy."

Hunter's cynical bark of laughter smacked with a discordant pitch against the faint cries of gulls over the ocean and the waves lightly slapping the side of the boat. "That *orgy* was me catching up with an old friend and her life partner. We left because we couldn't hear each other's yells over the techno crap the DJ kept blasting. Shelly might have been interested in sex that night, but not with me. Even if she had been, Lori sure as hell wasn't in the mood to share."

Jillian felt the heat of embarrassment flame in her cheeks. Served her right for listening to Deidre in the first place. But there was still this situation. She propped her hands on her hips and lifted her chin. "And what she said about fucking Saint Jillian? Did she get that wrong too?"

Hunter shoved his hand through his hair, pushing several thick strands of light brown hair out of his eyes that had been blown there by the wind. "No. She showed up at a bar a couple of months ago, pestering me and several of the guys to come this year. I'd had a little too much to drink to be dealing with her, and spouted off that the only reason I'd show up this year was to fuck Saint Jillian." He sighed like a poker player resigned to go *all in* on a losing hand. "Then she promised that you'd be here and the more I thought about it, the more I thought it would be a good idea."

He winced. "Shit. There you go with those big eyes again. Look, I was an idiot, acting out of a stupid ego trip from when you stood me up graduation night and sent Deidre to tell me that you'd never be seen with a loser like me."

"She said that?"

"Like I said. I was an idiot. Graduation was a long time ago and —"

"I didn't show up because she said you'd gone off with Penny Jackson. She said it was because you knew I wouldn't sleep with you."

Hunter dropped his head between his shoulders and let out a disgusted sigh. "I didn't sleep with Penny that night. I slept with Deidre."

"*What?*" Jillian had never before seen Hunter Scott self-conscious. He held his hands up and then dropped them to his sides.

"I was pissed about you dumping me. She offered. I was eighteen and stupid." He looked off over the railing as a rueful smile quirked the side of his mouth up. "Make that really, *really* stupid."

A long, quiet moment passed between them before he said, "Jillian, the reason I came to the reunion might have been some shit-for-brains idea about payback, but the reason I slept with you had less to do with a girl I knew twenty years ago, and more to do with the woman she'd become. The one who smiles first with her eyes and whose laughter stops my world. The woman I found in my arms last night when I kissed you in the hotel hallway."

Hunter was still staring out over the ocean, his features tight. Part of Jillian wanted to turn away. Prove to him that he just couldn't...couldn't...

Well, hell. It just wasn't worth it. So they both had been taken advantage of by a spiteful, teenage bitch that had turned into a spiteful, fully mature bitch. So what. She wouldn't change her life even if she could for a chance at a night going different so long ago. She had too good of a life to trade it in for a bunch of "what ifs". And then there was Meghan. Worth every decision — right, wrong, indifferent — that had led her to the place of having her daughter in her life.

Time to put high-school memories in the past where they belonged and get started making some new ones.

"Soooooo..." She waited until Hunter turned to look at her and then popped open the top button of her shirt. "I *still* haven't been ravished by a pirate."

Chapter 4

Jillian's startled scream bounced across the waves. She had no idea a man could move that fast. One moment she was staring at Hunter with a "come and get me if you dare" look, and the next she was flat on her back inside the cabin on the bed.

Between shrieks, laughter and being dumped on the bed, Jillian was still trying to catch her breath when Hunter speared her with a challenging look and asked, "So are you a meek, woe-is-me damsel or are you a determined-to-resist-until-you-come-screaming damsel?"

"Oh definitely the last one. In fact, I'm planning my escape right now."

A sexy grin lit up his face. "Good." He shifted and pulled a strip of material out of a cubbyhole next to the bed. "This pirate came prepared. And there's no way in hell you're escaping your fate this time." Holding her wrists together above her head, he tied them together and secured them to a metal bracket in the wall that looked like it was used to lock the bed into place.

When he released her, she immediately tugged on it. She wasn't going anywhere until he decided she was. Just the thought of being at his mercy sent a rush of anticipation tossing through her and making her wet.

Hunter had been watching her test her bindings and when she looked at him, his smile was gone. Replaced by blatant lust. He sat up on his knees, straddling her thighs. She twisted under him, trying to dislodge him. He grabbed one breast through her shirt and squeezed.

"You're not going anywhere, sweetheart. You're mine and I'm going to take you exactly how I want to." Seizing the shirt on either side just under the collar, he ripped it apart, sending buttons flying around the cabin and leaving her instantly exposed and incredibly turned on.

Jillian sucked in a deep breath as Hunter stared at her body. His gaze roved from her breasts, down her belly and over her hips to her mound and back up again. Just when she thought she'd come from the heat of his eyes alone, he leaned back over toward the little cupboard he had pulled the tie from. She frowned when she saw a plastic bottle of lube in his hand.

"Exactly how I want to," he repeated and moved to flip her onto her stomach. She tried to scramble away, but couldn't go far with her hands tied to the side of the boat. Hunter climbed back on top of her, holding her in place with his weight on her upper legs. He parted her buttocks and without warning, squirted some lube along the line between them. She gasped in aroused surprise and then a mouselike squeak eeked out when he rolled something solid in the slick gel and then started working it into her anus.

"Just a small butt plug," he explained.

It might be small, but it was sending huge ripples of novel sensations throughout her body. She was still trying to adjust to the invasion when he rolled her back over and she lost her breath again.

"Damn, woman. Do you know what those breaths do to your breasts?"

Actually, she was more concerned about her ass at the moment. Lying on her back with that inside of her was driving her need to come through the roof. With a soft moan, she closed her eyes and started rubbing her thighs together.

"Oh no you don't. Exactly how *I* want you to come." The bed shifted as he moved off her, but she wasn't paying attention.

She flexed her bottom, spiking the sensations swirling there and then pressed her thighs together harder. So close to coming, her muscles started to tighten towards release.

Abruptly her legs were pulled apart. She let out a sharp protest, but it was useless. Hunter was tying her ankles to keep her legs separated. She looked down at him as he was finishing the last knot. He stood there staring at her pussy, hungry desire sharp in his eyes.

When his gaze moved up her body, she was more than ready to be ravished. By a pirate or a fishing guide for tourists, she didn't care. Expecting him to climb on top of her any second, she was surprised when he just leaned over and tested the strength of her bonds. "That should hold you for a while."

Then he turned and was halfway out of the door before she got past her disbelief enough to voice a protest. "Wait! Where are you going?"

He turned and studied her over his shoulder with a look that scalded her with an almost tangible lust. "You're in no position to be issuing orders or asking questions. And if you insist on screaming, hoping someone will come to your rescue, I can easily gag you." A wicked grin crossed his face. "Though personally, I'd rather not. I'm looking forward to hearing you moan."

He didn't have to wait very long. His words spiked hard the need pulsing through her with every beat of her heart and she moaned his name. She couldn't help it. Not spread out before him like she was, with him looking at her with the full knowledge of what he was doing to her.

"But even pirates have compassion for certain things," he said, walking back toward the bed. "And this pirate has a particular fondness for a cunt that's open and slick.

As he reached over her, Jillian closed her eyes in relief—in *hope* of relief—and took a deep breath. "Oh thank god!"

Then Hunter pushed a dildo deep inside her and immediately the air rushed out of her lungs on a loud *whoosh*.

The rubber cock slid in easily thanks to her incredibly wet pussy, but against the heat of her inner muscles the coolness of the toy sent a shock through her system. Her entire body clenched and between the toys in both her cunt and ass, she started to shake as her body strained toward a climax held just out of reach.

She was so close.

Not until she heard Hunter say her name and his face swam into view did she realize she had opened her eyes. Blinking some of the sexual haze away, she bit her bottom lip and tried to calm her breathing.

"Don't come without me, Jillian," Hunter commanded. "I'll know if you do, and if you disobey me, I'll tease you all day and not let you come again." Gently, he smoothed a tendril of damp hair back from her cheek. "But if you're a good girl, I'll make you come." He dragged his lips sideways over hers. She opened her mouth but he pulled back. Whispered, "Hard. And repeatedly."

Jillian didn't know how long Hunter was gone. If measured in number of almost-orgasms, he was gone an eternity. Not long after the cabin door had clicked shut behind his retreating form, the boat's motor roared to life and soon she was fighting not to come against every rock and roll of the hull as Hunter took them out to sea. She had no doubt he'd carry through with his threat if she let herself climax on one of the swells of pleasure that kept surging through her body.

It didn't help that he had left the shirt she had been wearing torn open and hanging off her. An ocean breeze blew in through several open portholes to brush over her heated skin and her nipples remained tight and aching from that whisper touch of air.

When he turned into what felt like a particularly large wave and the bottom of the boat smacked down hard against the water, Jillian cried out as her body jerked with sensation.

From her ass to her cunt to her breasts, she couldn't take much more without giving in to the building pressure pushing her closer and closer to the edge.

Clamping her eyes shut, she focused on not breathing too hard around her moans and trying to keep her writhing in sync with the rocking boat. She didn't think she could take another sudden jolt and not come.

"Now there's a woman in desperate need of a fucking."

Jillian's eyes popped open. Hunter was whipping his shirt off over his head to reveal sleek, well-defined muscles wrapped by tanned skin. Fishing must be *really* good exercise for the upper body, judging by Hunter's chest and arms. Her hands flexed and pulled against the tie. She wanted to feel all that hard muscle under her palms, and trace the sinewy lines, explore to her heart's content.

He came to stand beside the bed and slid the dildo out of her. She gasped at the sudden emptiness deep inside of her.

"I love seeing you wet, Jillian," he growled, lust reeling through every word. He finished stripping and his cock thrust out from his body. Involuntarily, her pussy contracted fiercely as she remembered how it filled and stretched her. God! She wanted him inside of her. *Now!*

He slid a single finger into her open cunt. A dark, dangerous sound reverberated from Hunter's chest as he withdrew his finger and then slid it back in. His eyes narrowed as he watched his finger press deep inside again. "Christ, sweetheart."

With his other hand, Hunter started stroking his erection, firmly caressing it from base to tip and back again. Over and over as he continued to slowly move his finger in and out of her. It was just enough sensation inside of her to keep her hot and wanting, but not enough to push her finally to climax.

Even as her desire intensified until she trembled with it, she couldn't take her eyes off his hand on his cock. Outside of a movie she's seen at a bachelorette party, she'd never seen a man touch himself like that. She found it incredibly erotic. Seeing an utterly manly hand—strong, rough, large—working a hard, fully erect cock made her *need* to touch. To do more than watch.

Hunter widened his stance and she started to unconsciously twist against her bonds. He pulled his finger out of her cunt to use both hands on himself. The one still pumping his shaft, the other stroking his balls. She licked her lips. Stared. A soft whimper escaped.

"Open your mouth," he ordered as he climbed onto the bed. There wasn't even a thought of disobeying. Hunter leaned forward and guided the head of his cock past her lips. When she closed her mouth around him and sucked, he groaned loudly and pushed in deeper. With shallow thrusts he filled her mouth and she licked and sucked in time to his rhythm.

After seeing him stroke himself, after he had brought her so high and held her in a limbo of need between her ass and cunt, finally tasting him, feeling the heat of his cock in her mouth, the intimacy of being so totally at his mercy and yet being placed in a position where he was also at hers—she had reached her end. Swirling her tongue around the rim of his cock, she moaned and started to close her eyes to fly into her release.

Hunter's head snapped down. The ferocity of his expression sliced through the passion momentarily eclipsing everything else in her world. He pulled his cock out of her mouth and moved so that his hips were between her spread thighs.

"Exactly as I want, Jillian," he growled. The head of his cock butted up against her throbbing pussy, skyrocketing the sensations radiating out from her ass and into her cunt. She closed her eyes as the heat of pure need blazed through her. He lowered himself until his chest grazed her breasts, her nipples tightly puckered and responsive to every slight movement against them.

She whispered his name. A plea. A demand.

He answered, plunging inside of her. Driving in to the hilt with the first thrust. Jillian screamed and came in a thousand parts as he filled her. Took her. She rose to the crest, splintering, sparkling. Riding the wind and coming back together only to scatter in ecstasy once more as he pushed in again. This time he joined her in the free-fall to ecstasy, coming with an uneven, soul-grinding groan. The sound of his ultimate pleasure filled her heart and made her feel strangely complete. Expanding and warming places deep inside she hadn't even realized had grown so cold over time.

* * * * *

Later, much later, when the ties and toys had all been undone and tossed to the floor, Hunter held Jillian tucked against his body, planning again. Only this time, she was listening, helping, suggesting.

"I want to see you past this week, Jillian. Want to give what's between us a chance." He caressed the curve of her waist down to her hip. Drew a small circle there with his thumb. "But I can't move away from my son."

She tugged lightly on his chest hair. "I know. For years, I was dead set against moving until Meghan graduated high school and decided what she wanted to do next."

Hope soared. Hunter's hand contracted on her hip. "Was?"

Jillian looked up at him. Smiled. "Meghan's leaving for Berkley at the end of July and though I do like my job..." Her voice wandered off, leaving him waiting.

"What?" He never was a patient man.

"It's not the challenge it used to be. I've been thinking about a change of scenery for some time."

Damn. He wanted so much, knew he was asking a lot. A stacked deck never had deterred him though once he got his mind set on something. It had taken him from a part-time guide through the marshes, to the owner of a charter fishing guide business that had a fleet of boats docked in cities all along the east coast.

"Think you might be willing to consider Charleston?" he prompted, feeling like he was balancing on a tightrope above a very deep canyon.

"Perhaps." The warm, teasing in her answer said much more than the single word as she pulled on his chest hair a little more sharply. He pulled her hand away, lifted it to his mouth and nipped the tip of her thumb.

"My business is doing very well." He kissed her temple. "Could use a partner who understands how to run the books."

"Really?"

He frowned at the surprise in her question. "Yes, really."

With an affectionate laugh, Jillian pushed up on one elbow and looked down at him. "You've come a long way from Pier's Point most infamous Rebel. I mean you did—hey!" she squeaked as he suddenly rolled her underneath him. He silenced her with a kiss.

"And you've come a long way from your saint status." He bit her earlobe gently. She arched under him and he shifted to press her thighs apart and settle between them. "Not that I'm complaining..."

Jillian skimmed her hands down his back And grabbed his ass. "Maybe you should try to convince me over this next week that Charleston might be worth the trouble."

Hunter rocked forward, slid inside of her. "In that case sweetheart, you better hang on. That's the type of convincing I can do."

Also by Eve Jameson

ഔ

Bethany's Rite
Brooke's Sanctuary

About the Author

ഔ

I can't recall a time when I wasn't making up stories. As long I remember, they've played like movies in my mind and I love seeing what will happen next.

Why did I decide to become an erotic romance writer? Easy. I didn't.

One day I was minding my own business, writing a nice sweet story, and suddenly this incredibly sexy, all-things-fantasies-are-made-of man just jumped out of my pen. He smiled at me, winked and told me to follow him. What could I do? My feet were moving before my brain had a chance to lodge any reasonable objections. Thank goodness!

I've been on this journey with my muse ever since. And I gotta tell you, I'm loving it! He's introduced me to some gorgeous, alpha heroes and take-no-crap, sassy heroines and the adventure has just begun. I can't wait to introduce you to them and hope you'll have as much fun reading their stories as I have writing them.

Besides being whisked away by my muse, traveling, hiking and reading are in my top ten favorite things to do with a day, along with eating Mexican food and the most decadent chocolate dessert I can find. Drop me a line, I'd love to hear from you.

Eve welcomes comments from readers. You can find her website and email address on her author bio page at www.ellorascave.com.

WATER LUST

Mary Winter

Chapter 1

A heavy full moon hung over the Caribbean. The soft sounds of waves lapping against the shore and the waving of palm fronds in the breeze provided the soundtrack for Grace Edwards' own personal seduction. She lay there, thin bands of water pressing her wrists and ankles into the sand. Beneath her, a cottony soft blanket, far nicer than the 300-count Egyptian sheets on her bed, cushioned her from the grainy sand. Next to her fingers, a crab scuttled along, intent on returning to the ocean. If she had to dream, at least she dreamed in color.

"Listen to it, my love. Hear the ocean caressing the shore. Feel the water touching your body." At his words a wave rushed in, drowning first her toes, then her ankles, as it hurried to her hot, throbbing pussy. Over breasts, nipples drawn tight by the cool water, to kiss her chin before retreating. It was like this, always like this, an ocean-side seduction with her very own sea god.

Except he lived only in her mind.

Grace closed her eyes. This night, just like every night, he came to her in her dreams. She knew she dreamt. That was the torture of it all. In the morning, she'd wake, and he'd be gone. A fleeting touch against her cheek pulled her attention back to the water racing up her body before it retreated to the sea. She looked up at him, the moonlight casting a halo around his dark blue-black hair. The color of the sea at night, and she ached to trail her fingers through the silken strands.

Full lips smiled as he moved to straddle her. With his knees resting beside her slim waist, his cock jutted forward, pointing straight toward her mouth. Grace reached forward, trying to reach the succulent tip with her lips.

Her ocean lover smiled and shook his head. "Not yet," he whispered as he leaned over and pulled a turgid nipple into his mouth.

Grace moaned at the pressure. Her pussy ached, wet from more than the seawater, and she longed to feel him slide into her once more. He filled her, completed her, and not for the first time she wondered why the men she slept with in real life didn't feel like this. Then he bit gently on her nipple and the pleasure-pain of it had her arching her back away from the soft blanket and the sand. In the sea, a fish splashed. She looked over his shoulder to the ocean and watched a porpoise rise from the water, then dive into its dark depths again.

He released her nipple to press hot, wet kisses over her stomach. His tongue strayed into her navel, and as another wave rushed in, he pressed his face against her pussy.

"Yes, god, yes," she moaned, unable to stop herself as he licked her slit. The water washed over his face, up to her breasts, but it didn't matter. He lived in the ocean and the submersion in salt water only heightened the experience for both of them. The wave kissed her chin a moment before it retreated, and she found the rhythm of the sea mirrored in her blood. In and out. Up and down. The same motion she wanted to feel as he fucked her with his thick, hard cock. The sea made love to the shore as her dream lover made love to her.

He pulled her clit into his mouth and sucked gently. Grace clenched handfuls of blanket and sand, anything to anchor her as the desire rode her higher and higher. The tip of his tongue slid into her tight channel, and she cried out at the shudders racing through her body. This was how sex was supposed to be. All hot and wet and the slide of skin against skin and lips and cocks, all with the roar of the sea in the background. Grace allowed herself to sink into the sand. There was no use fighting her dream lover, and she didn't want to.

She'd come here to find him and be close to him. Did it really matter that it happened only in her mind?

Grace shoved against painful memories. So long as she didn't tell anyone it would be all right. If the outside world knew… She shoved the thoughts away. It was her dream. She didn't have to tell anyone.

Her lover pulled away long enough to stroke her clit and labia with his fingers. His digits slid into her slick folds, and she bucked against his hand. He finger-fucked her, leaning forward and capturing one of her nipples in his mouth. The dual sensations carried her to a fever pitch. She cried out, and convulsed around his fingers as her orgasm washed through her.

The waves ceased to roll over her. They'd done this many times before, and she lay there, waiting for his next command.

"Roll over."

His voice, rough with passion, compelled her to obey. She did, stretching arms and legs out until she lay facedown and spread-eagle on the blanket. A hiss of water sounded as the restraints closed once more around her wrists and ankles.

"Your ass is so pretty." He spanked it, his taps so light as to arouse. "I want to fuck you there, in your sweet little hole." He traced the puckered rosebud of her anus with his fingers. "Do you want me in there?"

In her pussy, her ass, Grace really didn't care so long as he was inside her. "Yes," she said, wanting to give her consent, though she knew he didn't need it. He had it. From the very first dream where she'd finally had sex with him, he had her consent, and he knew it.

He rubbed a moistened finger around her anus, slipping just the tip inside. He thrust gently, warming her up for his larger invasion. With his other hand, he stroked her clit and labia, eventually sliding first one finger, then a second inside her.

Grace writhed beneath his ministrations. She didn't bother muffling her cries. After all, she owned the island. Who was going to hear her?

With one finger up her ass and two in her pussy, Grace thought she would explode. She fucked his fingers, driving her clit against the blanket. "Oh god! Oh god!" she cried out, coming closer and closer to the peak.

He curled his fingers, stroking her G-spot. Grace exploded. She screamed, thrashing against the blanket as she came. Her pussy released its juices, drenching his fingers and the blanket beneath her. "Please," she begged. "I want your cock inside me."

"As you wish." He brushed his lips against the nape of her neck, the featherlight touch maddening on her sensitized skin. Her lover withdrew his fingers. She heard him moving behind her, imagined him coating his cock with her cream.

Something solid pressed against her pussy, and she squirmed, thinking it the stone dildo he used on her before. The polished ocean jasper held the swirls of the ocean. A long column of it sat on her desk, reminding her of this man, this place. Inch by inch he filled her with the dildo until she clenched her pussy around it in bliss.

The head of his cock pressed against her anus. She closed her eyes and lifted her rear in silent invitation.

His hands held her hips, their strong grip keeping her from moving. Not that she wanted to with his cock nestled between her cheeks. They'd done this before, many dreams, many times. Now he pressed the head of his cock against her hole, and she held her breath with anticipation.

A slight thrust, and he popped inside. He stretched her, the slight pain only adding to the pleasure of the thick dildo in her pussy. Slowly he moved, millimeter by millimeter as he sheathed himself inside her.

"More," Grace whimpered. She used her voice and her body to urge him on, pressing back against his penetration. At last his balls rested against her, and he sheathed himself completely within her body.

"Oh Grace, you're so beautiful." He smoothed his hand over the curve of her hip, palming her cheeks. "So damn beautiful."

His husky admission shocked her, and when he began to retreat, a slow and sensuous dance of flesh, she moaned. Each thrust brought her higher and higher, her body wound so tightly she doubted she'd ever come back down. He reached between her legs and fingered her clit.

Grace screamed. Her voice filled the night with the harsh cry of passion. "Oh god! Yes! Yes!" Her pussy clamped down on the dildo, and she rocked back against his hips. Her orgasm hit her with the force of a tidal wave. It rolled through her, threatening to tear her apart. Only his hands on her hips, his cock in her ass, kept her grounded. She clutched at the blanket and keened her pleasure into the balmy Caribbean night.

He thrust through her orgasm, triggering another one. She panted, her body convulsing around him. Always it was like this, and yet, this was stronger, more profound. She rested her forehead against the blanket, too stunned to do anything but enjoy the thrust of his cock inside her.

Behind her, he stiffened. His guttural roar signaled his own release, and he shot jets of come into her. The contact triggered yet another orgasm, and Grace slumped to the blanket with him wrapped around her.

Entwined, they lay beneath the stars. Grace felt him slip from her and gently remove the dildo. Where it went, she didn't know, and sated with a bone-deep satisfaction, didn't care. He was a god of the ocean, belonging only to the wind and the surf. He could be magic for all she knew, and he was all hers, for he existed in her mind.

He pressed a featherlight kiss against her neck, and slipped away with the tide.

* * * * *

Sunlight poured through the windows. The raucous cries of gulls woke her from sleep. Pulling the light sheet over her face, she yawned and struggled toward wakefulness. Once again he'd come to her, her dream lover from the sea, and once again he slid back into the sea when morning came. Her deliciously sore body testified to his presence, as did the sticky wetness between her thighs. She grinned and heaved a sigh, happy to remember the caress of masterful fingers. Tossing the sheet from her, she swung her legs over the edge of the bed. She stood and made her way to the bathroom and into a hot shower.

Wrapped in a towel and staring at her reflection in the mirror, Grace admitted her dream man spoiled her for anyone physical. Light red marks shone against her skin, love bites given in the heat of passion. The aching in her thighs told her she'd been thoroughly loved.

"I live on my own private island," she told her reflection. "Does it matter if the only man I fuck is imaginary? And maybe it's for the best..." She fought against the bitter memories of a child longing to share her "imaginary" friends with her nanny or her mother, and being denied. Her mother chalked up the tales of water sprites in the family pool as the ramblings of a child who had seen *The Little Mermaid* one too many times.

Grace closed her eyes against the pain she could never release. All she'd wanted was her parents' love and acceptance. She barely received dutiful attention. Her abilities held her separate, distant from those, and so she buried herself in work. "I'm here to enjoy the fruits of my labor, to finally have a place where I can be myself." Her words sounded hollow, and she wondered if it wasn't because every night she loved a man and every night he left her.

Grace shook her head. Along with her own island came a sense of peace. A desire to reconnect with her aquatic lover, and now, finally she felt as if she were coming close.

"So why do I feel like I should be hiding?" She slipped into a modest workout bikini in a blue the same color as the lagoon off her beach. After slathering herself with sunscreen, she grabbed her beach towel and headed outside. Sometimes things just needed to be contemplated beneath a cloudless sky. Warm sands, softly rippling water, what more did she need?

Her dream man in the flesh.

Grace tried not to frown as she settled her beach towel and stretched before her yoga routine. She could deal with his nightly visits. In fact, they might be better than the real thing. No worries about the toilet seat. No need to cook for two. Maybe it was better this way. She stepped easily into the Salutation to the Sun, felt the stretch in her muscles, and as she looked out over the bay, knew she could deal with having a nocturnal lover. Of course, having him in the flesh was better, but she wouldn't complain. Some things weren't meant to be.

In the sea, two dolphins splashed, and she smiled, and knew no matter what, she was incredibly lucky.

* * * * *

A short boat ride brought Grace to Eleuthera Island. Known for its serenity, Grace could see why people came here for freedom. Around her, the azure blue waters of the Caribbean promised wonderful fishing and views. However, she wasn't here for recreation. No, this was her weekly trip to town to get supplies, and although she loved the locals, she hoped to return to her private island as soon as possible.

As she strolled to her favorite market, she passed an elderly woman sitting on the corner. A shawl in the colors of the rainbow wrapped around her shoulders, and the woman's face held the lines of age and wisdom. She held out a gnarled hand. "Child," she said, her voice surprisingly strong. "Come here."

Grace stopped, her hand on her purse to extract a few Bahamian dollars to give to the woman.

She shook her head. "I do not want your money. Sit. There is something I must tell you." Clutching Grace's hand, the old woman directed her to the bench beside her.

Grace sat. She'd never seen this woman before in her life. It seemed incongruous that the woman might have something to tell her, though she knew the locals liked to share their stories with others. Still, it would be rude to decline, and the woman had done nothing so far to arouse suspicion. She supposed she could spare a few moments. After all, it wasn't like she punched time clocks anymore. She left that life behind when she bought her island and moved to the Bahamas.

"What you seek is within your grasp. Fill a cowry shell with rose petals. Put a white candle in it, light it, and set it out to the ocean at dusk. Then he will come." The old woman closed her eyes and wheezed. When she opened them again, she stared at Grace, her milky-white eyes unseeing. "Can I help you, child?"

"Thank you," Grace said. The old woman seemed to not know of what she spoke, and Grace didn't want to further disturb her by asking for clarification. Chills ran down her spine. Could it be that this elderly person knew of her quest to find the man of her dreams? She exhaled and stood, pressing several dollars in the old woman's outstretched hand. "Thank you," she said again as she closed the woman's fingers around the money. Releasing a sigh, she walked away from the woman.

Grace looked over her shoulder, half afraid the woman never existed. Behind her, the bench sat empty. Grace shook. She found a bench outside a flower shop. The scent of roses filled her nose, and she thought of the woman's words. What could it hurt to try out what she said? And if it brought him to her? She quaked with the thought. After all these years, could it be possible to conjure the man about whom she dreamed?

She went into the shop, marveling at the beautiful roses. Red, pink, yellow, they came in all hues. She touched one petal-soft flower and inhaled its sweet aroma. She quickly purchased two-dozen red ones, and then went to the market. Her purchases included not only her weekly groceries, but also several cowry shells from a street vendor. Beautiful, she thought to use the extra ones as decoration. With everything delivered to her boat, she carried the shells and the flowers back down the street. Soon, she'd return to her home.

Grace reminded herself of her earlier decision, that if he stayed in her mind she'd be content. After all, she didn't want to be disappointed if the crone's words didn't come true. But it wouldn't hurt to try, and it might yield results beyond her expectations. Besides, she loved roses and seashells. She had plenty of candles. And she always spent as much time by the ocean as possible, so it wasn't like she was doing anything beyond her normal routine. She kept telling herself that, and as she passed the bench, once more glanced around for the mysterious old woman.

Normally she lingered in her favorite café over a conch salad. Today, however, she hurried back to her boat. After tipping the delivery boy who secured her groceries in her boat, she waited her turn and propelled back out into the open sea to return to her island.

A slight breeze toyed with strands of her hair, and she inhaled the salty air. In the distance, cumulus clouds gathered, white and puffy against the horizon. The purr of the boat's motor filled the air, mingling with the cries of gulls. Grace turned her face into the wind and smiled. Here, on the water, she reveled in the sense of peace it brought to her. She debated about putting on her snorkeling gear and going out to explore the reefs around her island.

And tonight I might actually meet my lover in the flesh. She shivered and wondered how she would make it to dusk. Snorkeling. Most definitely snorkeling to get her mind off the coming night. She docked her boat and carried her purchases into the house. Tonight she would do the ritual and she would just see what morning brought.

Chapter 2

Wearing a sarong patterned in the deep blue and turquoise of the ocean, Grace stood on the shore. She curled her toes into the sand, still warm from the heat of the day, and watched as the sun painted the rippling water with shades of pink and orange. The deep indigo of the sea called to her, as it always did. She raised the shell above her head.

"I don't know if you're listening to me, Poseidon, but you're the god I feel most in tune with. If what the old woman said is true, and this will bring my love to me, then I ask your blessing." Grace stared into the ocean and tried to still the racing of her heart. She lowered the shell to heart-level and stared into its folds stuffed with rose petals. A white pillar candle rose from the curve of the shell. Grace studied it, the cowry shell shaped like the folds of a woman's pussy, the thick, white pillar candle rising from within it. With the rose petals surrounding it, the entire ensemble looked like homage to a god of passion, or fertility.

Grace smiled. She strode closer to the sea. The surf washed over her feet, a gentle caress that reminded her of last night's dream with her lover. Closing her eyes, Grace wished she even knew his name. That way, she'd know whom to ask for. It didn't matter, she supposed. Either whatever benevolent deities that listened to her prayer knew whom she dreamed about or they didn't. Either way speaking his name probably wouldn't help one way or the other.

She waded deeper, until the salt water came to her calves, then her knees. She stopped, not wanting to go farther out without some kind of protection on her feet. Bending over, she set her shell on the surface of the sea. She expected it to sink. It didn't. Instead, it floated, drifting gently with the current away from the shore.

Grace watched the shell. It floated like a boat, and she wondered if it were part of the spell that it didn't sink. After all, the shell alone should have been heavy enough to sink. She watched it, bobbing along with the suddenly still waves, until it disappeared into the distance and out of sight.

Her feet chilled from the water, Grace backed up a few steps. She sat down, clutching her knees to her chest. A crab scuttled along the sand next to her, heading to the sea. A few gulls sat on branches, uncharacteristically silent.

After long moments, Grace stood. She stretched and removed her sarong to reveal the bikini beneath. Standing on the beach, she moved into her evening yoga pose, and as the sun slipped beneath the horizon, she kept watching the ocean, expecting her lover to appear.

* * * * *

After a night of dreamless sleep, Grace tried not to get mad at the old woman. When her lover didn't even appear in her dreams, Grace feared she'd driven him off with her need to actually feel him. She doubted him, and if he existed on some level, certainly he wasn't happy with her uncertainty. She stretched out on the lounge next to her pool and leaned back. Covered with SPF30, she basked in the sun's rays. A nearly cloudless sky hovered overhead. In the bay, dolphins splashed and played. She watched them, wondering if she shouldn't put on her swimsuit and go snorkeling. Of course, dolphins could be dangerous, though she'd never had any problems with the ones near her cove.

A romance novel lay spine up on the stone next to her. Reading about fictional heroes who made her toes curl only conjured images of her dream lover. She nestled her head against the pillow, let her arms drape at her sides, and prepared to worship the sun. Her eyelids drifted closed.

A shadow fell across her face. Grace ignored it, still half asleep. The sun had moved, coming from behind her, and the slight rustling of leaves suggested that the trees might be causing the shadow. If she waited, it would move.

It didn't.

Fingers reached for her sunglasses. Finally, her dream lover had returned. It had to be him. She lived alone, so no one would be there to remove her sunglasses. She smiled as anticipation sent goose bumps skittering down her arms. With her sunglasses off, she didn't dare open her eyes, but as strong, warm fingers massaged her temples, she didn't want to either. If this were only a dream, she wanted it to last.

The calloused pad of a thumb brushed across her lips. Grace opened her mouth, her tongue darting out to taste the sun-warmed flesh of her dream lover. He tasted like salt and heat. His scent, crisp like the wind unfurling sails, filled her nostrils. She breathed deeply.

Knuckles brushed against her throat, down to the hollow between her breasts. Grace sucked in a breath as his fingers traced the flimsy straps of her bikini up to her shoulders, then down again. For a moment she regretted not sunbathing in the nude. Then again, make him work for her body. He'd kept her waiting. She grinned.

"You're back," she whispered.

"I am." His voice, rich and deep like expensive chocolate, sent shivers all the way to her toes. He brushed his lips across hers.

In his gentle touch she sensed his restraint. When he pulled away, she licked her lips, hungry for more. She knew what he could give her. She sat up.

And realized she wasn't sleeping.

Grace's eyes flew open. She stared at the man before her, from his thick, dark hair, to the white shirt, open to reveal his tanned, muscled chest. Casual pants, also white, only emphasized his tanned skin and muscular physique. Sandals revealed a pair of the most perfectly formed male feet she'd ever seen. Reluctantly, she dragged her gaze back to his face.

"My dream lover," she breathed. Grace struggled to pull her gaze away from his chest. Just a little bit closer and she could lick her way between his pecs down over luscious abs. "You're here." *And you can stay.* Silently, he moved behind her chair, sat down on the cement with his long legs so close she could touch them, and gently touched her forehead. He walked his fingers along her hairline until he reached her temples. He picked up the massage where he left off, and the heat from his fingers threatened to burn her.

Waves of pleasure roared through her body. Grace moaned at the fingers stroking her skin. Tension she hadn't known she had, released from her body, leaving her boneless on the lounge. His thumbs dug into the muscles along the back of her neck, working out each little twinge and stutter. For living a life of leisure, sometimes she found it hard to relax, and her mysterious dream lover certainly helped.

His hands slid down to her shoulders, massaging along her collarbone and the sides of her neck.

"That feels heavenly," she whispered.

"I'm glad you think so." He shifted position, leaning forward to brush his lips across hers. "I want to make you feel good, very, very good."

Her own private genie, come to grant her some wishes, Grace thought. He smoothed his hands along her arms, then the sides of her breasts. Her stomach fluttered at the intimate contact, and within the confines of her bikini top, her nipples hardened. A few strings separated her from his gaze, yet he made no move to release them.

Grace fought against the urge to shift on her chair. Her legs parted, an insistent ache roaring to life from his magical fingers. She licked her lips. Her mystery man touched like her dream man, and she struggled against becoming lost to his touch. It seemed highly unlikely she'd have two separate secret lovers. What if her spell worked?

Grace's eyes flew open. "Who are you?" Sure, she'd said he was back, but it seemed the right thing to say. What if he wasn't a dream lover? What if he was a complete and total stranger?

He skimmed his fingers along her shoulders, shoving the thin straps of her bikini top aside. "I am the man who will make your dreams come true."

The husky confidence in his words sent a flood of moisture to her pussy. Oh yes, stranger or not, she very much wanted this man to make her dreams come true. She reached behind her and pulled the tie on her bikini. "You are, are you?" She grinned at him, loving this cat and mouse game with her senses. A quick glance along his body showed him as affected as she. His cock bulged against the fabric, a package she would love to wrap her lips around and suck until he roared with pleasure.

"What's your name?" *I want to know whose name to scream when I come.*

He brushed his thumb across her nipple, making her gasp. Dear gods, with him so near and just touching her, she felt ready to come. Just thinking about what it would be like to feel his cock inside her made her bite her lip.

"Chemal." He slid her bikini down, revealing her breast.

The sea breeze caressed her body, making her hot and wanton. She turned toward him, and the other half of her bikini fell, baring her breasts to his hungry gaze. In eyes as deep blue as the sea behind them, a storm raged. Hunger, need, desire, churned in the depths of his eyes, and Grace's lips parted. Her hand fell to the ties on the side of her bikini bottoms.

"Not yet." His hand covered hers, warm and comforting. "I want to worship you, my sea goddess."

He knelt beside her and brushed his lips across hers. Gentle touches like the lapping of waves against the shore. His kisses reminded Grace of the dreams she had, bound to the sand while the waves and this man made love to her, and she arched her body against his. More. More. She'd had time to savor the moment, been seduced in her dreams. Now she wanted to wrap her arms around him and feel him hot and hard inside her.

She clamped her hand on his biceps. Rock-hard muscle met her grip, and with her other hand, she splayed it on the tanned skin revealed by his open shirt. Heat seared her palm, and still she explored him. Palming his male nipples, she ran her tongue along his lower lip. Not content to be passive, she slipped her tongue past his lips.

Chemal groaned. He tasted like the sun on a balmy, tropical day, like drinks with little umbrellas in them, and suddenly, she couldn't get enough. Cupping the back of his head, she held him to her, kissing him, drinking from him. Her breasts flattened against his chest, the delicious friction making her ache.

She pulled away long enough to draw in a breath of air, then kissed and nibbled his neck, his chest, down to circle her tongue around his flat, male nipples.

With one hand, he tunneled his fingers through her hair. The other pressed her back onto the lounge. He nipped her shoulder then laved the spot with his tongue.

Grace clung to him. Her pussy ached, so much so that when he put a trouser-clad thigh between her legs she rubbed against him. A hand slid to her hip, to where the tie of her bikini waited. A quick tug, then another, and cool air brushed against her fevered skin.

Chemal laved a nipple with his tongue. He licked her then pulled it into his mouth, the wet suction sending heat straight to her core.

"Oh god, Chemal," she gasped.

Palming her other breast, he worshipped her skin, acting as if he had all the time in the world.

Grace shoved his shirt from his shoulders. She needed to see him, to view his masculine beauty, to know this was the man about to fuck her. And, oh yes, she wanted him to fuck her. Her channel clenched, already imagining the length of him inside her. To be possessed, to be his just for these moments, Grace knew it would be the best experience of her life. Her dream lover in the flesh. The spell must have worked.

And suddenly she couldn't wait to experience him firsthand. If it was true, if her spell had worked, then she would have all the time in the world to be patient. Another poolside lounge chair sat beside her. She gently shoved him back until he climbed into the chair. Then she straddled him.

"Two can play at this game," she said, heedless of her nudity. On a private island, who cared, and if a passing boat happened to see them, well she hoped they got a good show. Just thinking about others seeing them, watching them, perhaps even getting off on the sight of her and Chemal making love, only heightened her arousal.

She curled her fingers into the waistband of his pants. Gently, she unbuttoned them then slowly lowered the zipper. His cock rose through the opening, fully erect. Chemal lifted his hips, allowing her to slide the pants over them and down his legs. She removed his sandals, then his trousers, and soon he lay there as naked as she.

Grace couldn't pull her gaze away from his cock. A small trail of hair led from his navel down to the mat of dark curls around his cock. Thick and long, she doubted she could have circled it with her hand, and just the sight of it sent a flood of cream through her. "Oh yes," she said, her hands on his thighs, also lightly dusted with hair. The contrast of tanned, hair-roughened male skin with her own silky smooth limbs made her feel all the more feminine.

Crawling over his body, she stopped at his cock and stroked it from base to head with her fingers. A small pearl of fluid emerged from the end. With her thumb, she massaged it into his skin, eliciting a groan from him. She lowered her head, her hair sliding over her shoulder to brush his thighs, and wrapped her lips around him.

She took him as deep as she was able, then worked her way back to his tip. Up and down, pausing to lick the length of him with her tongue or swirl it around his head, until he bucked beneath her and she had to press her legs together to ease her need. Fingers tangled in her hair held her close while he fucked her mouth.

"This was supposed…to be…for you," Chemal growled. The cords in his neck stood out, and sitting back on her heels, Grace looked down at him. Magnificent, with his cock slick from her saliva, his gaze fixed on her breasts, and lower, where her pussy rested against his leg. "Come here."

Grace obliged, more than ready to have her share of the action. She moved until her pussy brushed the head of his cock. Such sweet torment. She cupped him, guiding him to her center. She was on the pill, had been clean, and here was her sea god ready to please her. The last thing she wanted was a scrap of latex between them.

Chemal cupped her hips, his grip urgent. He eased into her, inch by erotic inch, until his balls rested against her ass. He filled her so exquisitely she tilted her head back and moaned, squeezing her vaginal muscles around him. Taking it slow flew right out the window as he closed his eyes and thrust even deeper into her.

Guided by his hands on her hips, she rode him like waves on the sea, rising until he nearly slipped from her, then gliding down to join their bodies once more. The give and take, the thrust of his hips beneath her, all of it spiraled pleasure through her. Then, he reached between their bodies to touch her clit.

Grace screamed as pleasure rocketed through her. One touch, two, and then her pussy clamped around him and she came. Stars burst behind her closed eyelids. Spasms rocked her body. She slumped forward, and still Chemal thrust. His hand slid around to her ass, fingers close to her puckered hole. His hips increased their pace, and all Grace could do was lean forward, grab his biceps, and hang on for the ride.

Over and over he pounded into her. Grace struggled to keep her gaze focused on the man beneath her. So beautiful, and all hers. She couldn't quite believe it, yet as his finger pressed against her anus, she knew he was hers. He knew everything she liked and played her body like a virtuoso. He thrust harder, faster, and she knew he neared his own climax. She reached between them, stroking his cock where their bodies joined. And then, with a roar, he came.

His hot seed pulsed into her, triggering her own orgasm, and Grace cried out as she exploded above him. Her pussy milked his shaft, her cream washing over them. She stiffened, feeling him still in the throes of his release beneath her. And then, she collapsed against his chest. Chemal wrapped an arm around her as she listened to his panting breaths and pounding heart.

Inside her, his cock remained hard. She squeezed him with her muscles, and he grinned. "Not yet, my siren." He brushed a strand of hair from her forehead and pressed his lips to her skin.

Grace grinned. She snuggled closer against him, prepared to enjoy her dream lover for as long as he lasted.

Chapter 3

The need for food and a growing chill forced Grace indoors with Chemal right behind. Sitting in her dining room, the curtains pulled back from the French doors to reveal the sun setting over the sea, she stood at the central island in her kitchen and sautéed vegetables for kabobs. Chemal stood beside her, his breath warm on her neck. He stared intently at the skillet, watching as she cooked their meal. With one arm around her waist, he pulled her against his hard body, reminding her how it felt against her. "Smells wonderful," he said.

Not as good as you. Grace bit her lip to keep the words from emerging. It seemed so natural to have him in her kitchen, so right.

The skillet sizzled. She added chunks of beef and chicken, unsure which he would like, and added several pinches of herbs. The heavenly aroma filled the kitchen, and she glanced at Chemal to see him smiling at her.

"Is there anything I can do?" he asked.

"You cook?" Grace arched an eyebrow and smiled. "You truly are a dream man, aren't you?" Reaching into the counter, she pulled down a wooden bowl and began to mix greens in it. "I have everything covered. Just sit there and enjoy."

"The view certainly is worth admiring." Deliberately, Chemal didn't look toward the Caribbean.

A hot flush crept over her cheeks. Blaming it on the stove, she finished tossing the greens with light vinaigrette dressing. Grace set the bowl on the counter, quickly adding plates and silverware. She didn't expect to use it, except for the salad, but didn't know how Chemal felt about finger food. Actually, she hoped they'd be feeding each other. She topped off both their wineglasses, arranged the kabobs on a platter, and then motioned for him to sit at the counter. "Help yourself," Grace said as she sat, and watched him add a beef and chicken kabob to his plate along with a generous serving of fresh fruit. She grabbed a piece of pineapple with her fingers and popped it into her mouth. She closed her eyes in ecstasy as the flavor burst inside her mouth. Sweet and tangy, she savored each delectable bite. When she opened her eyes, she saw Chemal staring at her.

He picked up another piece of pineapple and brushed it across her lips. The juice dribbled down her chin, and he moved the fruit just enough to kiss the liquid away. "Do you know you have the same look on your face right now that you did when I fucked you?"

His low voice sent a shiver of awareness down her spine. Grace opened her mouth. Chemal slid the fruit between her lips, pausing to rub it across her lower lip before sliding it over her tongue. He drew his fingers from her mouth and watched as she chewed and swallowed.

Grace forced her eyes to remain open. Her breathing hitched in her throat. A storm darkened in Chemal's eyes, a storm of passion that sent a rush of moisture to her pussy. Her nipples beaded inside her bikini top, and not even the cover-up she'd thrown on over her bikini could hide them from view.

"We, uh, should probably eat." Grace reached for a kabob.

Chemal's fingers closed around her wrist. His thumb stroked the sensitive underside. "We need to keep up our strength for tonight."

His words evoked images of the two of them, bodies entwined, skin slicked with sweat, fucking on the beach, in her bed, anywhere they could reach, all night long. Grace sucked in a harsh breath. She pressed her thighs together to try and stop the throbbing in her pussy.

"Because tonight is all we have." He picked up a cube of steak and held it to her lips. "When the sun rises above the horizon tomorrow, I'll be gone."

"Gone?" Grace whispered.

He nodded and slipped the tender morsel into her mouth. "I want to do everything with you tonight. Spend as much time as I can buried in your hot, tight pussy, because I don't ever want to forget what it's like to live on land with you."

Grace took her time chewing and then swallowing to process his words. In the morning, he'd be gone. Her dream man would return to the ocean from which he came. She closed her eyes, hating the sting of tears. Why would she finally get her wish only to have it taken away from her? Had she done the spell wrong? Had something happened? She picked up her own kabob, staring at it for a moment before replacing it on her plate. In the wake of his news, her appetite fled. "Why?" she asked. "Why would you have to go?" *And why did I think this time would be different? Everyone I love leaves me sooner or later.*

"My beautiful Grace, I am a creature of the sea. A minor god, if you must call me such things. I cannot live on land separated from my beloved water for long." He thought for a moment, and then reached for more food. "But let's not waste the time we have in conversation. I want to taste every inch of your body." He brushed the cool pineapple down the column of her neck, following the fruit's trail with his lips and tongue. He kissed her, tiny licks and nibbles that had he squirming in her chair.

Grace clung to his shoulders as he shoved the flimsy cover-up over her shoulder.

Chemal caressed her with the fruit, licking clean everywhere the pineapple touched her. Finally, he slid it into his mouth and chewed. "Mmm," he breathed against her skin. "It tastes like you."

Grace pulled off her cover-up, letting it flutter to the floor. If Chemal looked hard enough he'd see the damp place on her bikini bottoms where her pussy soaked the fabric. Emboldened by his words and actions, she reached behind her neck. Two quick pulls released the ties, and she tossed her bikini top down to the floor with her cover-up. She sat before him with bared breasts and had never felt so sexy in her entire life.

Chemal brushed a strawberry over the tip of her nipple. Leaning forward, he licked off the dewy juice before mashing the fruit against her chest. He nibbled it off, then went back to her breast and drew the nipple into his mouth. He sucked, alternating between hard pulls against her breast and flicks of his tongue.

Grace moaned, her fingers tunneling through his hair to hold him in place. He moved from his stool to stand between her thighs. Too many clothes separated them, and yet, she couldn't muster the energy to move.

With his other hand he palmed her breast, toying with her nipple until it stood out in a hard stiff peak. Each pull went straight to her pussy, drawing something high and tight within her. A slight bite, then soothing the hurt with his tongue, Chemal knew exactly how she liked to be touched. Of course he should. They'd been fucking in her dreams for too many months. And now she had him in her arms, in the flesh.

She trailed her fingers from his hair, to his shoulders, then down his arms, caressing everywhere she could reach. His tanned skin and hard body called to her, invited her to taste and lick every inch of him. The barstool suddenly seemed to be the worst place to have sex, and she clutched his shoulders. The floor was close and freshly waxed. Or maybe the patio with its hot tub overlooking her beach.

Chemal slid his hands under her ass and squeezed gently. He pulled her toward him, and her legs wrapped around his waist instinctively. The hard ridge of his cock pressed against her pussy. She rocked against him, fueling the shudders of need racing through her. Enough with the foreplay. She wanted him now, hot and hard inside her, filling her with his cock.

"Mmm, baby, you taste so good." Chemal slid his hands beneath her rear and massaged gently. Her legs lowered, and as he lifted her against him, Chemal pulled down her bikini. It slid down her legs, falling off when he put her back on her perch. "Spread your legs for me." His gaze dropped to her pussy, slick from wanting. "Yeah, just like that." Grabbing another piece of pineapple, he dropped to his knees.

Grace looked down at him, his head dark between her thighs. Oh god, he couldn't be doing this, could he? Then she didn't care as he trailed the pineapple along the inside of first one thigh, then the other. Licks and nibbles led him straight to her core, and the first touch of his tongue against her labia sent sparks shooting through her.

Her nipples puckered into tight peaks. Her breathing came in shallow pants, and Grace curled her fingers around the edge of the barstool to keep her balance. No one had ever shown such reverent care for her body before. No one had ever touched her like this. She closed her eyes and let the sensations wash through her. A lick, a nibble, a caress, they all combined to focus her attention on the man between her thighs.

He slid the piece of pineapple between her lips.

"Oh," Grace gasped, feeling his tongue slide in after it. She succumbed to the sensations in her pussy, closing her eyes and letting her head fall back.

Wrapping his lips around her clit, Chemal sucked. He flicked the tiny bud with his tongue, making it plump and swell.

Rocking her hips, Grace strained toward his mouth. Just a little more, and then, oh yeah. Her orgasm slammed into her hard and fast, her pussy rippling as it convulsed around the fruit. Between her legs, Chemal groaned. Her fingers clenched into his shoulders, her cry of release a keening in the air. She sucked in a deep breath as he ate the fruit.

She looked down and saw his cock tenting the front of his slacks. "My turn," she murmured, caressing the side of his face and tilting his chin up to look at her.

Effortlessly, he rose to his feet and grabbed the bottle of wine. Holding out his other hand, he helped her off the stool. Grace looked up at him and knew this was going to be a night she wouldn't forget.

Just twenty-four hours with Grace. Chemal swallowed hard and vowed to make every minute of it last. He'd come to her in her dreams, their minds merging as their bodies came together. He knew what she liked, what she wanted, and worked to enact her every fantasy. Now that he had her in the flesh, he wanted to do the same. Because then, perhaps, she could accept his aquatic existence.

He couldn't tell her the truth. Chemal wrapped his arm around her waist and pulled her against him. Her curves pressed snugly against his side, the curve of her bare breast tempting him. He led her to the patio, opening the French doors and stepping through. Out here only the sound of the breeze in the palm trees and the ever-present surf filled the air. Birds roosted for the night, and not even a crab scuttled across the sand. Out here was his world.

His chest tightened as he thought about showing her his underwater realm. Corals and sea fans among which little brightly colored fish played. It was truly paradise, and one he longed to share with her. The terms of his existence bound him to silence, though he wanted to tell her the truth. She'd accepted him in her mind. That's what opened the doors to the spell working. If she accepted him in her heart, then maybe, he could come to her in this form during the night, instead of only in her dreams.

Drawing Grace into his arms, he pulled her tight against his body. He set the wine on a table by the door, deciding he needed nothing more than the woman in his arms. Resting his chin against her temple, he inhaled the floral scent of her shampoo. For tonight, he'd forget about their separate lives and simply enjoy the woman in his arms. He felt her snuggle into his embrace. Over her shoulder he saw her hot tub and smiled. Scooping her into his arms, he carried her across the patio to the hot tub. A quick press of the button and the jets churned the water into frothy bubbles of relaxation.

Grace shuddered as the jets began whirring, and Chemal knew what she was thinking because he was thinking it too. Them, naked, in the hot tub together. His cock throbbed with the need to be buried inside her, but as much as tonight was for him, she came first. Always, Grace had come first. As a child, she'd flitted and played with the spirits of the water, and those spirits drove her to a successful athletic career as a swimmer. She'd missed the Olympics by a few hundredths of a second. And as she matured, the spirits began to dissipate, leaving only him prominent in her fantasies, until they shared minds and bodies like longtime lovers.

A soft caress along the length of her spine coaxed a blissful sigh from her throat. He cupped her bare ass, kneading the cheeks, as she pressed closer to his cock. Her stance widened, invited him closer. He nibbled her neck, her chin, inching them closer and closer toward the hot tub. She bumped against the stairs, and then sat down, legs spread.

. "I want you inside me." She captured his gaze with her own, and the hunger and need he saw in the depths of her eyes mirrored his own.

Chemal shed his clothing.

She gasped at the sight of his naked body, her eyes lingering on the length of his cock. It jutted from his body, long and hard, and he curled his hands under his balls just to watch her squirm. Once, twice, he stroked himself, certain she knew he was thinking of being buried balls-deep inside her the entire time. Then, he strode forward.

"I want you in the hot tub." Deliberately, he mirrored her words then motioned to the water.

"Only if you come with me." She turned and sashayed up the stairs giving him a view of her rounded ass. Knowing what it felt like to be buried between those cheeks, to feel her take him deeper than she'd ever taken anyone, he swallowed hard and hoped to Poseidon he lasted long enough to come with her.

"Oh, I'll come all right, but so will you." He followed her up the stairs, watching as she settled into the water. Eyes closed, arms floating on the surface, she looked like a mermaid come to life. He paused at the top of the stairs, just watching her. Gods, he could watch her for hours. Slowly, he descended into the hot tub and sat down across from her. Stretching out his legs, his feet brushed against hers.

Grace opened her eyes. She settled deeper into the water, a grin on her face as she caressed his foot with her toes. Inching from her seat, her digits moved over his leg. They curled into his skin. She floated toward the center of the whirlpool and inched her toes higher up his leg.

She disappeared under the water.

Chemal sat rigid with anticipation. A graceful turn, and then slender fingers closed around his cock.

Grace's head broke the surface, and he realized she straddled his legs. With her fingers she squeezed his shaft, working it up and down, from the head down to his balls, and then back again. Long, sure strokes that had his balls drawing tight against his body. The base of his spine tingled, and if she kept that up, he'd come.

"Grace, please," he groaned, moving to intercept her hands.

"Please what?" She braced her knees on either side of him on the bench. Her pussy hovered tantalizingly close to his cock.

"If you keep doing that I'll—"

Grace squeezed his cock then reached down to fondle his balls and the sensitive skin behind. She trailed her fingers over his chest, wrapping her arms around his neck, and she impaled herself on his shaft. Inch by heavenly inch, he filled her, and with one arm wrapped around her waist and looking out over the Caribbean Sea, he wondered how he could return to his aquatic world. And then Grace began to move and he forgot conscious thought at all.

Water churned around them, the jet hitting him in the lower back adding stimulus to the woman straddling his hips. He rose to fill her, his balls slapping against her, and with her hands braced on his shoulders, Grace began to move. With her eyes closed and her head thrown back in passion, he thought she was the most beautiful thing he'd ever seen. He surged into her, wanting to brand himself on her soul. Each stroke took him higher, deeper, until the tip of his cock brushed her cervix. He reached between them and caressed her clit.

Her husky cries enflamed his desire. Uninhibited, she moaned, her voice rising to a keening wail as he pressed her up and over the edge of release. Her pussy milked his cock, the ripples bringing him perilously close to his own climax.

She gloved him so perfectly, her slick heat a counterpoint to the warm relaxing water around them. Like an inferno she burned around him, and even as she came down from her orgasm, he pushed her onward.

At last, he released the rein on his passion and fucked her. Their cries joined, his deep moans a counterpoint to her higher whimpers. Water sloshed over the edge of the hot tub.

And then with a breath, Grace screamed her release. She slumped against him, head resting against his shoulder as her body convulsed around him. Chemal surged once more and with a guttural cry spilled his seed into her. He held on tight, never wanting to let go. Their panting breaths mingled, and as the jets silenced in the tub, Chemal could do nothing but stare out at the bay and figure out how the hell he was going to leave her behind.

Chapter 4

After Chemal carried her from the hot tub into her bedroom, they spent the rest of the night making love. Fierce need gave way to tender exploration, and by the time the night grew late they'd known each other's bodies in many different ways and positions. Sitting there, on the beach, the sand cool between her toes, Grace leaned into Chemal's warmth. She didn't want to think about what would happen in an hour or so, though she knew she needed to. When the sun breached the horizon, he'd be gone, and she would return to loving him only in her dreams.

She trailed her fingers in the sand, making little furrows into which the surf rushed. The cool water chilled her toes, and although she had put on a sarong skirt and wrap, she welcomed the shivers. Every moment had to last.

"You look troubled." Chemal smoothed his thumb over her chin then leaned forward to press his lips against hers. "Do you regret bringing me to join you on land?"

His words, so tender and worried, brought a sheen of tears to her eyes, and she blinked it away. "No, not at all." She brought his fingers to her lips and kissed each digit in turn. "I just wonder what will happen when you go back to the sea. Will you forget me?" She searched his eyes for the truth. In so many tales the lover returned to the sea, forgetting about those left on the shore. If Chemal were to forget her, better to know now, than to foolishly believe he'd pine for her.

"I'll never forget you." He pressed his lips to her forehead.

For long moments she sat there, wrapped in the warmth of his embrace. The surf tickled her toes, before rushing out again, and she exhaled. "Never?" This time, she let a tear run down her cheek. She buried her face in his shirt, not wanting him to know about the soul-deep grief that filled her at the thought of his leaving. She glanced toward the sky at the first streak of pink and knew their time drew to a close.

"For as long as I live, and that will be far longer than you, I'm afraid, I'll never forget you, Grace." Chemal paused, and Grace sensed he weighed his words. "I love you. I always have from the time when you were a little girl playing in the surf. As you matured, so did my affections, and when you came to me, started dreaming of me, you can't know how happy it made me. If I had it to do all over again, Grace Edwards, I'd still fall in love with you." He glanced toward the horizon. "But now my time grows short. Do you love me? Could you live with a lover who spent part of the day in the ocean and the other part by your side?"

Grace stared at him, his words rendering her speechless. Living with him part of the day didn't seem fair. She wanted him all day, every day, beside her all the time. The selfish part of her wanted to spend her days with him at the beach and make love to him all night. And love, what did she know of love? An only child growing up with parents she knew loved her in their own way, for whom sports and academic achievements were the only way she could curry favor long enough to pull them away from some social function or board meeting. She knew nothing about love, yet feared she loved Chemal.

"I don't know," she whispered, everything suddenly too overwhelming, too much for her at the moment. Closing her eyes, she swallowed hard with the fear her words might drive him away.

More pink lightened the sky.

Grace searched Chemal's face in the hopes of not seeing the hurt she saw reflected there. He looked away, but not quickly enough. A glance out to the sea, a longing, heartfelt glance, and she knew she'd wounded him.

"I'm sorry," she said with the sudden need to heal the pain. "I just don't know. Books speak about love, and in college girls talked about love, but what do I know of it? You were there. You know how I grew up." Grace bolted to her feet. Restless energy poured through her. "What if I say I do love you and this turns out to be a wonderful, beautiful dream? What if I live here forever knowing that the only man I love lives in my mind? I thought I was ready. I prayed I was ready to accept that, but after holding you, how can I let you go?" Crossing her arms over her chest, she stared at him for a long moment. Hating the tears choking her throat, she whirled and ran.

She was a coward, a horrible, hideous coward. Heedless of her bare feet, she raced down the beach, past the outcropping of rocks where she liked to sit and watch the dolphins play, down to the dune where sometimes she went snorkeling, nearly to the cove where sharks patrolled the waters. She stopped, rested her head in her hands, and let the tears flow.

Chemal stopped behind her. He wrapped his arm around her shoulders and turned her so she rested her head against her chest. "Is it enough?" he asked after long moments. "Just to know I'm there."

Grace nodded. She sniffed and dashed away her tears with the back of her hand. "It's enough. It's going to have to be, isn't it?" She hated goodbyes. They always seemed so final, even when she knew she would return.

"Oh, my sweet Grace. I've lived so long without you, and now to finally know you, I'm selfish. I don't want to let you go to this world of land. But I have to, and know every moment I'm in the ocean, I'll wish I were on land." Chemal reached down and grasped her hands. He glanced over his shoulder at the rising sun. "My time grows short. Walk with me."

Bone-deep weary from the night's exertions, Grace nodded. She slipped her hand in his, loving the way his warmth surrounded her. They walked slowly with no particular destination in mind. Back down the beach to where they started from, and then Chemal stopped.

He turned to her. "You know I'll think of you every moment of every day." Reaching up, he brushed a strand of hair off her forehead, his touch lingering.

Grace nodded, not quite trusting her voice. She gripped Chemal's hand as the sky lightened, spelling his doom.

He cupped her chin and tilted her head up to look at him. "Remember last night. Cherish it always. I know I will." Without waiting for an answer, he dipped his head and kissed her. His lips brushed across hers, a gentle touch filled with promise. As his mouth settled against hers, his tongue brushed the seam of her lips.

Grace swayed into him, leaning against his hard frame for the strength she needed. Her mouth opened, and she moaned as his tongue plunged inside. With her eyes closed, she concentrated on every nuance, on his flavor, his scent, the feel of his tongue stroking against hers. Warmth filled her, chasing away the chill of knowing he would be leaving. She kissed him back, wishing she could pour her heart into her mouth and give it to him. Perhaps with her actions she could say the things she couldn't with words.

His arm wrapped around her waist. Held between his hard chest and the hand splayed on her lower back, Grace felt comforted, protected. Maybe her heart would be dashed on the rocks like a boat during a storm, but standing here, with Chemal holding her, kissing her, she believed perhaps there might be a way for them to work.

Overhead the flapping of wings announced the first arrival of the gulls. Their raucous cries filled the air with noise announcing the coming dawn. Grace squeezed her eyes closed, not wanting to look over the sea and watch the bright orb of the sun rise over the horizon, for when it did, it would take Chemal from her.

The need for air parted them, and for long moments, he stood with his forehead resting against hers. "Do you know what I fear the most?" he asked.

The raw vulnerability in his voice shocked her. Looking at Chemal, Grace doubted he feared anything. The sharks that sometimes patrolled these waters probably didn't even bother him. She'd stumbled upon a moray eel while snorkeling once and swam hell-bent back to the shore. She doubted such things worried him.

"That when I return to the ocean you'll find someone else to hold you, to stay in your bed. If I could take you with me, I would, and if I could stay, I would. Tell me you won't find another, that you'll dream with me for as long as you live." Chemal swallowed hard.

It sounded a hell of a lot like a permanent goodbye. "Will I never see you again?" She risked a glance at the horizon where the edge of the sun rose to light a new day. "Will you not return to me except in my dreams?"

Chemal shook his head. "I don't know. We were granted this night. Tell me there won't be someone else."

"How can there be when you're the only one I've dreamed of? How can there be someone else when no one compares to you? Gods, if I live a hundred years, you'll be the only man for whom I'll yearn." She pressed her face against his chest and wrapped her arms around him. Releasing him, she stepped back. "But you have to go now, don't you?" Thankfully, she kept her voice from wavering. She willed herself to be strong, to watch him go without a tear in her eye. Breathing deeply, she looked out over the Caribbean.

"Yes, I have to go," Chemal said. He reached for her hand, twined his fingers with hers, and gave them a gentle squeeze. "I love you." He slid his fingers from hers and stepped toward the surf.

Grace forced herself to watch, damning herself for the words that wouldn't spring to her lips. "I'll never forget last night," she said at last.

The surf curled around his ankles, dampening the legs of his trousers. He stood there, looking back toward the shore, and her, for long moments. Then he blew her a kiss, turned, and walked into the ocean.

Tears streamed down Grace's cheeks. She watched as the water surrounded his knees, then his thighs. He seemed to be simply walking into the ocean. With the sea around his waist, he held his hands over his head, and dove into the water.

Grace stood there for long moments half expecting him to surface again. He didn't, and as the sun rose fully above the horizon, she realized he was gone.

Exhaustion weighed on her. Sinking to the sand, she sat, arms braced on her knees, and watched the steady roll of the surf. Overhead gulls played on the warming air currents, and a fish splashed not far offshore. Still, Chemal didn't return.

When the air warmed and her tears dried on her cheeks, Grace gave in to the need for sleep. She wobbled to her feet, certain he wouldn't be coming back, and strode into the house. The bottle of wine still sat on the porch, and partially eaten plates of food sat on the counter. She picked up a chunk of pineapple and pressed it to her lips. The sweet flavor filled her with longing, and she chewed thoughtfully as she strode upstairs to her bedroom. Taking a shower and changing into an oversized T-shirt, she crawled into the bed, still able to smell him on her pillows. Cuddling one to her chest, she gave in to the need for sleep.

* * * * *

Waking to the sunlight streaming through her bedroom window, Grace reached for Chemal's pillows. She ran her fingers over the soft fabric. It didn't even bear the imprint of his head anymore, and when she brought it to her nose, no longer did his scent linger. She looked out the window, at the constant view of the Caribbean and sighed. Chemal was gone.

Where had she gone wrong? Grace padded into the bathroom and turned on the shower. She stepped beneath the stinging hot spray, closing her eyes as the water eased away aches and pains, all of them except the one in her heart. Could she have kept him with her, and if so, would she live with the consequences of her folly forever? She squeezed her eyes closed as she washed her hair and lathered her body with rich, French milled lavender soap. The aroma was supposed to be relaxing, but all it did was remind her of everywhere Chemal touched her, kissed her. She turned off the shower and wrapped herself in a fluffy robe.

Before she executed the spell, she thought herself strong enough to handle a lover who existed only in her mind. That's why she went to town, and that's why she accepted the old woman's advice. Grace stared in the mirror at the woman who returned the intent gaze. *I don't know you. I don't know who you are.* She exhaled and the woman in the mirror did too. *Just because our parents loved us the only way they could doesn't mean we can't accept love.* She thought of Chemal's words, so giving, so true, and how she couldn't return his simple declaration of love.

She dressed in another two-piece, this time the top a simple black tank top. Slipping her feet into sandals, she hurried downstairs to clean up the aftermath of last night. If only her heart could be cleaned as easily as her kitchen. She stepped outside long enough to grab the bottle of wine from the porch. In their lust, they'd forgotten to cover the hot tub, and she did so, not wanting to look at the blue water or remember how easily she'd straddled him and rocked them both to satisfaction.

The wine went down the drain. A few moments of cleanup, and soon her kitchen looked as if she had never invited Chemal inside. And if she hadn't, would that have been better? Grace didn't know, and it hurt too much to probe for answers.

Grace leaned against the counter. She didn't like it. She hated how easily she'd erased him from her home. She grabbed the wine bottle, though it still dripped water, and set it on the counter. There, if she could stare at it long enough maybe she could believe last night had happened. She touched the side of her neck where she'd noticed a love bite and sighed. "I never meant to shove him out of my life. I never meant for last night to be a goodbye." She sank onto a barstool, trying so hard not to remember his dark head between her thighs, his mouth at her pussy.

She went out to the patio where she sat so many times looking out into the sea in the hopes of finding him. She searched the cerulean blue waters, though this far away she saw only the soft white-tipped waves as they rolled toward the shore. Just thinking about Chemal drove some of the loneliness away. In her office, business paperwork awaited, deeds and contracts her parents wanted her to review for their company. It could wait. Out here, the sun and the surf came first, never business. And when she walked toward the ocean, Grace smiled.

Memories of their night together filled the void she feared never would go away. In her heart, the place where she feared she might never be loveable, where she knew she was to blame for her parent's disinterest, she heard only the whispered words of love Chemal offered. Where he came from and how he lived mattered little. He could be a beggar on Nashua's street corners, or the owner of the finest resort on the islands, or simply a minor sea god. It mattered little to her, for he loved her, and she loved him.

Grace's hands fell to her sides. She toed off her sandals, feeling the sand warm and soft between her toes. A gull flew over, its boisterous cries mocking her with avian laughter. A fish splashed in the ocean, and a crab walked across the sand. Her world. His world. Here where the surf met the sand the two worlds collided. Somehow it worked, with the surf giving way beneath the ground, and the sand tumbling after the water into the bay. Creatures lived in both worlds, as testified by the crab. A wave came in, picking up the crustacean and carrying him out to sea. He'd return, Grace knew, he and hundreds like him. Watching the play of nature, her answer became so easy. No one ever leaves forever. Eventually they return, just like her parents, and just like Chemal.

"I love you, Chemal," she said. She thought about yelling, perhaps then her voice would carry and he'd hear. She sensed, somehow, that he knew, and he'd known all along. "I love you."

Land and sea, they'd make it work. Maybe she could only have him one night a year, maybe every night, but not the days, and maybe only during certain times, like high tides, it didn't matter to her. So long as sometimes, he came to her world, and maybe, just maybe, if she came to his, he would join her.

Grace waded into the ocean. Tiny fish darted around her feet, their tickling nibbles widening the smile on her face. She watched for anemones, and when the water was deep enough she began to swim. Like the collegiate champion she was, her strokes cut through the water. She broke the surface, a whoop of joy on her lips. In the distance, dolphins jumped and played. Grace dived deeper and swam toward them.

Hands clamped around her waist.

Grace stifled a shriek. She twisted in the water and grinned when she saw Chemal behind her. He hauled her against his body and nuzzled her hair.

"I missed you."

Grace turned in his arms. "I missed you too. I love you." She cupped his cheeks in her hands and pressed her lips to his. "I love you so much, and I'm so sorry I didn't tell you last night. Why are you here? Why have I never seen you in the water before?"

Holding onto her waist, he propelled them toward the dolphins. "You love me, so when you visit my realm, you can see me. By night, I can walk the land beside you, but every dawn, I'll return to the sea."

"The only thing that would sound more perfect would be to have you by my side forever." She pressed her lips to his cheek. Then a dolphin bumped her with his nose, and with Chemal's arm wrapped around her waist, she knew she'd be safe forever.

"I love you, Grace."

"And I love you, Chemal. You're really the man of my dreams." She pressed her lips to his, sealing her words with a kiss.

The dolphins circled, herding them toward safer and shallower waters, and soon Grace forgot about everything else but the man in her arms.

Also by Mary Winter

∞

Ghost Redeemed
Ghost Touch
Once Upon a Prince (*anthology*)
Pleasure Quest (*anthology*)
Prodigal Son
Snowbound

About the Author

∞

Mary Winter began writing when she was 16, using it as an excuse to skip gym class. She currently lives in Iowa with her pets and dreams of writing full-time. Ghost Touch was her first published novel, and her advice to anyone is: "Persistence pays off. Don't ever give up on your dreams!"

Mary welcomes comments from readers. You can find her website and email address on her author bio page at www.ellorascave.com.

Tell Us What You Think

We appreciate hearing reader opinions about our books. You can email us at Comments@EllorasCave.com.

Why an electronic book?

We live in the Information Age—an exciting time in the history of human civilization, in which technology rules supreme and continues to progress in leaps and bounds every minute of every day. For a multitude of reasons, more and more avid literary fans are opting to purchase e-books instead of paper books. The question from those not yet initiated into the world of electronic reading is simply: *Why?*

1. *Price.* An electronic title at Ellora's Cave Publishing and Cerridwen Press runs anywhere from 40% to 75% less than the cover price of the exact same title in paperback format. Why? Basic mathematics and cost. It is less expensive to publish an e-book (no paper and printing, no warehousing and shipping) than it is to publish a paperback, so the savings are passed along to the consumer.

2. *Space.* Running out of room in your house for your books? That is one worry you will never have with electronic books. For a low one-time cost, you can purchase a handheld device specifically designed for e-reading. Many e-readers have large, convenient screens for viewing. Better yet, hundreds of titles can be stored within your new library—on a single microchip. There are a variety of e-readers from different manufacturers. You can also read e-books on your PC or laptop computer. (Please note that Ellora's Cave does not endorse any specific brands. You can check our websites at www.ellorascave.com

or www.cerridwenpress.com for information we make available to new consumers.)

3. ***Mobility.*** Because your new e-library consists of only a microchip within a small, easily transportable e-reader, your entire cache of books can be taken with you wherever you go.

4. ***Personal Viewing Preferences.*** Are the words you are currently reading too <small>small</small>? Too large? Too… ANNOYING? Paperback books cannot be modified according to personal preferences, but e-books can.

5. ***Instant Gratification.*** Is it the middle of the night and all the bookstores near you are closed? Are you tired of waiting days, sometimes weeks, for bookstores to ship the novels you bought? Ellora's Cave Publishing sells instantaneous downloads twenty-four hours a day, seven days a week, every day of the year. Our webstore is never closed. Our e-book delivery system is 100% automated, meaning your order is filled as soon as you pay for it.

Those are a few of the top reasons why electronic books are replacing paperbacks for many avid readers.

As always, Ellora's Cave and Cerridwen Press welcome your questions and comments. We invite you to email us at Comments@ellorascave.com or write to us directly at Ellora's Cave Publishing Inc., 1056 Home Avenue, Akron, OH 44310-3502.

erridwen, the Celtic Goddess of wisdom, was the muse who brought inspiration to storytellers and those in the creative arts. Cerridwen Press encompasses the best and most innovative stories in all genres of today's fiction. Visit our site and discover the newest titles by talented authors who still get inspired - much like the ancient storytellers did, once upon a time.

*Discover for yourself why readers can't get enough
of the multiple award-winning publisher*

Ellora's Cave.

Whether you prefer e-books or paperbacks,

*be sure to visit EC on the web at
www.ellorascave.com*

*for an erotic reading experience that will leave you
breathless.*